D1021915

Moonscape

A NELLIE BURNS AND MOONSHINE
MYSTERY

MOONSCAPE

JULIE WESTON

FIVE STAR
A part of Gale, a Cengage Company

WITHDRAWN

GALE
A Cengage Company

Farmington Hills, Mich • San Francisco • New York • Waterville, Maine
Meriden, Conn • Mason, Ohio • Chicago

Copyright © 2019 by Julie Weston
Map of craters of the moon, copyright © 2019 by Poo Wright-Pulliam
Five Star Publishing, a part of Gale, a Cengage Company

ALL RIGHTS RESERVED.
This novel is a work of fiction. Names, characters, places, and incidents are either the product of the author's imagination, or, if real, used fictitiously.

No part of this work covered by the copyright herein may be reproduced or distributed in any form or by any means, except as permitted by U.S. copyright law, without the prior written permission of the copyright owner.

The publisher bears no responsibility for the quality of information provided through author or third-party Web sites and does not have any control over, nor assume any responsibility for, information contained in these sites. Providing these sites should not be construed as an endorsement or approval by the publisher of these organizations or of the positions they may take on various issues.

LIBRARY OF CONGRESS CATALOGING-IN-PUBLICATION DATA

Names: Weston, Julie W., 1943- author.
Title: Moonscape : a Nellie Burns and Moonshine mystery / by Julie Weston.
Description: First edition. | Farmington Hills, Mich. : Five Star Publishing, a part of Gale, a Cengage Learning Company, 2019. | Series: A Nellie Burns and Moonshine mystery ; [#3]
Identifiers: LCCN 2018050004 (print) | LCCN 2018052055 (ebook) | ISBN 9781432858230 (ebook) | ISBN 9781432858223 (ebook) | ISBN 9781432858216 (hardcover)
Subjects: | GSAFD: Mystery fiction.
Classification: LCC PS3623.E872 (ebook) | LCC PS3623.E872 M659 2019 (print) | DDC 813/.6—dc23
LC record available at https://lccn.loc.gov/2018050004

First Edition. First Printing: June 2019
Find us on Facebook—https://www.facebook.com/FiveStarCengage
Visit our website—http://www.gale.cengage.com/fivestar/
Contact Five Star Publishing at FiveStar@cengage.com

Printed in Mexico
1 2 3 4 5 6 7 23 22 21 20 19

For Gerry and Melanie

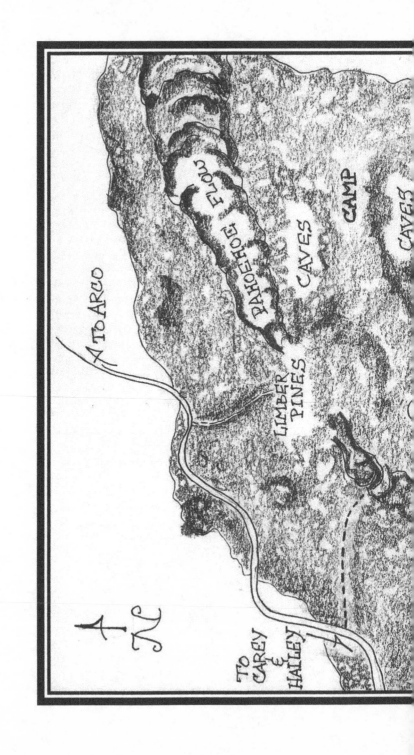

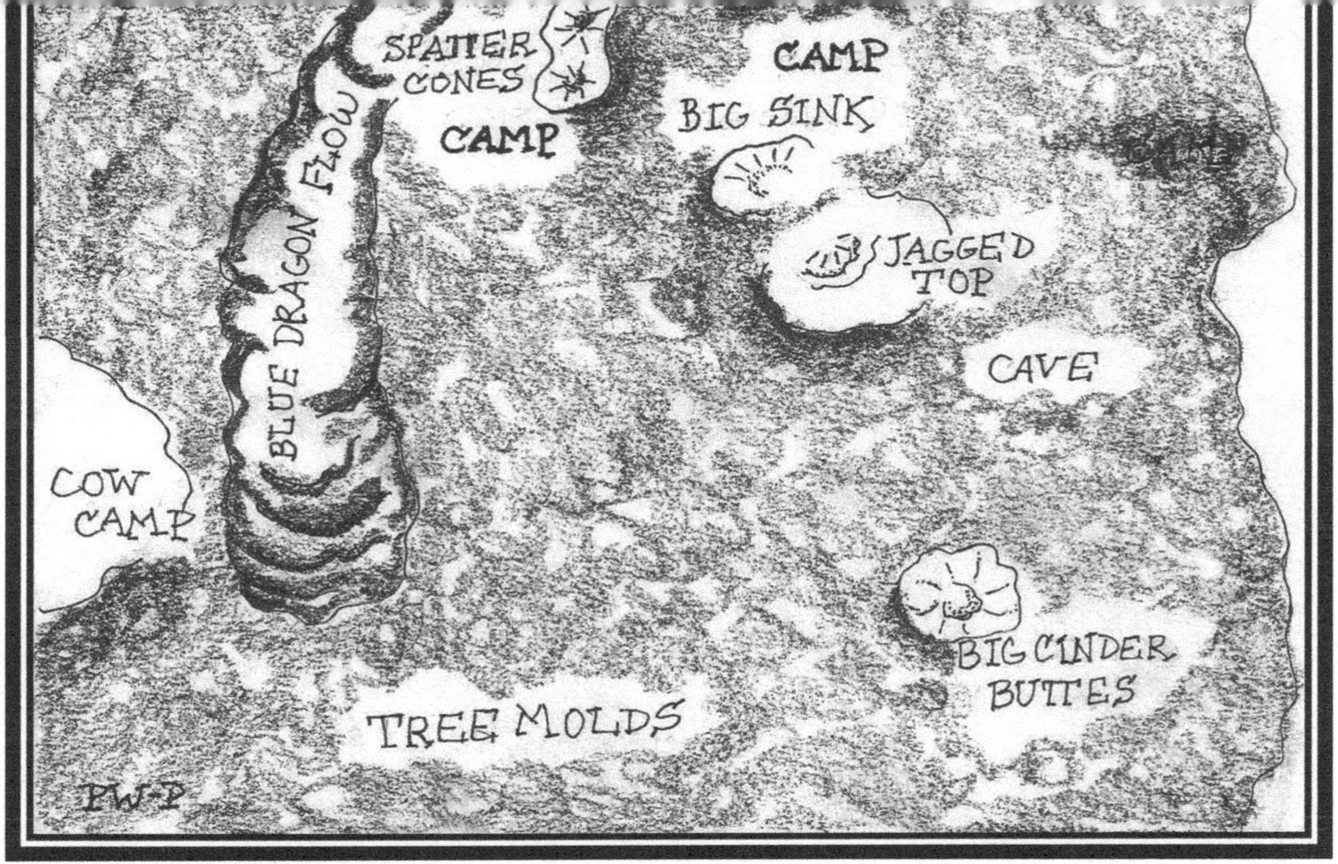
SPATTER CONES
CAMP
CAMP
BIG SINK
JAGGED TOP
CAVE
BLUE DRAGON FLOW
COW CAMP
BIG CINDER BUTTES
TREE MOLDS
PW-P

ACKNOWLEDGEMENTS

In southwest Idaho lie the strangest geologic remainders of thousands of years of lava flow found anywhere in the continental North America, known as "Craters of the Moon." For eons, these lands were unexplored except by indigenous peoples. After Europeans arrived in the area, their maps still contained the words "unknown" or "unexplored," as few people risked wandering into the twisted and contorted heaps of black lava and the forbidding tubes and caves, where roofs and walls might collapse at any time.

In 1920, R. W. Limbert and his fellow explorers traversed the area from south to north over two weeks, climbing into and out of caves, dropping down into spatter cones, and naming many of the formations. In 1924, Limbert penned an article published in *National Geographic:* "Among the 'Craters of the Moon': An Account of the First Expeditions Through the Remarkable Volcanic Lava Beds of Southern Idaho" (*National Geographic* Vol. XLV, no. 3, March 1924). That year as well, Calvin Coolidge designated Craters of the Moon as a national monument under the Antiquities Act (the same act that Theodore Roosevelt used to preserve other magnificent areas of the country, such as Devils Tower, Chaco Canyon, and others). In 2000, President William Clinton expanded the area included in the monument.

My husband and I have often visited Craters of the Moon, Gerry taking photographs and I noting birds and flowers and stepping carefully on the various kinds of lava. Even though we are familiar with many aspects of the Craters, it was Limbert's article that guided me while writing this book about the adventures of Nellie, Moonshine, Sheriff Azgo, and Rosy in this most forbidding of landscapes.

Limbert's article provided information about several of the caves and tunnels no longer accessible, and Todd Stefanic, wildlife biologist with the National Park Service at Craters of the Moon, National Monument and Preserve, furnished maps of several of the caves and a tunnel. The Regional History Department and Mary Tyson of The Community Library in Ketchum, Idaho, also assisted me with articles from both magazines and newspapers. I used my own imagination (and fears) for several aspects of the caves and the specific dangers of this moonscape. Once again, my husband, Gerry Morrison, helped with photography techniques and mechanics. Any errors in the geography, geology, and photography are mine. I should note that in 1969, NASA's Apollo astronauts learned basic volcanic geology here as they prepared for their moon missions.

As always, other writers and readers helped with my manuscript, including Belinda Anderson, Mary Bayley, Charlene Finn, John Rember, and Connie Loken. Their assistance and advice helped me continue the adventures of my characters in this one-of-a-kind wilderness. Poo Wright-Pulliam, birder extraordinaire and artist-in-residence at Craters, guided us on several explorations for birds and plants. Information I learned from her is also in this story. She is the artist who created the map included with this book, and she, too, used the Limbert map to inform her choices.

My thanks again to Tiffany Schofield and Five Star Publishing for choosing my Nellie Burns and Moonshine mystery and this story of a bleak landscape in Idaho. Hazel Rumney, once more, helped me solve several problems with my story, and her editorial savvy is much appreciated by me. Elizabeth Trupin-Pulli is my able agent and has been encouraging and helpful to me with this latest mystery.

My husband is still my first and last reader. I thank him, as well as my daughter, for patience and love during a difficult year of personal downs and ups and for always being there as my bulwark and support in my writing endeavors.

PROLOGUE

Long black cloaks shrouded the two women. The man with them blended in, his dark suit leavened only by a white shirt with a narrow black tie. Veils on the women's hats covered their eyes. The man's hat, also black, drooped low to shade his face. All three paused in front of a stone and mortar church, where a minister raked red and orange leaves off the sidewalk.

"Sir, we are looking for the lava fields." The man took off his hat. His voice rumbled in his chest. "We understand they are here in Arco, Idaho, but, so far, we have been unable to find them."

The minister leaned on his rake and studied the three people. "The lava lies out of town," he said, pointing west. "About a dozen miles or so—too far to walk. What do you want the lava fields for? Desolate country and not much to see except black cinders. Looks like someone's version of Hell if you ask me."

The man stood a good six inches taller than the priest. "We have God's work to do." He replaced his hat.

"In the lava fields?" The minister waved his hand. "What kind of God's work?" His face flushed.

"I am not at liberty to say," the man said. He turned to the women and made as if to walk away, one hand on the elbow of each. They were both small, but one was almost round while the other wore her clothes as if she had a broomstick hidden under the folds of the coat.

"If you want to know about the lava fields, you should talk to

Mayor Tom," the minister said. "He has spent considerable time there—even guided an explorers' party a couple years ago. You can find him at the livery—automobile garage—on Main Street." The minister gestured to the corner and then returned to raking, shaking his head.

At the gasoline station around the corner, the three dark spectres opened the door and stepped in. A barrel-shaped man stood looking out the window. There was no custom. "Sir, we are looking for the lava fields. A man in the next block said Mayor Tom could help us. Do you know where we can find him?" The man's voice had no softness to it, but he was polite enough.

"I'm Mayor Tom. What do you want to know? It's a stark place and no touring facilities, although that might change in the years to come. Word is, it might become a national monument because it is so strange. Nothing like it, except maybe on the moon." He motioned the two women to chairs against the wall. They remained on their feet. "Are you visiting here?"

"Are there roads or walking paths into the rocks? We want to visit the caves, and we've heard there are petrified trees. These aspects are of interest to us. Is any of the lava flowing?"

"There ain't no real road, but there is a wagon track part of the way. No auto could travel it. You'd have to leave yours and walk. That wouldn't be easy. I know some of the caves. I've been in most of them. I've seen the trees you mention, but they aren't petrified. They look like they were cast in hot rock. No lava flows any more, but there's plenty of cold lava of all kinds and some different colors. The blue lava is downright pretty."

Mayor Tom was curious about such a trio. He looked at their feet. "There's some Indian trails, but mostly the walking is over lava ropes and cinders. Your shoes wouldn't be suitable. When I helped a party in there a couple years ago, their poor dog's paws got cut up, and I doubt he ever walked the same again."

"God will guide us," the man said. The lumpier of the two women raised her hand to his sleeve. He shook her off. "Can you explain to me where the nearest caves are and also where the petrified trees can be found?"

"I can draw a rough map, but the trees ain't petrified, like I said." Mayor Tom shifted to the cash register desk and pulled out a wrinkled Idaho map. He opened it on the counter. "See here? This is the wagon track, right off the main road. You'd have to leave your auto there. Then you got to bushwhack through this area." He pointed with his finger. "To go from one area to another might take a whole day. The party I led was in there over two weeks."

One of the women followed with interest what he was saying and where he was pointing. The lumpier woman had seated herself in a chair and stared out the window. "Can one camp in this area?" the interested woman said. The man let the question stand.

"Wal, you can camp, but you might better take in water 'cause it's been damn . . . oops . . . darned dry this summer and fall. Sometimes, there's water at the bottom of some deep holes, but you can't count on it. It's gettin' cold at night now, too. You need tents or a lot of blankets." Mayor Tom began to fold up the map. "And leavin' your auto out on the roadway is a little chancy. Thieves and things. Some people don't want the lava fields to be a monument, so they make trouble when they can."

"I would like to buy this map from you," the man said.

"All I got. You can make a drawing of it, iffen you like, but I need the map. There's wild animals, too."

"What kind?"

"Mountain lions and bears. Coyotes, too, but mostly smaller stuff like marmots and porkypine. Some deer. They'll be attracted to any food you take, so wrap it up good and hang it on trees, if you can." He opened the map again and pointed to

15

another area. "Off past the lava, there are fields with cattle grazing. Don't fool with those, or you'll get the cattlemen after you."

A small noise came from the sitting woman. The man turned his head, and she lowered hers.

"Reckon I could guide you, if you like. I could even take you out and pick you up so's you could leave your auto here." So far, he hadn't seen an automobile, but he assumed they had one. They were strangers in town.

"No, we'll go on our own. Effie, would you copy out the part of the map he showed to us? I'll bring our automobile around, and we will travel to the lava fields." The man buttoned his top coat. "We'll be back in two days."

Mayor Tom walked outside with the man. He noticed the women consulting with each other as the one called Effie pulled paper from her bag and a writing tool and worked with the map. He waited outside until a dark automobile pulled up with the tall man driving. It was an older model, dusty, with dents here and there. The two women climbed into it, the plumper woman in back. The man almost shoved her past the front seat. Mayor Tom warned the trio again about needing water, but they drove away.

CHAPTER 1

Ever since Sheriff Charles Asteguigoiri engaged Nellie to be a crime photographer, she had taken few photos of anything other than people charged with petty crimes or automobile crashes. True, she was paid, but as there weren't many crimes or automobile crashes in Ketchum and Hailey, Idaho, she did not make much money. On the other hand, the photography provided a base line of income for her. Still, she was bored, feeling a cipher in a world where adventures shied away from her. Perhaps it was time to move on, to Twin Falls or Boise or even farther west. She liked working with Sheriff Azgo—everyone called him that or plain Charlie—but he was all business. She missed the earlier camaraderie they had shared. She missed Rosy, too.

On the days she devoted to portrait photography, she waited in the morning for customers. While she waited, she dusted, looked at earlier negatives that she had developed but not yet printed by holding them up to the window, and wandered around the room. A few leaves like gold coins in the morning sunlight dropped past her view outside. Rosy, her miner friend who had left to retrieve his sons in the East, was framed in a photo with his wife, Lily, who had died of a growth. It was not Nellie's photo, but she kept it on the piano that was used for a prop.

Mrs. Bock, her landlady at the boarding house, came in with a steaming pot of tea and two cups. "I have news," she said, as she poured and then sat down in the gossip chair. Nellie picked up a cup and perched on the piano bench. Moonshine, her black Labrador retriever, lay under the chair but only moved his feet and then went back to sleep.

"What news?"

"Rosy is on his way home with Matt and Campbell." Moonshine lifted his head to look at Nellie, then lay down again.

Nellie perked up. "Wonderful. I can hardly wait to see him and the boys, too." She glanced at the photo. "How old are they?"

"Let's see." Mrs. Bock pondered a moment and counted on her fingers. "I think Matt is eight and Campbell is six. About that."

"They're school age. Will they still live out at Last Chance Ranch?" She sipped the tea, savoring the aroma. Thinking of the boys in the deep snow of winter at the ranch was more than she could picture.

"No, they'll stay here at first until Rosy can find a place to live, probably in Hailey. He needs a job, too."

"I don't see how Rosy can cook, wash, and keep house, too. Who will take care of the boys while he works?" And what would he do, Nellie wondered. She doubted his former job at the mine office in Triumph would still be open.

"Rosy's sister is coming, too."

Both contemplated the addition of a new member of Rosy's family.

"Do you think—" They said at the same time. Nellie laughed. "Go ahead."

"Do you think he still drinks moonshine, was what I was going to ask," Mrs. Bock said.

"I was thinking the same thing!"

"I kind of doubt it," Mrs. Bock said. "Where would he get it back East?"

"If he was in Chicago, it would have been no difficulty at all."

Nellie heard the front door open. Maybe a customer?

A throat clearing and then Sheriff Azgo appeared in the studio door. "Good morning. Ladies." He removed his Stetson and held it in his hand. A hint of a smile crossed his face, lighting up his dark visage. His black hair was creased where the hat had rested.

"Well, I gotta get back to my baking," Mrs. Bock said. She nodded and retrieved the teapot and left. Moonshine crawled out from under the gossip chair and sat by Nellie's side.

"Good morning, Sheriff. Do you need photographs? There isn't exactly a line-up of customers." Nellie placed her cup on the piano. "Or maybe you would like a portrait."

"No. No, I need more than just a photograph. I am traveling to the lava fields, past Carey, and I would like you to come with me. There is a . . . situation there that may need your expertise. I will not know until we get there." His Basque accent had lessened over time, but his formal style of language had not. He turned serious again.

"Lava fields?"

"Some call them Craters of the Moon, near Arco. People think they appear like the moon does upon closer study. Instead of white, the rocks are black lava. Several tourers are missing out there. It is not my county, but there is no sheriff in Butte County, so the federal marshal asked me to go and find out what I can."

"All right. Sounds interesting. I'll pack up my camera and tripod. I assume the photographs will be outdoors?" She stood up. Moonie yawned. "How far is it?"

"Yes, outdoors but possibly in caves." He paused and looked around. "We may be camping out. And we will be hiking unless I can locate some horses."

Nellie shivered. Caves. It was turning to fall, and the nights were cold. "What about a tent for me?" She began packing clothes in her mind—boots, sweater, pants, jacket. "I can be ready in about an hour. Can we bring Moonshine? Shall I ask Mrs. Bock to pack food for us? Will there be a place to eat?"

Sheriff Azgo's lips curved again, maybe a slight smile. "Yes, see if Goldie will pack a couple of sandwiches. I am not sure what we can get in Carey or Arco. I expect someone from Arco will be there to guide us into the area. I will return for you, as soon as I telephone the marshal." At the door, he turned back. "I think your dog might chase animals, which would not be good."

After he left, Nellie packed up her Premo camera and tripod and closed the studio. She hurried to her room upstairs, changed, and rounded up extra clothes in a satchel, then went to the kitchen to tell Mrs. Bock of her plans.

"Is this safe?" Her landlady had taken to acting like Nellie's mother.

"Oh, I'm sure it is. I'll be with the sheriff."

Mrs. Bock sniffed. "I'll pack a couple of ham sandwiches and cookies and potato salad. I had planned ham and salad for dinner. You may as well take some. Where you gonna stay?"

Nellie shrugged. "I think we'll be camping out."

Mrs. Bock struggled with a smile that turned into a grin. "Not sure that's safe."

"I think it will be." Nellie tried not to show her disappointment. The sheriff had been all business, as usual.

Back in the studio, she wavered about flash materials. They were bulky and hard to use. Better take enough for three or four photos in caves.

The sheriff's automobile was cozy and comfortable. After an argument, the sheriff agreed Moonshine could accompany them, as long as he was on a leash or stayed in the auto. The drive to the lava fields didn't take long—about two hours. Along the way, the landscape changed from sagebrush and rabbitbrush, some of which was still in yellow bloom, to harvested fields with golden stubble and a few farm buildings. They left the mountains around Hailey behind them and motored along flatter and flatter country. The white rock Lost River Range towered over a valley to the north, but lower mountains bare of trees and wrinkled like army blankets served as a backdrop to the sage. Buttes dotted the landscape as they neared the lava, which indeed was black rock that lay twisted and humped like an imagined moonscape. Black stacks stood out like chimneys from an underground world. Nellie looked forward to taking photos of the rocks, if nothing else. Unfortunately, foot travel looked to be strenuous and time-consuming, but, worse, painful. Bringing her dog was not a good idea.

Just as the sheriff said, a man in an auto waited. There were no horses.

"Two women and a man left Arco, saying they'd be back in two days," the man told them as he stepped out. "That was five days ago. We don't know if they went away in another direction, but I thought I should report them gone to the marshal. This area is about to become a national monument, so I figgered that was the right place to call. 'Course, there's a big fight about it becoming a monument."

"Why so?" the sheriff asked.

"No more grazing." The man swept his arm in a wide arc. "Cattlemen are up in arms. So is Arco."

"And who are you?" Nellie asked, since the sheriff didn't seem like he would.

"I'm the mayor, I guess you'd say. Mayor Tom. Someone had to take the job. Soon as I find another fool, I'll quit."

"What are we here to see?" The sheriff gestured toward the inky landscape.

21

"First off, you should see their auto. It's down the wagon trail a ways. Then, thought I'd show you some caves. That's what the folks said they wanted to see. I showed 'em a map. It's a bit of a walk and darned easy to get lost." He scratched his head full of ginger hair, grabbed a hat, and closed the auto door. He eyed the dog. "On an expedition through here a couple years ago, the dog we took hurt its feet real bad."

Nellie looked at Moonie, glanced at the sheriff and back at the dog, who sat waiting on the ground. Wrong decision. "How long will we be?"

"I'd guess an hour or two to get there and same to get back."

"Bring him. If his paws get scraped, I will carry him. Or make coverings from my handkerchief." The sheriff opened the boot.

Nellie pulled out her pack and donned the straps so the pack was carried on her back. The sheriff went to take it, but she shook her head. Her camera, her pack. "Ready."

They walked first along a rough wagon road where the parties' auto sat tilted in a rut. The men looked it over, and then the three of them and Moonshine trudged up and down lava flows, picking their way. It was like walking over broken dishware half the time, slipping and sliding on rock or cinders, as if they were hiking along a coal bin, and the other half on an easier surface, but one with hills and slopes and treacherous footing. The sheriff and Mayor Tom conversed as the sheriff asked questions about the missing trio. The mayor didn't know much, only that one woman's name was Effie and they were religious, but he didn't know what religion. "Could be a regular one or an irregular one," he said. "We got lots of both around."

Nellie would have liked to stop and take photographs but knew that would have to wait. She spent most of her time being careful where she placed her boots. She regretted not permitting the sheriff to take her pack and regretted bringing

Moonshine. So far, though, he seemed to move across the lava better than the three humans. When they approached an area with many trees, "limber pines" Mayor Tom called them, she wanted to stop and rest, but the men kept walking.

After almost two hours from where they left the autos, the mayor—who was more agile than Nellie would have supposed, as he was wide but compact with thin legs and arms—stopped. He stepped off the narrow trail they had been following and led them to what appeared to be a cave entrance in the lava. A rock fall led to the opening and climbing down across the chunks looked difficult but not impossible. Moonshine circled the opening and tentatively stepped down a few of the rocks. He sniffed and then barked.

"That's it?" she asked. "That's a cave?"

"Don't look like much, do it? Still, once you get in there, it opens up." Mayor Tom stepped carefully around rocks and brush. "There's more. They might've gone to another one up the way but could've stopped here. I marked several on the diagram they drew from my map." He ducked to go in but turned his head back. "Kinda smelly down here."

"Tie Moonshine to the boulder over there," the sheriff said. "We do not know what we will find here."

Nellie did as instructed. The sheriff followed the mayor readily, but Nellie wasn't so sure. Dark, tight spaces had no appeal to her, reminding her of the horror house at a carnival. Once she had been stuck in a darkened room with floors that angled every which way, unable to find the path out. She called and screamed, and, eventually, someone came to get her. Embarrassed and frightened, she left the carnie and never returned. The rocks leading to the dark hole suggested heavy going to her, even with boots on.

"Wait for me," she called to the sheriff. When she had clambered down, she grabbed his arm. "I'll just keep hold," she said. He didn't shake her off, and she vowed to herself not to scream.

The air was dry, and a moldy, dank basement smell hung around the entrance. Mayor Tom had a flashlight, as did the sheriff. Their lights helped to dispel Nellie's nervousness. The mayor crouched low under a rocky overhang and waddled forward and then disappeared. Sheriff Azgo took Nellie's hand and said, "Hang on to my belt." He crouched, as did Nellie, and both squat-walked past the overhang. Around a sharp corner, they stepped into a large space lit close around them by Mayor Tom's flashlight, but midnight dark around the edges. They cast huge shadows. As near as Nellie could tell, the space was half the size of her studio in Mrs. Bock's house. They could stand upright. The smell worsened and hung like fog in the cave. The floor was the smoother kind of lava they had just covered, but with piles of rocks here and there.

It was then Nellie saw a bundle of clothes at the rocky, dark edge. It moved as she watched. She screamed—not loud and long, but still a scream. The sheriff looked to where she pointed. He and Mayor Tom strode to the bundle. The sheriff turned it over, and a small creature dashed away. There lay a body, its shadowed face eaten half away, and dried, black blood clamping its neck.

CHAPTER 2

Sheriff Azgo and Mayor Tom dragged the body outside, because, even with the flashlights, it was too dark in the cave to inspect it and take photos. Nellie preceded them, pulling herself up the rocky entrance and then setting up her camera after she made certain Moonshine was secure. She had seen a number of dead people, but none as mauled as this one was. She wasn't even sure if it was a man or a woman at first, but, outside, she could see pant legs under the coat and men's shoes, and shoes they were, damaged with the soles bent and scratched and the leather torn. The clothes were ripped and pulled, but the animal had not succeeded in getting to the flesh, except around the face and head. The eyes were gone, as was the nose and most of both cheeks. One ear dangled. The hair was so matted with dried blood, she couldn't tell what color it was.

The sheriff was matter of fact as he examined the body. Nellie tried to act the same way, but she struggled to keep herself steady as she focused, inserted the film holder into the camera, pulled out the black slide, and released the shutter to expose the film. Judging by the pale color of Mayor Tom's otherwise ruddy face, she suspected he was struggling, too. The rotting odor was not as strong as in the cave, but, still, she fought not to gag.

"I need you to get as close as possible, Miss Burns. Can you do that?" The sheriff had placed the body face up and lifted the head a little to situate it on a stone. "He appears to have been hit with a heavy instrument, but sometimes we see something more in your photos that we miss with our eyes." He paused while Nell took the photo. "Good. Now come around to the top side, and then we will try the back."

As Nellie followed his instructions, she calmed down. This was police work. What did she expect? The surface upon which she set her tripod caused some difficulty. She spent time steadying it before she could take a photo. After the head, she photographed the clothed body front and back and then the shoes. She winced as the sheriff probed the man's face and head. She turned away, stopping to rub Moonie's head. He didn't seem bothered at all, although he sniffed the air several times. Mayor Tom sat on a boulder with his face turned toward the lumpy expanse of lava. An afternoon breeze rustled the sparse amber grasses, and small black pebbles skittered past. A chipmunk peeked out from behind a piece of lava and then dropped out of sight. Moonie saw it and strained at his leash.

"All right, Mayor Tom. We need to take this body to Hailey. There is a morgue, of sorts. Any ideas how we do that?" The sheriff walked to where Tom sat.

"That's the man who came into my station, Sheriff. I recognize his clothes. I can round up a stretcher in Arco or Carey and perhaps a crew of men. All we'd have is a truck bed. Maybe someone in Hailey can figure out that part." Tom stood, while Nellie slid her tripod closed. "At the same time, mebbe I can get their auto moved back to my station in Arco."

"What about the two women? Do you suppose they're still around and in the same shape?" she asked.

"It is too late to search more today," the sheriff said, "and get this body to town." Tom nodded his head. "Maybe the best bet is to move the body back to that area with pines that we passed. Think we can do that, Tom?"

Tom scratched his head and sighed. "Guess we could. Sure

would make it easier for whoever comes with a stretcher, not to have to climb over all this lava here." He leaned over the body. "The man's coat looks big enough to carry him that far."

Nellie stayed to one side while the sheriff covered the man's head and rearranged the coat. He and Tom managed to lift the body using the coat as a hammock and began the task of transporting him. She had no intention of offering to help. She released Moonshine and followed, barely able to keep her own balance. Watching her feet helped her lose the images of the man's face. The lava was a myriad of colors, not just black: burnt red, pale gray, sometimes green or yellow with lichen. Before long, they were back among the limber pine. Both men sweated profusely. "Stuck pigs" was Nellie's thought, echoing Rosy's one-time description.

"Let us head back to the road," the sheriff said. He swabbed his face and neck with a red handkerchief. "Nellie, would you wait and see that the body is not disturbed again? I am glad now that we have your dog. I will get back as soon as possible with our camping gear," the sheriff said and looked at Tom, "along with water and food. We can search tomorrow, if, Mayor Tom, you will give us more directions for where else we might look. Or come and join us."

Stay alone? With that body? Nellie shuddered. This was much worse than staying with a dead man in an abandoned cabin in the night—one she thought then had frozen to death. Even with Moonshine, she did not like the prospect. "Couldn't we put rocks around it or something so no animal can get to it again? I think I'd rather come with . . . with you." It wasn't only the maimed body that bothered her. "What about bears or mountain lions?" She looked at Mayor Tom. "Would they attack me?"

"Normally, I'd say not, but with this body here . . . It ain't exactly . . . fresh."

"If the dog is with you, I doubt you will be bothered. I can leave my gun. I think you know how to use one, as I remember." The sheriff's face relaxed from its stern visage. "At least enough to scare anything off. I and a crew should be back before it gets dark." He turned as if there were no question she would stay. "And you can take photographs of the scenery." The sheriff fiddled with the man's coat again, so that the gnawed face was fully covered, and then handed his revolver to her. She stuck it in her jacket pocket. "See you in a while." He and the mayor headed back the way they had come.

Nellie waved. She set up her tripod again and placed the camera on top. Moonshine lay in the shade of a pine. She might as well see what kind of photos she could take. The sun was still high, and her surroundings were mostly dark, although the limber pine lightened the background and danced whenever the wind blew. "Let's scout around, Moonie. As long as we don't go too far, the . . . the body should be all right, for now."

They traveled a hundred yards east, along ground that was crumbled lava and flat, rather than the waves of lava farther out. Then Nellie spied a long stretch of smooth lava and climbed onto it. A deep crack cut the surface, each side with a raggedy edge matching the opposite. Inside the crack, the darkness was complete. In the distance she saw where the ground rose to a large cone, covered with dried brush and bright red hanging leaves, ready to drop with the slightest push. Along the ground extended a series of small, purple flowers, low and out of the wind. Bunchgrass turned gold grew near the pines, so Nellie sat down with her legs stretched out in front of her. She studied the whole area from her resting place, trying to visualize photographs. Maybe later in the afternoon, there would be shadows to make the vistas more interesting. Right now, the cone and a faraway butte and surrounding rocks would not have much definition on her film. She decided to stay nearer the body, but not too close. She moved and found a rock out-cropping to lean against.

The afternoon sun and the quiet surroundings lulled Nellie to a doze, even sitting up. She was startled awake by Moonie's deep-throated growl. "What is it?" Nell scrambled up. She pulled the sheriff's gun from her jacket and called Moonshine. She was still a ways from the dead man, so she hurried closer to it. Still, nothing. Moonshine's growl grew deeper, and then he began to bark.

A horse and man appeared from the east, walking from around a series of boulders. The man wore a Stetson, a red flannel shirt, and chaps. He led the horse closer to Nell.

"Howdy, Miss. I thought I saw several people up yonder so trotted over to see what was going on." He leaned forward in a friendly way. "Is your pooch gonna attack?"

"No, my dog won't attack unless you come after me."

"Better watch my step, then." The man winked at her. "I'm Ben O'Donnell. I'm with a herd of cattle back beyond the lava fields."

Nell glanced past him but could see only the black rock she was getting too familiar with. Some distance away, another rider waited, it appeared. Too far away to identify, she thought there was something familiar about the way the person sat the horse.

"What are you doing out here? You look like you're all by yourself—except for that dog there."

"I'm Nell Burns." She glanced over at the body, looking like a dead black crow in its shroud. "Are you related to a rancher up north?"

"That's my pa. He owns all the cattle out this way and up there, too." He let the reins drop. "Mind if I join you?"

Nell wasn't sure if she minded or not. Moonie wasn't either. He barked once and then backed up to stand in front of her. "No. Maybe you have some water with you?" If she was thirsty, so was her dog. "Is that other rider with you?"

A frown crossed his face, and then he smiled. He didn't look back. The cowboy untied a canteen from the horse. "Sure thing. Take a swig, and I'll pour some onto that lava over there a ways for your dog. It won't soak in there." He reached out with the canteen. "That's a wrangler who comes from up north some-times."

Nellie kept Moonie in front of her, took the canteen, unscrewed the top, and took a long draught and handed it back. "Thank you." The cowboy walked over to a small depression in the lava and poured a small amount. Moonshine immediately slurped it up.

"You know my pa?" The cowboy kept his distance.

"Cable O'Donnell? Yes. I met him this last summer—up in the Stanley Basin. I was with several sheep herders." She thought she would get that out early, so he might leave. Dealing with strangers didn't appeal to her after her adventures in the Basin. She had shoved the gun back into her jacket when the horse and man appeared. She walked over to her camera on its tripod. "I would like to take your photograph up on your horse. Would you mind?"

The cowboy studied the camera and then Nell. Then he glanced around and seemed to see the shroud for the first time. "What's that?"

"A dead person. Sheriff Azgo and I and a man from Arco found it in the cave over there. The sheriff is going after some men to help take the body back to town." She fiddled with her camera and placed her black cloth on her head. "They'll be back soon." She had a good view of the cowboy, upside down. He walked toward her, so she pulled the cloth off.

"I don't want my pitcher taken." Moonie again placed himself between the cowboy and Nellie. He growled when the man stepped closer. "Oops, sorry, pooch. I just don't like my pitcher taken." He stepped back and then walked over to the dead man.

"Don't touch it." The sheriff would not want the body disturbed.

"Who is it?"

"We don't know. Someone who came through Arco almost a week ago." Nellie wasn't sure how much information to give out.

"Are you that pitcher lady that caused all the trouble in the Basin around the fourth of July?" He stayed by the body.

"I am a photographer. I didn't cause any trouble. It was other people who caused the problems. I only took photos."

He leaned down. This time, Moonshine jumped across the space between the dead man and Nellie, barking. "Thought I might know him," he said but stepped back.

"When did you see the people around here? Today?" She wanted to distract him and gestured back toward where she, the sheriff, and Mayor Tom had found the body.

"This morning but saw some several days back. I had my hands full with the cattle. There'd been a thunderstorm in the afternoon, and they was nervous. I saw what looked like three or four people up here then but figured they was some of the Indians from nearby or prospectors or somethin'."

Nellie said nothing. She wondered how much Mr. O'Donnell had told his son about the summer's doings—the sheep herding, the moonshiners, the dead Basque. This man made Moonie nervous and therefore made her jumpy. The sheriff had been gone quite a while. She wished he would make his appearance. The ground over which he had retreated was filled with swales and valleys, so she could not see him from a distance, even if he were there. The afternoon shadows lengthened.

"May I take a photo of your horse? He's a beauty." She walked over to where the horse's reins dropped to the ground and patted the horse's nose.

"Want to take a ride?" Ben turned toward Nellie and seemed to lose interest in the body.

"No, I want a photograph. The scene with the horse and that dead snag would be a nice one. Better without the saddle, of course." Nellie bit her tongue. She didn't want to keep him there any longer than necessary. She felt braver alone, even if there were wild animals around.

"How did he die?" The cowboy gestured toward the dark bundle.

"That's something for the sheriff to determine," she said. To divert him, Nellie lifted her camera and tripod and stepped closer to the horse, working around to get the snag off to one side. It was an old tree, gnarled and crooked, as if it had weathered in place for eons. The remains of what might have been a bird's nest hung from the joint between two lengths of branches. The gray and textured wood advertised its age. As she moved, so did the horse. Moonie kept pace with Nell. "Whoa, now." She turned back to Ben. "Could you keep him still, please? I'll tell you when I'm ready, and you can step out of the scene to one side."

The cowboy did as asked and stepped away when Nell motioned. When she was finished, he took the reins in his hands. "I'll be off," he said. He raised his Stetson, guided the horse in a turn, and left without another word. The horse stumbled once, and the cowboy turned back to stare at Nell. She was afraid he would come back, but he continued and met up with the other rider. Nellie felt a sense of relief even though he hadn't actually threatened her. The riders both moved away and soon disappeared behind the lava structures.

CHAPTER 3

Voices preceded the appearance of several men. Maybe the cowboy had heard them coming and she had not. Two of the men had a canvas stretcher slung between them. It looked like an awkward burden. She walked forward to greet the sheriff. Moonshine stayed by her side and did not bark or growl. He was the same color as most of the lava and could blend almost to being invisible. She wondered about a photo that would show only his teeth and eyes like a Cheshire cat. Another time.

Sheriff Azgo carried a pack on his back and a bag that she hoped was food. Two canteens were slung in opposite directions around his chest.

"I'm glad you're back," she said after he introduced the other men. Their names immediately slipped her mind. "We're thirsty!"

The sheriff deposited his pack and other gear near the wood snag and handed Nell a canteen. She drank from it and poured water out in a lava depression for her dog. The men and the sheriff lifted the dead man onto the stretcher, and one of them circled the body with narrow rope so it wouldn't fall off on the trip back.

After the stretcher group left, Nell asked the sheriff: "Was it difficult to find help?"

"No, Mayor Tom rounded up the men and stretcher and called Hailey to come get the body. He arranged for these fellows to push the automobile to the road and get it to Arco, so it should be safe there. I can look at it later." He held up a sack. "I have the rest of Goldie's food here and some additional offerings from Tom. He will return in the morning to help out." The sheriff sat down on one of the boulders. "How did you get along? Any photos? See anyone or any animals?"

"I didn't get many—the light was too harsh. I did have a visitor." Nell pointed toward where the riders had disappeared. "You won't believe who it was! Cable O'Donnell's son, Ben. He said he's with some cattle over yonder." She tried to see if she could see the two people on horseback. "Another rider stayed back. He didn't come close enough to talk to."

"Hmm. Did he say why they had come? I think it is strange that cowboys would leave their herd, although the weather is calm, and few animals prey in the daytime." He frowned. "The cattle must be quite a distance. This lava extends a long way."

"He said he saw people here this morning—presumably us. He also said he saw people here a few days ago. He wanted to look at the body, but I cautioned him not to touch it." She joined the sheriff and sat on a rock nearby. "Moonshine didn't like him, but maybe he was only protecting me." She looked around. "Now where did he go? I let him off his leash when he growled as the cowboy rode up."

"He will show up when I get the fire started and food begins to smell good." The sheriff raised himself with effort. His boots were scuffed and dirty, and he looked tired. "One of the men helped us move the auto to the road and then drove it back to Arco to Tom's station."

"I hope the women don't return and find it gone." Nellie worried that thought for a moment, then stood up. "I can get wood. Why don't you work on our shelter?" Nell hoped there were two tents. She wasn't prepared to share one with this man—not yet, at any rate. And not while they were looking for what might be murderers. "Can we stop with the 'sheriff' and

'Miss Burns' titles, now that no one else is around?" She left him.

There were plenty of dried wood and rocks, so it took little time to find a likely fire pit and circle it with stones. She had helped with a number of camps in July and felt practiced enough to do her share as evening drew in. She stowed her camera and tripod under a tree for protection if it rained, which was not likely in the arid, stars-beginning-to-appear late evening.

A short distance away, Charlie Azgo erected one tent on a patch of dry, dusty ground. Closer to the fire, he spread out a sleeping bag and settled his pack next to it. The tent appeared to be the same one Nellie had used in the Stanley Basin when she stayed at a sheep camp for a couple of weeks. This ground looked much harder, but, if Charlie could sleep outdoors on it, she could make do in the tent. Their surroundings conjured up nightmares of rocky shapes and swirls in the evening shadows. The setting sun turned the red shades to vermilion and yellow lichen to brilliant green. Her film could not show the colors, but the shapes could be outlined against the still-light sky. Nellie retrieved her camera and tripod and set up quickly to see what she could capture. While she moved around to change angles, Moonshine trotted up to her.

"Where have you been, Moonie?" She placed the black cloth over her head.

The dog made a strange mewling cry, so she pulled off the cloth to look at him. "Oh dear! What's in your mouth?" She squatted down and in the light from the campfire could see a multitude of what looked like needles stuck in his nose. Moonie cried again.

"Charlie, Moonshine's hurt. He got into something." Nell wrapped her arms around the dog's chest to keep him close but kept his face clear of her shoulder. He was in such obvious pain, she began to cry, too. "What did you do?"

Charlie jumped up from where he was squatting by the fire and rushed over. Then he laughed.

"It's not funny! He's in awful pain."

"Moonshine tangled with a porcupine. He will have learned a painful lesson. I have pliers I can use to take out the quills. That will hurt, too, but we need to get them, so they will not work their way deeper." He circled over to his pack, dug into it, and came back with pliers. "Hold him steady."

Such a round of grunts from the sheriff and cries from the dog, Nellie wanted to close her ears. She held the dog instead and tried to soothe him. In all, there were at least a dozen white quills in a pile when Charlie finished. "Now," he said. "I have some jerky for you, Moonshine. That will make you feel better."

He fetched a cloth wet down from his canteen and held it over Moonie's nose and face, rubbed some salve on him, and then handed him the jerky. Moonshine ate it with gusto and then curled by the fire, next to Nellie, who was dishing out beans and biscuits that Charlie had cooked. The two of them had eaten most of Goldie's sandwiches earlier, and Nellie was hungry. They ate without talking, filling inner needs first.

After Nell scraped the last bit of beans off the tin plate, she said, "I guess we need to keep him on a leash. I'm sorry I insisted on bringing him. He would have been better off with Goldie—and Rosy and the boys when they arrive."

Charlie looked over at her. "Rosy is returning?"

"Oh, I forgot to tell you in the rush of leaving. He, his sister, and Matt and Campbell are due in shortly on the train." Nellie wanted to bite off her tongue. Mrs. Bock—Goldie—should have told the sheriff first. He had a special interest in the boys, or at least one of them. Blurting it out by accident was stupid, if not hurtful, and probably that, too. "I'm sorry. That is what Mrs. Bock was telling me when you came to the boarding house."

Charlie nodded, his face a mask in the firelight. He gathered both their plates, used sand to wipe them clean, and stacked them to one side with the pot he had used to cook. "Once a sheepherder, always a sheepherder," he said, as much under his breath as aloud. He turned to her. "I will sleep by the fire and keep it going during the night. The tent is for you. The flashlight is by my bag if you wish to use it in the dark." He walked off into the night. "Take Moonshine into the tent with you," he called back.

As tired as she was, Nellie stayed by the fire ring until Charlie returned. Stars sprinkled the darkening sky and soon lit up with shining lights, a field of glitter. No moon stole their thunder; only the dwindling fire competed.

"Why aren't you in the tent?"

"I wanted to talk." She was silent for a few minutes, trying to think of what to talk about. The murder, obviously. "Do you think this murder is part of a religious ritual?" she asked. Charlie didn't answer for a long stretch. The flickering flame tongues seemed to mesmerize both of them.

"I do not know. There was nothing that seemed ritualistic about the man's death. I would guess he was killed in anger, pounded by a piece of lava or heavy stone. Until I see the report . . ." He shrugged. "And your photos."

An ember in the fire dropped, and sparks flew up and then faded.

"What about Matt?" There. She had waded into deep water where she didn't belong. Last winter, she had learned Matt, the older boy, was actually the sheriff's from an almost-elopement with Lily, later Rosy's wife.

More silence.

"He is Rosy's son." Both stared into the fire. The last flames disappeared, and red embers like rubies shifted again. "When I left the valley, I left in a rage. I thought I would show Lily's father, Gwynn Campbell, I was more than a sheepherder. I

37

would make my way and come back for Lily."

Nell waited and poked at the fire with a stick. A flame licked up from a half-burned branch. The yellow light lit Charlie's face, frozen into a mask of tragedy.

"I cut sagebrush, loaded railroad cars, worked as a clerk, and saved my money. I made enough with odd jobs to attend school and then a police academy out of state. I heard from no one about Lily, and told no one where I was. I came back when I heard Hailey wanted a deputy. By then, Rosy and Lily were married, and Matt was born. Rosy did what I should have done—protected and cared for Lily." Charlie's recital contained no emotion. It was as if he had said the facts over and again many times, and it had become a litany to himself if to no other.

Only the sounds from the fire filled the silence. Nellie didn't think Charlie would say any more. She wasn't sure how to respond. "I left, too," Nellie said. "But I left because I didn't want to get married—unlike Lily."

"You left a . . . a man?"

"There was no one to leave, except my mother." She would not mention the man killed in the war. He had been married to another. "I left to find a different future than one tied to a man, any man. I wanted—do want—to lead my own life, make my own way, see what I am capable of doing." She wanted to say "like you did" but did not and did not add "alone." Everyone she met in Idaho, including Charlie, thought she should get married, settle down, be a wife and mother. Not for her.

Charlie added the word: "Alone?"

She didn't answer. Charlie stood and added more branches to the fire. "Time for sleep. Tomorrow won't be any easier than today."

Nellie pulled herself up. "I wonder what tomorrow will bring. Good night, Charlie." She could find her way to the tent by starlight.

"Thank you, Nellie, for your work today."

So tired, she could hardly walk, Nellie was still gratified. The sheriff rarely expressed a word of thanks. At the tent flap, she stopped and looked up. She wished she were sleeping outside so she could watch the sky. It was awash with a universe of milky star clouds and studded constellations. It would be impossible to count them or even to try. The leftover sky was black as a raven's wing and surrounded her, wrapping her in ink. The significance of their travails today, their dreams, their sorrows, their needs—all faded to naught, even as she herself was caught up and swept away in the beauty of the night.

Moonshine trying to creep out under the tent flap woke Nellie up. She hadn't slept well, and her back ached. She also needed to find a private spot. Her clothes were inside her sleeping bag with her, so she pulled them out. At least they weren't cold. The sun was not quite up, but a pink blush covered the eastern edge of the sky and even tinged some of the rocky cone tops. The sheriff's bag was rolled up, and there was no sign of him. She gathered up Moonie's leash and clipped it on his collar. "Come on, Moonie. Let's find a place that is hidden."

Nell found a secluded glen and did her business, then returned to camp and met the sheriff returning from the opposite direction—from the cave. "Did you go down into the cave again?"

"Yes. No light reaches it, but I looked as carefully as I could with the flashlight. I could see no sign of anyone in there but us and the body. We may have tracked over prints from someone or something else. There were a couple of canine prints near the edge, so it was probably a coyote that ate on the man. A green branch had been leaning against the outside of the cave, one that would not have fallen there naturally." He pointed. "All the green is here."

"So someone tried to hide the entrance?"

"That is my guess. Or brushed away any tracks. Mayor Tom said he pointed out the caves to the travelers, so trying to hide the entrance does not make sense, unless someone else came along."

"Or someone didn't want anyone to find the . . . the man. That cowboy said he saw people up this way. Maybe we should find him and ask how many he saw."

Charlie nodded. His mind seemed to be on something else. He made no move to follow up on Nell's suggestion.

"If we are going to search farther out, we should eat and move along. Speaking of Tom, is he coming back?" Nellie hoped he was. They could get lost forever in the twists and turns of lava and the ups and downs of the landscape. "Do you have a compass in that grab-bag of yours?" She smiled so the sheriff would know she was joking. He was such a serious man.

"I always have a compass." At last, he smiled, too. "Biscuits and gravy for breakfast?"

While they were eating, sounds of someone coming from the direction of the road, not from the fields, reached them. Soon Mayor Tom appeared. He held the reins of a horse with lumpy side saddles. Nell looked to see if it wore shoes, and it did.

"Hiya spelunkers!" He waved and tied the reins to a branch. "Thought we could use a horse, if for no other reason than to carry one of us out if we got tired bushwhacking or slipping and sliding over the *pahoehoe*." Tom rubbed his hands together. "Brought water and rope and a few odds and ends."

Nellie laughed. "I might need the horse today! Or Moonshine might. He had a run-in with a porcupine yesterday." Moonshine lifted his head. He had not been lively that morning, and no wonder—his muzzle was swollen. "What is *pahoehoe*?" She mimicked Tom's pronunciation: *pahoyhoy*.

"That's the smooth, ropy looking lava. Hawaiian word. The

rough, cinder type rock is *a'a*. It's the hardest to travel on, and, with this horse, I need to avoid it." He leaned down to pet the dog. "More than one dog gets into a porcupine around here. And they don't never learn. Best to keep him on the leash. How're his feet?" He picked up one to look. "Not bad. I brought some leather shields in case he needs them." He pulled these from his pocket and slipped one on Moonshine's left front paw and tied it tight.

That endeared Mayor Tom to Nellie Burns forever.

While Tom tied on three more shields, he talked. "Sheriff, I heard from the morgue in Hailey this morning. Is that at the jail or at a hospital?"

"Neither. It is a separate, iced area in a meatpacking location."

Nellie turned to him. She didn't know about the "morgue," even though she had known someone who had stolen a body from it. She wrinkled her nose.

"Anyway, the man who called said it looked like the body had been beaten pretty badly, maybe with a rock or some hard instrument. He said it was hard to tell because of the animal chewing . . ." Tom looked at Nellie. "Sorry, uh, Miss Burns."

"I am a crime photographer," she said. "I have seen worse." Although she hadn't.

Tom continued, ". . . because of the animal chewing off his face. There were marks on his body, too, but he thought the man died from blunt trauma, he said." He waited a space. "Sure looked like that to me. I figured either a coyote or a bear might'a done the chewing." Again, he glanced at Nellie. "Sorry."

Nellie packed up her camera gear. "Let's go. Where are we going?"

"There's more lava tubes not far from here—caves like we seen already. The lava cooled on top, but the hot stuff kept going underneath and left those tubes. Some caved in, but not all of 'em did." He loosened the horse's reins and walked south. "Follow me."

Mayor Tom led, followed by the sheriff, with Nellie and Moonshine in the rear. Because the horse tended to pick its way, their cavalcade moved slowly, but Nellie didn't care. That gave her time to pick her own way and also to take in the scenery. To the west she saw what looked like miniature volcanoes, but no fire or smoke emitted from them. Everywhere she saw globular shaped rocks on the ground in various sizes. Tom identified those as lava bombs—lava that had blown out of the spatter cones, the forms that were volcano shaped, but smaller.

"Just imagine what it looks like in Hawaii, where the lava still flows. You've seen pictures from there, haven't you?"

"I suppose I have, but a long time ago. I never would have thought there would be anything like this in Idaho. As we motored this way, we saw huge ridges of black lava that looked impossible to walk on."

"No one else thought that neither. The maps used to mark this area as 'unexplored' and 'barren.' " Tom pointed to one of the cinder type formations. "Now that's *a'a*." After they crossed another slick black rock formation, he stopped and once more tied horse reins, this time to a dead, twisted tree. "Here's some more caves. These here are lava tubes, and they can be dangerous to climb into 'cause they might 'cave in,' " he said and chuckled again. "I been down these ones several times. They're kind of spooky but seem okay. We don't want the horse to cross on top, and probably keep the dog out for now. Follow me." The entrance to this cave was a dark hole at the bottom of a rock slide.

The sheriff motioned for Nell to stay on top. She wanted to ignore him but decided she would rather wait where she was. Sliding into that hole didn't appeal to her at all. She couldn't take many photos inside anyway. She had not brought enough flash materials to waste any, and she had not liked the feeling the day before when they found the body. This one looked like a tight squeeze. Instead, she wandered on to where she could see a dark, flat plain of cinders, dotted by low, dead clumps of leaves, almost as if they had been planted in neat rows. How desolate! Why would those people come this way? Indians had been through here, but Tom had mentioned they didn't spend a lot of time on the lava. They thought it was sacred, he said. Still, the Indian trails were noticeable, especially when the sun was overhead. They looked like white stripes along the black ground.

No sound escaped from the lava tube. As she tracked back to where both the horse and Moonie were, Moonie barked twice. She glanced around and saw two deer in a green area some distance away. Could he see that? One of them peered around to watch her but apparently decided she wasn't a danger and lowered its head again to graze. Moonshine lost interest, too. Large birds flew overhead in a long *V* aimed south. As the *V* drew closer she could hear squawks and what sounded like voices. Geese, she surmised. Even in Chicago, she had seen skeins of geese migrating in the fall and spring. Their familiar sight and sound comforted her.

CHAPTER 4

Rosy bounced off the train. He looked as grizzled and unkempt as when he had left Ketchum in May. The spring to his gait belied the first impression. When he turned and two young boys appeared on the top step, Mrs. Bock understood. Behind them, a bony woman appeared, dressed as if she came from the last century with a face-framing bonnet, a long hemmed gray dress, and gloves, a small purse in one hand and a weighted satchel in the other. She looked like a cloudy day.

Uh-oh, Mrs. Bock thought. What has Rosy done now? Surely, he didn't get married again.

"Well now, Goldie. Here we are!" He helped the young ones down as she walked up.

"Matt and Campbell, do you remember me?" She knelt. "No, Campbell, you were too young, weren't you?"

Matt, the older boy, whispered, "I do, Auntie Bock."

"Why so you do, Matt, even to naming me." She opened her arms, but he didn't come closer. Instead, he glanced back at the gray woman.

"This here's Esther, my sister, from Chicago. She took care of the boys while I was . . . gone."

Mrs. Bock stood and gave a slight curtsy. "How do you do, Mrs.—"

"I'm not a Mrs.," the woman said. "My last name is Kipling like my brother here." She lunged off the last step. "Shake hands with Mrs. Bock, boys. You know to be polite to your elders. Just

44

don't talk to strangers."

Each boy stuck out his hand. Mrs. Bock wanted to grab them up in her arms and hold them but did not. She could see the resemblance between brother and sister and decided brother was much the handsomer of the two, even with his bad eye, the result of a mine accident. Her hand made up two of one of the boy's hands. They both looked as if they needed hugs with their uncertainty evident in their hesitant steps and almost unwillingness to leave the other woman's side.

Rosy gave Mrs. Bock a huge hug, and she felt vindicated. "We all missed you, Goldie. Sorry I didn't give you much warning, but we had to sell my sister's house before we came West again."

That meant the tall woman would be staying. Mrs. Bock tried to smile. "Welcome, Miss Kipling. I'm sure you will love the West."

"I doubt it. But what choice did I have? Those boys need a woman to look after them, and we all know Ross's weaknesses."

Mrs. Bock straightened her shoulders. "Come, boys, I made a peach pie for you." She grabbed one hand each and began to walk away.

"They don't get sweets except after church on Sunday."

"Well, they get a piece of pie today because it is as special as a Sunday is," Mrs. Bock said. "Rosy, you, too. If Miss Kipling doesn't want pie, she can have . . . coffee."

"Boys, you go with Goldie. Esther and I'll get our luggage. Goldie's pies are the best in the valley—and lots better than any in Chicago." Rosy waved after them.

Miss Kipling huffed. "Don't you let her undermine everything I taught them, Brother. Or I'll go back to Chicago."

Mrs. Bock heard the last statement and smiled.

CHAPTER 5

Nellie carried her camera and tripod and walked, gazing at the scenery, studying possible photos, either up close or far away. The sky was blue and cloudless, which did not make for interesting photography. On the other hand, she would not wish for clouds. Being stuck out in rain, or possibly even snow, held no attraction. She came to a round, deep depression in a rocky area. It was open to the air but looked as if it might lead to a cave or "tube" of some sort. She set up the tripod with the camera and then pulled Moonie over to the lip of the depression. It wasn't all that deep, so she sat on the edge and jumped in, stumbling forward as she landed. It was deeper than it looked. Moonshine had no choice but to jump down, too. The leather shields on his feet protected them from the rocky surface.

Along the floor of the depression, she found dried grasses and wildflower seed heads. As she neared what had appeared to be the opening of a cave, she almost stumbled over a skeleton with half the bones scattered in the amber colored grass. "Oh!" Moonshine nosed a few of the bones but did not pick up any. "I think it's an animal of some sort," Nellie said. "These bones are so dried, they must have been here a long time." Her habit of talking to Moonshine suited them both, she thought. The dog looked at her. "Look, horns." Nellie knelt in the grass to touch the thick, almost rock-like curls. "This must be a big horn sheep. I've never seen one before." She glanced around. "I wonder why it's here."

Moonie pulled on the leash, moving toward the opening. He growled low but kept moving, and, this time, Nellie followed him. "Maybe it's a bear's cave," Nellie whispered to him. "I don't think we should go in."

Part of the opening was in shadows, but sunlight lit the upper portion. Nellie tried to climb one side, but it was too steep and the lava rock there was slick with no foothold. Even Moonshine couldn't get a purchase. Then it hit her. Maybe the sheep was in this depression because it couldn't get out. This time, she looked around and studied the sides of what might have been a crater in times past. If a big horn sheep couldn't climb out, neither could she. No one knew where she was.

"Charlie," she called. "Tom." Silence as overpowering as the white sun above met her efforts. Her voice probably didn't extend up and was crushed by the walls around her. She had even left her canteen next to her camera. Ah! Surely, someone would see that and wonder where she was. She moved over to the shady side of the opening and sat on a boulder almost as big as she was. Maybe she could push it to the edge and climb out on it. No, too far. And way too heavy. The lack of water made her aware of her dire thirst. Moonshine nosed into the cave opening, sniffing. He growled again and the hackles on the back of his head rose.

Necessity is the mother of something, Nellie thought. She pulled on Moonshine's leash and hurried back to where they had jumped down. "Let's pile up rocks. We can get out that way." She looked around to find rocks she could lift. "Stay," she ordered Moonie, unclipping his leash. Back and forth, she hurried, each time carrying a heavy rock and keeping an eye on the cave opening. If a wild animal came out, she could try to protect herself with the rock in her arms.

Before long, she had built up a scramble of stones. "Okay, Moonie, you go up." He climbed but stopped to look back at her. "I'm coming," she said and began making the climb, using her hands to hold herself steady. "I think." All the rocks shifted. She stopped and held herself still until they steadied. She could reach the top but couldn't quite get the leverage to pull herself up. Slowly, she stepped backwards until she reached the floor of the crater. More rocks. Moonshine barked, and his muzzle pointed toward her. "I can't, Moonie. I need more rocks!"

This time, she not only carried one rock at a time but had to climb her pyramid-like structure to place it on top of the others. If one slid, the others would tumble down, probably with her in the middle. Moonshine jumped up over the edge and lay down with his nose toward her. One, two, three, four. The last didn't look stable, so she decided to try again before adding another. This time, she came up to her chest on the edge. To pull herself out, she had to bounce the bulk of her weight up and over. As she did just that, she felt the rocks give way, but, this time, her arms held her, and she swung one leg over the top. Grunting, Nell managed to swing her whole body up. She lay prostrate, breathing hard and sweating. Moonshine licked her face. She crawled to her knees and looked down. Most of the rocks had tumbled back to the bottom.

Her camera was where she left it, of course. Now, which way back? Perspiration still dripped on her face and down her back. She opened the canteen, which was lighter than she remembered, and then she noticed a puddle of water. Oh no! It leaked. "Here, Moonie. You drink."

Only piles of sharp cinders offered a place to sit down, so she sat on the ground. A breeze blew, chilling her as her sweat—no, horses sweat, men perspire, and women glow, her mother had often reminded her—evaporated. The sun was so high, she couldn't tell which direction might be north. And, Charlie had the compass. As Nellie looked around, trying to see which direction she might have come from, looking for a familiar boulder, dead tree, or pile of rocks, a movement in the corner of her eye drew her glance back to the depression. Two small critters, about as big as rats in Chicago, but furry and light brown with large ears, crept out of the opening. They squeaked to each other. Moonshine barked, and they skidded back to the dark.

Nellie laughed. "You saved me, Moonshine!" She hugged her dog. "Here, sit by me, and let's just wait a while. Maybe the two explorers will show up." Moonshine curled around and put his head on her lap. His nose showed less of the effects of the quills. He slept. Nell was aware of a few bird chirps but saw none. They must nest in a sagebrush patch nearby. Something skittered on the ground but disappeared before she could find the source—maybe a lizard. The silence enveloped her. She wished she had binoculars, so she could see farther than just her surroundings. A drink of water would be nice. So would an apple. Or a slab of ham on one of Goldie's bread slices. Her mouth watered. A few late fall insects buzzed, and she felt her eyes close.

In a dream, Nell heard bird songs. Moonie's head lifted under her hand.

"Nell!"

"Miss Burns!"

She stood up and saw two figures approaching from a direction she had not even considered following. Before long, Mayor Tom and Sheriff Azgo met up with her. "Are you all right?" the sheriff asked. He looked into the depression, the crater, as Nell had decided to call it.

"Yes." No reason to go into her lame-brain adventure.

"We thought you were lost," Tom said. "Guess you were!"

"I wasn't sure which way to go back to the cave," Nell admitted. "I'm glad you came this way. What did you see in the lava tube?"

"Looked like someone stayed there for a bit," Tom said. "We

couldn't tell if it was an animal's den or there were people. Could we?" He turned to the sheriff, who had wandered around the side of the crater.

"How did you get in there?"

"We jumped. Moonshine came with me. It looked as if there was a cave down that way." She pointed to the other end. "There was, and Moonshine growled, so it seemed better not to explore on our own. Turns out, it was two little furry animals. They looked like small rabbits, but not quite."

"Pikas." Mayor Tom shrugged his shoulders. "They's all over the place. About the size of a packrat."

"How did you get out?" The sheriff persisted.

"Climbed." Nell busied herself with packing up her camera. "I'm thirsty. Do you have any water left? My canteen leaked."

The sheriff shook his head but offered his canteen. "Please do not explore on your own again. We cannot spend time searching for you as well as for what might be lost tourers." He turned to the mayor. "Are there any more lava tubes in this area? We could search another hour or so, and then I need to return to Hailey. First, I want to stop in Arco and see if we could round up a group who knows the area to look again and in places we have not."

"I could stay and search with a crew," Nell said. "I don't have anything pressing in Ketchum." Then she remembered Rosy. "Or else I can come back with you. There are some people I would like to see."

Mayor Tom led them to another cave area, not far removed from where Nellie had dropped down into the crater and explored on her own. This one had a rock slide leading down to the entrance, too. The sheriff motioned Nellie to join them and suggested she leave her camera outside. Moonie kept pace with her, as they stepped on and over the rock pile. At the bottom, they discovered there were two tunnels, one going to the right

and the second to the left. The right one looked more accessible.

"That left one is pretty much plugged in a ways, is my
memory," Mayor Tom said. "This one keeps goin' for a long
ways. Both of 'em have ice inside, leastways part of the year." As
they moved toward the overhanging lava edge of the right one,
they slowed. This tube area also appeared plugged with falling
rocks and slabs, as if a giant had shaken it all up in a tumbler.
Some of the jumble grabbed at her boots, and others were slick
rock. Here and there bright yellow lichen shone against the
black background. Even a few wisps of faded tall grasses waved
in the afternoon breeze.

Once again, Nellie stirred herself to be brave and follow the
men into the dark. Their flashlights looked like small spotlights.
This time, the sheriff stayed in the lead and also scrambled
along one edge. Nellie felt the roof of the tube pressing on
them, worried that the giant might try another shake or two.
She slipped and fell to one knee. The sheriff stopped until she
pulled herself upright. "I'm all right." They moved deeper into
the maw, which opened into a larger tunnel.

Even Mayor Tom stopped chattering. He stayed right behind
the sheriff. Nell wondered if he felt a little nervous, too. Nell
couldn't remember when she had been in such a spooky, black
place. A ghost could fly out, and she would expire from fright.
Moonie, beside her, was as invisible as the way ahead. "Who
would go in here voluntarily?" she asked. No one answered.

The sheriff paused, turned, and placed a finger on his lips.
He turned off his flashlight. Tom did the same. A Stygian black
surrounded them, and Nellie felt as if she might suffocate as the
darkness wrapped around her like a veil being pulled tighter.
Then she heard what Charlie must have heard—a steady drip,
drip, drip. It was such a strange sound in this driest of all
deserts, that she almost exclaimed. She felt rather than saw

Moonshine leave her side. She heard his progress along the slick rock toward where she thought the sheriff stood. But when he said, "Stay," in a low voice, the sound came from yards farther in. Again, drip, drip, drip.

"That's just a stalag . . . static . . . you know, one of them icicles." Tom's voice jumped at her like a carnival barker. He stood right next to her, much closer than when they had all stopped. He turned on his flashlight. It felt as if the sun had risen in the cave, it was so bright.

Sheriff Azgo was not even in sight. "Charlie!" Another light came on somewhere ahead and around a corner.

He appeared at the bend. "We might as well be in a circus, what with the talking and the lights." He looked back from where he had come. "Never mind. We have another body here. Come ahead, Tom. You, too, Nellie. We'll need help getting this one loose. Moonshine, stay."

"Loose?"

"A stalactite pinned the body to the ground."

CHAPTER 6

Mrs. Bock showed Rosy and the two boys Gladys's old room. She had removed the double bed and all her belonging when Gladys, the former roomer, left. Three single beds jutted out from one end of the room, and a small table and chairs as well as an overstuffed couch filled out the other end. A long bureau rested against the hallway wall. She turned on the overhead light, and the bright-colored bedspreads cheered her. The walls were now bright yellow, and several Oriental rugs covered most of the parquet floor. "You boys and Rosy stay here."

She turned to Esther. "I have a room down the hall for you. It's not as big, but . . ." She wanted to say "beggars can't be choosers," but didn't want to hurt Rosy's feelings. "You all can stay here until—" she said and led Esther to a cubbyhole of a room past the bathroom. "Bathroom is shared with everyone. No one should dawdle.

"School's started already. It's just down the street. There's about two, maybe three classes. Matt can get in the middle class and Campbell in the younger one. I already talked to the teachers. If you decide to go to Hailey, there's grades."

"Is Nellie Burns still living here?" Rosy asked. He had given a cursory look at both rooms.

"Yes, she's in her usual room, right across from Room Six— your and the boys' room."

Miss Kipling harumphed. "Is she that camera lady you keep talking about, Ross?"

"Yep. Saved my life." He ruffled Matt's hair, and then the boy scooted back to his and Campbell's room. "In more ways than one. She here?"

"She's off somewhere with the sheriff."

Rosy grinned. "Ah, that the way it is?"

"No, they're down at the lava fields finding dead bodies."

Miss Kipling gasped. "That's not something to say in front of these boys. What if they heard you?" She glanced back to Room Six, but the door was closed.

"What if they did? They're in the Wild West now. Got to get used to bodies and all manner of goings-on." Mrs. Bock walked to the stairs. "You get settled now and come down for some pie." She could hear Esther yapping behind her but ignored it. Getting used to Esther was going to take some doing.

Rosy was first to enter the kitchen. "Hiya, Goldie. Did you miss me?"

"Are you still drinkin' like a fish?"

"Nope. I give it up. My sister said it wasn't fittin' to be drinkin' around the boys. And I knew Lily wouldn't like it." He sat at the table, where Mrs. Bock sliced generous pieces of peach pie and slipped them onto plates.

"Those boys have grown so much. What are you going to do with them?" She looked up and studied Rosy. He had always been ornery after his wife Lily died. That was not a match made in heaven, but it seemed to work, even given the difference in their ages, almost twenty years.

"I don't know, Goldie. I couldn't leave them back in the city. I knew Lily would want them home, but we can't live out at Last Chance Ranch, what with school and winter comin' on and all." He lowered his head and heaved a big sigh. "Does the sheriff know I'm back?"

"I didn't tell him, but I suspect Nellie will say something while they're out at the lava fields."

The boys came running down the stairs like two young ponies. They found their way into the kitchen, chasing each other with cap guns. "Whoa!" Matt said.

"Sit down," Goldie said. She placed an ample piece of pie in front of each of them with a fork and a glass of milk. "Now, don't shovel it down, but eat up!

"I expect they'll get back tonight or some time tomorrow. Charlie can't stay out of the office too long. Too much goin' on here and in Hailey, what with hunters comin' in to slaughter elk and deer. I'm hopin' I'll get a venison from one of the miners boardin' here, but Henry is gettin' too old to shoot straight. Still, someone out at Triumph might get lucky. Will you get your old job up there back?"

"Dunno. I'll head out there tomorrow, I guess. Is my auto around somewhere? Did Nellie run it into the ground, or did it give up the ghost?"

"She put a lot of miles on it this summer. She went up to a sheep camp with Gwynn Campbell and got mixed up with moonshiners and cowboys. That girl doesn't have a scared bone in her body, near as I can tell."

"Moonshiners? Not that gang of robbers up there at Fourth of July Creek, did she?"

"Those're the ones. Bad business. One of 'em got shot. Not before he tried to slit her up one side and down the other."

"Who got slit up?" Matt asked.

"Oops, little pitchers have big ears." The boys might need to know some bad things happened, but they didn't have to know how they happened. Goldie cut up two more small slices and added them to the empty plates. "You want more, Rosy?"

"Was she hurt?"

"She survived it. Gwynn sewed her up. Not a bad job either."

"I would like a cup of tea." Esther strode into the kitchen

55

and plunked herself down on the only remaining chair. "If you please."

"I'll get it for you this time, Miss Kipling, 'cause you're new here. Watch close so you know how to do it yourself next time. I ain't nobody's servant."

CHAPTER 7

Nellie and Mayor Tom followed Sheriff Azgo around the bend. With both flashlights on, the interior of the next section of the cave glistened. The lights reflected off thin icicles hanging from the ceiling in prisms of color—red, orange, yellow, blue. Nell wasn't sure she had ever seen anything so beautiful in her life. Until she saw the dark lump with what looked like a sword sticking out of it. No scream, but she heard herself gasp. This time, no animal had plundered the body or face. It was upturned and looked beatific in the light—like a frozen Madonna.

The sheriff, Nellie, and Mayor Tom paused in stunned silence. Around them, Nellie heard again the water dripping and wondered where it was. The sound echoed, almost like footsteps. She glanced up, not wanting to look at the sight and hardly able to look away.

"Do you have your camera, Miss Burns?" the sheriff asked.

"Ye-es. No, it's outside."

"Mayor Tom, can you retrieve Miss Burns's pack and tripod? I think we should have a photograph here."

"No, I'll get it. I can't—" Nellie backed up and stumbled toward the entrance. "Moonshine, come here." After the two of them rounded the corner again, she stopped and choked, trying to keep her food down, but she was not successful.

"Mayor Tom. Get her pack and tripod." The sheriff must have heard her.

Nellie pulled herself together, wiped her mouth with her sleeve, and hung on Moonie's collar to guide her. The sunshine was so white, she blinked and covered her face. Moonie barked and waited for her as she climbed back up the rocks. Her pack and tripod were where she had left them. She found the leash for Moonshine and tied him to a rock. "I'm sorry, Moonie. You must stay here." She knelt and circled his body with her arms. He felt so strong and warm and brave. She must be, too. She gathered up her equipment and re-entered the cave. The flashlights still reflected off the icy walls, making her feel as if she were in the middle of half a dozen rainbows, except for the deep dark behind it all.

"Sheriff, I need your help with the flash." Nellie wished Rosy were with them. He had done this for her in the mine last winter. "I'll explain what to do." She secured her Premo to the tripod and placed it close to the scene—the body. She poured flash powder into the inverted narrow length of the tray. "Hold this tray steady. Wait until I get situated. Here are some wood matches and a strike pad. When I tell you 'now,' light the match and touch it to this powder. It will explode in light but keep hold of the tray here." She demonstrated. "At the same time, Mayor Tom, you should keep both flashlights just behind and above . . . her. Not directly on . . ." They did as told.

Nellie pulled the black cloth over her head and concentrated on the view through the ground glass, the upside down and inverted image. A doll, she told herself. A play. She lifted the black cloth and swung it over her shoulder and set up the film and shutter release. Nell motioned Charlie and Tom to stay still. "Now!"

The explosion of light blinded all of them. Nell, at least, had closed hers in anticipation. "One more. Wait until I move about to get a different angle, Sheriff," she said and turned to him. "I should only take one more. Do you want to direct me?"

"I still cannot see. Take the view from the feet toward her . . . head, and include the stalactite as much as you can."

Nell detected the crack in his firm voice. She moved with care to the different angle, helped fill the flash tray, pulled on the black cloth, and proceeded as before. After the flash exploded, she thought she heard Mayor Tom gasp, but she didn't stop her end of the photo procedure—placing the film in the carrier, releasing the camera from the tripod, folding up the camera, re-packing the flash tray. As soon as she was finished, she looked at Tom. "Please help me out of here." He did.

Outside, Nell waited for the two men to return. "What are we going to do with . . . ?" she asked when they appeared at the entrance. She wanted to sit but was still too upset.

Mayor Tom looked as sick as Nell felt. "Jesus, Mary, and Joseph!" Mayor Tom rubbed his mouth. "How are we gonna get this . . . this . . . out of there?" He motioned behind them.

"I do not know. Just the three of us probably cannot do it. We need another stretcher and rope and couple of men." The sheriff stared at Nell and then looked elsewhere. "I tried to move her, but her clothes are frozen to the ground." He squatted down. "And a shovel so we can pry her loose."

"I don't think I will be any help at all," Nell said.

Neither man said anything for a spell.

"We must do what we did before," the sheriff said. "We'll have to ask for a stretcher and several men to help remove the body and take it to Hailey."

"I'm purty sure this was one of the women with the man, but her face was covered mostly with a veil. She didn't say or do anything, like the other one. This must be the one that looked so plump and didn't say much. Can't tell now. So what about the other woman?" Mayor Tom's jollity had disappeared long since. "Do we keep lookin'?"

"Not now. I have to return to Hailey and enlist other searchers." Sheriff Azgo did not get to his feet. His voice had lost most of its strong timbre.

"I am not waiting here this time," Nellie said. "I can take the horse back and—"

"No, we are not leaving you behind again. We will all leave. Tom, can you come back again with a stretcher team in the morning? You are the only one I know who can find this cave again. This is much to ask, and, if you do not wish to do so, I understand."

Tom sat on one of the large boulders in front of the cave. He dropped his head between his knees. He said nothing for a moment. "Guess I'll have to, won't I?" He looked up at the sheriff. "I'd sure rather you come back, too." Another pause. "I don't think I got the heart to push and shove . . . her like might be needed."

Sheriff Azgo sighed and stroked his chin. A dark shadow had begun to grow. "All right. Let us do this. I will take Nellie back to Hailey and round up a stretcher and team. You can go back to Arco and meet me here tomorrow morning. We can use your horse to load our packs and camera," he said and gestured to Nellie, "and Nellie, too, if she wants to ride. I do not wish trying to sling this dead body over the horse. I would like to see what I can see once we get it out into the sunlight." He glanced between Nellie and Tom. "If she . . . it may have been here for days, so one more day will not make a difference. But," he said, as he pushed himself up to standing, "I want to stack rocks in front of the entrance to reduce the chance of animals getting to it."

Nellie felt as if moving rocks were a Sisyphean task after her morning's experience. The two men were much more efficient and with their strength could move larger rocks as well. When the cave front was mostly closed, all three made their way back to the camp, picking up the horse where Tom had tied it to a tree near the cave Nellie didn't enter. The sheriff carried Nellie's tripod, and she carried her camera. No one spoke until they reached the tent and then only to share the dismantling and loading. Nellie said she would walk, at least over the roughest surface, so the horse's feet would be saved. Moonshine was as quiet as they were.

Much later at the road, the sheriff and Nellie climbed into the sheriff's automobile, and Moonshine curled himself around at her feet. Mayor Tom waved good-bye and turned his auto to face Arco. They left the horse hobbled with a long lead and feed near several trees. Mayor Tom said it would be all right another night. "I'm sorry I wasn't more help," Nellie said.

"No matter, Nell. It was as distressing a sight as I have ever seen. I would have followed you out, but the county pays me to handle distressing sights."

"If you want photos, I should come back with you. It might be easier once she is outside." Brave words, she thought. The icicle in the woman's body would bring her nightmares, perhaps forever. Portraits grew more appealing by the minute. "What time do you want to leave in the morning?"

"Early." He didn't argue with her, so she supposed her services were needed.

"Maybe Rosy could come with us, too. He used to be very strong, and I suspect that hasn't changed. As long as he doesn't bring his jar along with him. Don't you think?"

The smile on the sheriff's lips was the first good sign since they entered the auto. "I think that is a good idea."

The sheriff drove Nellie all the way to Mrs. Bock's boarding house. She was relieved because she didn't want to have to find a ride from Hailey to Ketchum. She knew he was as exhausted as she was and probably more so. "Come in," she said.

"Not tonight. I will come to pick you up at 7:00 o'clock. If Rosy wishes to go, he should be ready too, with sturdy shoes and warm clothes, gloves, a hat—"

"I think he probably knows how to dress for cold, Charlie." She patted his arm. "He may even have been to the lava fields for all I know. Maybe he looked for gold there." As she swung her legs out the door, Moonshine crawled out, too. Then Nellie leaned back. "Thank you for understanding how I felt."

Nell could hear noise all over the house. Pounding on stairs. A woman shouting. Clattering pans in the kitchen. Nell quickly walked back to the kitchen, where Mrs. Bock was by herself. "Anything left to eat?"

"Lord a mercy, child! You scared me to death!" Mrs. Bock looked as frazzled as Nellie felt. "I can fix something up for you quick as a wink."

Her landlady looked so undone, Nellie rushed to her and hugged her hard. "Oh, Goldie. This has been an awful day, and it looks as if it were for you, too. Are Rosy and the boys back?"

"Can't you hear them monkeys on the stairway? I should slit my throat for saying they could stay here. They were quiet and shy when I met them at the train. And now, listen to 'em!"

"They're happy to be here, I'm sure." Doors slammed upstairs and downstairs, and then the noise stopped. "Where's Rosy?"

"He said he was going out to see about his automobile. I told him you left it at the motor garage. He hasn't come back, and I'm afraid he stopped to fill up on liquor." Mrs. Bock pulled a big haunch of lamb out of the refrigerator, where it took up most of the space. "I can fix you a lamb sandwich. The boys ate like birds, and Miss Kipling looked like she would never stop." She took a quick glance to the door. "That's Rosy's sister, who says she is here to stay." Mrs. Bock wrinkled her nose. "She's as priggish a woman as I've ever met. I don't want her around any longer than necessary. I'd move her out tomorrow if I could."

The back door slammed open, and Rosy stepped into the kitchen. "Nellie!" In three steps he had his arms around her and held her close. "I thought you'd never get back!"

"That's what I thought about you! It's been—what? Five months? Six?" She threw her arms around him, too. He had gained weight from the time at Last Chance Ranch and looked about ten years younger. And then she felt shy. He was a handsome man, something she had never thought before, perhaps because of his one bad eye. And, maybe for the first time since she had known him, he was not drinking and didn't smell of it.

"Sit and eat, cookie," Mrs. Bock said. "Rosy, go calm those boys down, get them to bed, and come back, so we can talk." She motioned to the three of them. "And don't bring your sister down with you, please."

"I had to bring her, Goldie. She ain't easy, but she's got a good heart." He left the room, letting the kitchen door slam behind him.

CHAPTER 8

"First," Nellie said, "the sheriff and I are going out to the lava fields again, the Craters of the Moon. We have found two bodies, and there supposedly were three who are there. Charlie needs people to help carry the newest one back to the road and get it transported to Hailey. And to find the third person. I hope this one isn't dead, too." The vision of the ice sword still wouldn't leave her, and she curled her shoulders up and in.

"Charlie, eh?" Rosy puckered his lips.

Nell could feel her face flush. Mrs. Bock heaved herself up from her chair. "Nell and Charlie," Mrs. Bock said, emphasizing the name, "spent quite a lot of time in the mountains in July, Rosy. They're good friends. Don't interrupt."

"I work for the sheriff now," Nell said. "I'm his crime photographer. He doesn't have much of a staff, not even a deputy. The federal marshal asked him to investigate out on the Craters, and a man from Arco is helping out—Mayor Tom. I don't even know his last name."

"Tom Thompson, I bet," Rosy said. "He's a good ol' boy from way back. I used to do some explorin' out in the lava with him a long time ago. We tried to find gold." He shook his head and chuckled. "Lost cause, that."

Finished with her sandwich, Nellie stood up, too. "Do you want to come help search, Rosy? Charlie said it was all right to ask you. If you know the area, you would be a huge help."

"Don't know it much anymore. What's Charlie say about—"

he said and gestured toward the ceiling.

"He didn't even know you and the boys were coming back until I said something yesterday." She remembered his mumbling about being a sheepherder and his story about leaving town but decided not to say anything.

"What's 'second?' " Mrs. Bock asked.

"I don't know. I'm too tired to think. Charlie is coming by early, around 7:00. I'm going to bed." Nell placed her hand on Rosy's shoulder. "I hope the auto was in good shape, or at least as good shape as you left it. I'm so happy you are home, Rosy. I hate to ask you to go out with us right away."

"Weekend tomorrow," Rosy said. "I can't do nothin' about the boys in school until Monday. Esther can take them around. There ain't much to see anyway. I can take 'em out to the ranch on Sunday, if we're back." He hung his head and fingered his hat. "Not sure what I want to do about that anyway. They don't remember Lily. Don't know if that's bad or good."

"Matt remembers her." Mrs. Bock put the lamb away. "I don't think Campbell does, but then he was pretty young when . . ." She fastened the icebox and rubbed her hands on her apron. "I'm going to bed, too. I'll get breakfast for all of you."

Next morning, Charlie, Nell, Rosy, Mrs. Bock, and the two boys sat around the dining room table. The mine workers had already left. Moonshine sat next to Matt. "Two men are waiting for us in Hailey. Tom lined them up. They will bring a paneled truck to carry the body back to the morgue. Then the three of us and Mayor Tom can go about searching the other caves. They seem the most likely spots." The sheriff turned to Rosy. "Nell said you spent some time in the lava with Tom. Do you remember much about the area?"

"Can I come, too?" Matt asked.

"Me, too!" Campbell said.

"No, you boys need to stay here. Your Aunt Esther will show you around town."

"Does Moonshine get to go?" Matt asked.

"Esther don't know anything about town," Mrs. Bock said. "I'll show 'em. We can take the train to the hot springs, maybe go for a swim. How'd you like that, boys?" When they jumped up, ready to leave immediately, Mrs. Bock motioned them down again. "Do you have somethin' to swim in? Go sort out some shorts, if you have 'em, and get dressed in some longer pants and shirts. We can't go 'til after lunch. In the meantime, go sit on the porch and watch people go by."

"Hmph. Not many people in town no more," Rosy said. "Do what she says." He turned to Goldie. "Do you have an extra blanket or two?"

"I do, but I don't want 'em all muddied and ruined."

"No mud out there, unless it's changed a lot," Rosy said. "Sounds like we might be out all night, so I need somethin' to sleep in."

"I fixed up some cut lamb and trimmin's so you can all eat. I don't know how you're gonna carry everythin' though."

"Tom has a horse," Nellie interjected. "Ready to go?" It felt as if she were always spurring them on. She didn't want to find another dead body. She hoped the last woman was still alive and only in need of food and water. "Do we have enough canteens?"

"I want to be a sheriff when I grow up," Campbell interrupted, not quietly. "Can I hold your gun?"

"Not now. Maybe when you are a little older, I will teach you and Matt how to shoot and handle a rifle. Then you and your dad can go hunting." The sheriff tousled the hair of each boy. "Let us go."

Nell climbed in back of the sheriff's automobile. Moonie jumped in with her, his leather footpads back in place. Neither the sheriff nor Rosy objected. "You two might want to talk. I want to rest my eyes."

Her gesture was wasted. They didn't say anything to each other all the way to the lava fields. Mayor Tom waited for them. The horse grazed on grass next to him.

"Say, I asked around to see if anyone knew anything more than I did about those three people. The minister said they said they were doing God's work."

"Some God's work," Nellie mumbled.

Rosy lifted a pack out of the boot and slung it around his shoulders. "Here's your camera, Nellie. Want me to carry it?"

"Do you think she would let that go?" the sheriff said.

"Thanks, but I'll carry it," Nell said.

The paneled truck pulled up and parked behind the sheriff's auto. "Okay, we are all here. We can talk about the search after we get the first job done."

"I almost forgot," Tom said. "I looked in that automobile, and there were three packages in the boot. I took and put 'em in my station and locked the door, like I always do."

"I will pick them up after we finish our search today, or tomorrow, depending on what we find." The sheriff loaded his pack and gestured for Mayor Tom to lead the way.

As they walked, Nellie kept her eye out for photographs. She fell farther and farther back until she realized she couldn't see anyone, not even the horse. Moonshine stayed with her, so she didn't feel lost. But then, nothing seemed familiar from her treks into and out of the lava fields from their first camp. Or maybe it was that everything seemed familiar, the dark ropy swells and curves with some of the broken pieces looking like brown, broken wood, the cinder stacks, the spatter cones. This time, she saw the blue lava, a deep cobalt blue in some areas and brighter, almost teal blue in others. What turned it blue? It shone like glass along some facets. She liked the cones best, and each one carried a different shape, probably depending on how much lava had bubbled forth. What a strange place this was. She wondered what it would have been like when everything was red hot. The ice cave had felt like a tomb. And it was a tomb for that poor woman. Had the ice spear killed her, or did someone spear her after she was dead? It resembled a religious tableau in some ways, although what religion, she couldn't guess. Maybe the Aztecs in Mexico.

"Nell!" The sheriff appeared on the horizon. "Miss Burns," he corrected himself. "Come along, please. You are holding us up."

Relieved that someone had realized she lagged behind, she hurried to catch up. "I was just thinking about what we found yesterday. Do you suppose that poor woman was already dead and then someone speared her with the ice?"

"I thought about that possibility as well. Until I can look closer in the area and at the woman, I cannot know. We now have a lantern, so that with the flashlights and the lantern, I can inspect the whole scene. Maybe then I will know more." He stopped. "I do need more photos, if you can get them, preferably inside."

"I brought more flash powder. Rosy helped me with powder in the past, so he will know what to do." Nell dreaded going back into that cave, but, this time at least, she would know what to expect and steel herself ahead of time.

The sheriff gave her a questioning look.

"In the Triumph mine. Do you remember that photograph? It was accepted by the gallery in San Francisco." She found it difficult to keep the pride out of her voice. Her photograph would be in a gallery! "I heard from them when I returned from the Stanley Basin."

"Have you sent any of your Stanley photographs to the gallery?" They clambered along again.

"No, those were mostly for the railroad brochures. They were picture postcard images. I would like to get something while we are out here, but everything is the same color from the camera's viewpoint. In a photo, it will all look black or gray with very little white as a contrast, unless we get a cloudy day. Then, I might be able to take an unusual photo with clouds that I could send with some confidence."

They passed the area where the sheriff and Nell had camped and continued on to the cave where they would do their work. After close to another hour of hiking, and of Mayor Tom leading the horse afield to avoid the worst *a'a* lava, they arrived at the cave site.

"Oh, oh." Sheriff Azgo stumbled down the rocky stairway and almost fell in his haste. "Someone or something has been in the cave." The rocks they had piled around the entrance were scattered, and the small, dark entrance revealed itself. He removed another layer of stone, asked for a flashlight, and called for one of the men to bring a lantern as well. Nell hadn't noticed anyone with a lantern, but one appeared as if by magic. Rosy took it in hand.

Moonshine had followed at the sheriff's heels and climbed down and in before Nell could stop him. She wasn't going to be left behind, so she, too, stepped down the rocks but carefully enough so she didn't stumble. She carried her camera pack and tripod and held them close as she half slid through the entrance. "Wait for me! Rosy, I need you to help me take a photograph with the flash powder."

Nell followed the light from the sheriff's flashlight. Rosy held the lantern behind them both. When she rounded the bend into the deep dark, she stopped. There were stalactites and a few stalagmites as well as rock stalactites. Ice glittered in the light. The body was gone.

"Did we imagine it?" If they couldn't move the body

yesterday, how could someone else, and when?

"No, we did not imagine it. We have three witnesses." The sheriff sounded as surprised as Nell felt, although she suspected he didn't feel relieved, as she did.

Moonshine sniffed his way around and stopped right where the body had been. He barked.

The sheriff knelt down next to him. He inspected the ground using the flashlight, and he felt the area with his hand. He took out a pocketknife and scraped up some of the icy ground. He had placed the lantern close to where the body's head had been and moved it closer to where he was scraping. "Blood."

Nell knew what that could mean: the body was not dead when the ice spire had been pushed through it. Dead bodies don't bleed. And the blood could have frozen the clothes to the ground, holding the woman like a trap.

"Call in the others with their flashlights so I can get as close a look as possible."

Rosy stumbled backwards and around the bend and gave out a yell. "Come on in here. We need more flashlights!"

Soon, everyone crowded around. Mayor Tom held his flashlight as close as possible to where the sheriff continued to scrape the ice and rocky surface. He said little, and, when the sheriff rose again and flashed his light around the cave, he did the same. "The cave goes back a ways. Maybe we should look that way."

"You and I and Rosy will go. Nell, you wait here and hold Moonshine. You others—Max and Trapper—you wait here, too. No sense in all of us tramping the ground and other tracks."

This was the first Nell had heard the other men's names. They seemed happy to wait, but she wanted to explore with the sheriff and Rosy. "Stay, Moonshine." He sat next to her, but she began to follow the explorers. The ground was slippery in places, and the noise they made covered hers. She did not have a flashlight but could see well enough from the light of the others, until they seemed to disappear completely. Another bend? A hole? Now what? This time, she couldn't even see. Again, she felt as if covered in a shroud herself. The deeper she went, the more slippery the floor grew—more ice. She waved her hand, hoping to find the wall to steady herself, but there seemed no wall at all. She stepped carefully to her left side and swept her arm up and down. "Ow." The wall found her. At the same time, a very faint light appeared in front of her. They were returning. She turned herself around and tried to hurry back out, willing herself not to slip.

"Do you ever follow instructions?" the sheriff asked as he neared.

"Only when I agree with them."

Rosy snorted. "The cave ended back there. Nothin' more to see. I'm thirsty!" Rosy caught up with Nell. "I didn't take this body." He laughed fit to kill.

CHAPTER 9

Outside, the group sat in a rough circle, eating the lunch Mrs. Bock had packed and sent with them. Mayor Tom ate the fastest. "The other entrance here is plugged." He gestured vaguely to the side opposite the entrance they had quitted. "But there's more caves. One ain't too far, but the rest are half a day's walk from here."

Rosy patted Moonshine, who seemed to enjoy the attention. The dog sat between him and Nell. "How about the tree mold area? Didn't you say they wanted to see the 'petrified wood'? Maybe someone is still there."

"That's even farther away," Tom said. "We could get there, but by then it would probably be dark. Do you remember how to find 'em?"

"We could explore the rest of the caves and then decide about the tree molds," Nell said. "I'd like to see them. Could we do that in the morning?"

Max and Trapper looked at each other and seemed to come to the same conclusion. "We'll head back to Hailey from here," one of them said. Nell wasn't sure which was which.

"Yeah. We came to carry out a body, not explore more caves. How much are ye payin' us, Sheriff?"

"Depends on how long you stay with us. I doubt you can find your own way back, and I cannot spare the others." The sheriff continued to munch on a sandwich. When he finished, he folded up the wrapping and stuck it in his pack. He took a

72

long pull from a canteen. "All right. We will explore the other side of this cave and then look for the others. Rosy, Nell, Moonshine, and I will camp the night and aim for the tree molds in the morning. Mayor Tom can take you two back when we finish with the caves."

With that pronouncement, the sheriff climbed back to the second entrance, barely large enough for him to squeeze through. He disappeared but reappeared within a few minutes. "This one is blocked, as Tom said." As he climbed back up, there was a little moaning and grumbling, but the two helpers gathered themselves up and joined the rest as they moved off once again over the tortured lava fields. Nell noticed a small dark cloud in the west. She glanced at Mayor Tom, but, if he had seen it, he said nothing. Onward, she thought.

Mayor Tom set the pace, a much faster one than the day before. They had reached an area where much of the ground was dirt or sheeted lava and not the irregular lava, so they made better progress. Before long, he called a halt. "This here area has several caves—lava tubes. I'm not sure how far in they go, but we could try them out. There's more ice in some of 'em."

"Tom, will you lead?" the sheriff asked. "Rosy and Nell can follow me. I think we leave Moonshine behind. Rosy, bring the lantern. Nell, bring your camera and flash equipment. Max and Trapper, wait for us, if you want to get paid."

Mayor Tom led the way down what looked like just another black hole, but, at the bottom, there was a fork, with one branch going west and the other northwest, according to him. Again, there was ice dripping down and growing up toward the ceiling. Rosy pointed out bear tracks. Nell hurried her own pace so she wouldn't be left behind. The floor was relatively flat, but still there were rocks and piles of stones to hike over. Two flashlights and a lantern created light that shone and reflected on the colors on the walls: green, yellow, brown, red. On closer inspection, the green was algae or lichen growing.

Except for their own murmuring and the sounds of their feet as they trudged forward, there was only silence. The depth of the silence seemed to discourage talking. Rocks sometimes rolled as one or the other person stumbled, and the sound echoed, making it seem like a landslide, and then all quieted again. No bodies lay under the stalactites in this cave. After one hundred yards or so, the cave or tunnel narrowed so much, they would have had to crawl to go any farther. Tom and the sheriff consulted and then turned around. They would leave, much to Nell's relief. Between a possible bear attack and the possibility of another dead body, her senses were so heightened, she wondered if her head would split.

Outside, the two men from Hailey had found shade in which to rest. They appeared to be playing a game of cards. They looked up when the cave party arrived. "You done?"

"Nope. There's one more cave, a big one just east of here. You might like to see it. Nothin' else like it in the world, I'd bet."

"Is there bears there?"

"Maybe." Tom turned and again led the expedition. This time, Moonshine was allowed to come. The two men went back to their game of cards.

As the group of four walked, they came upon a natural bridge of rock that arched between two cliffs of lava. The natural formation impressed Nell. She wondered if wind or weather might eventually knock it down. A twisted pine tree grew at one end. It was probably hundreds of years old already, she thought. She wanted a photograph, but no one would stop. "On the way back, Nell." Sheriff Azgo knew her penchant for photographing as much as possible.

The next cave was one where a portion of the roof had caved, but it was immense. Part of a domed ceiling remained, and, at

74

one end, there was what looked like a stage. "We could present a play here," Nell said. "Look at that big rock. It's a wing." Her voice echoed and seemed to carry, just as an actor's would in a dramatic piece. "Rosy, you could be Hamlet, and I, Ophelia." She pretended to be throwing flowers around herself.

Even the sheriff smiled as Rosy climbed onto the stage and threw his arms out. He dropped them. "What did Hamlet do?"

"He talked a lot," the sheriff said. He continued to explore the length of the cave under the domed roof that still stood. The others quieted and followed down a tunnel that led away from the back of the stage. They walked and sometimes crawled. The space was lit at first by the hole in the dome where sunlight flowed down. Farther along, the darkness again surrounded them. No one pointed out bear tracks, and, although Moonie sniffed here and there, he didn't raise any alarms. When they reached a point where the roof had caved in, they could go no further. There was ice in the nether reaches, again, making their exploration difficult and sometimes even painful. Another tunnel slanted off to one side. The floor was slick with ice. Between the lantern and the flashlights, Nell thought she might be able to take a photograph of the scene. She asked the sheriff to stop while she set up her tripod and camera. He didn't object this time.

After she pulled the black cloth over her head and looked at the image, she stood up. "Could you all put the lantern there," she said and pointed to an especially icy area, "and then point your lights to the same area, but a little higher and a little lower." She decided to move the camera just a small step or two. But her foot slipped, and she felt herself losing her grip on the icy floor. She began to slide down an incline into the dark. "Grab the camera!" Moonshine barked, and he, too, began to slide after her.

Nell didn't know how far she slid before she hit what felt like a wall, a rock wall. Her head banged on the side, and she saw stars. It took her a moment to realize she had stopped completely. Then a soft bag hit her: Moonie. She had no light, but she could feel his fur. He made his strange *arp*-ing sound, so she knew he was alive. "Are you all right?" She wasn't certain she was all right, but she moved her arms and legs, and nothing seemed broken. She felt an ache all over, beginning with her head.

Moonie tried to stand up but kept slipping into her. She felt around, touching rocks, icy spires above and one or two near where she had landed. She seemed to be in a narrow end of a tunnel that had collapsed, all that had saved her from sliding further into the earth. She held herself still to see if she could hear anything above her. Nothing. She tried to stand on the rocks at the bottom, but there was nothing to grab to pull herself up. Instead, she felt around with her feet to see how wide her dead-end was. One foot hit something soft. "Moonie, is that you?" Moonie whimpered next to her ear, not at her feet. She pulled her boot back as if scalded. "Ack! What is it?" She curled herself up into a ball. What if it was a bear?

Nell gathered up as much courage as she thought she would ever possess and turned herself around so she could touch whatever was soft with her hand. It was not furry. Not a bear. She felt material, cloth. As she groped with her hand in wider circles, she touched flesh. "Oh, no!" Cold, cold flesh. This was not something that was alive.

"Sheriff! Rosy! Where are you?" Her calls were loud to her ears, but the black tunnel swallowed them whole. She was going to have to figure out how to scramble back up the tunnel. She placed her feet on the rocks at the bottom and pushed her body up as far as she could. Then she swept her hands to her left and right, looking for something other than ice—and found it. Along one side wall was a narrow strip of rock or lava and a crack that felt as if it were filled with dirt.

"Come on, Moonshine. I'll boost you up. You see if you can climb out." She hugged her dog and shoved him over to the side wall. She took one paw and moved it along the dirt. He knew immediately what to do. She felt him grab hold in the non-icy patch and begin to move out of her reach. She followed with a touch on his leg as long as she could, and then he was gone.

Nell's head hurt and began to throb. She lay still, trying not to imagine what was there with her in the bottom of the tunnel. After a long while, she thought she saw the darkness grow a little less intense. Was it her imagination? She closed her eyes and then opened them again. No, it wasn't. "Sheriff? Rosy?"

"We're comin', Nellie. You hold on." Rosy's voice, rough as always, felt as if it could pull her out on its own.

"We will send a flashlight down to you, so you can see if there is a way to get out, a bigger trail than Moonshine was able to negotiate." The sheriff's voice comforted her. "It has to come slow because we can't see where it is going or if there are rocks in the way."

"All right. There is something down here with me." She tried to keep the tremble out of her voice but failed. Then a lit flashlight inched its way toward her at the end of a rope. "I have it!" She loosed the rope and flashed the light around her. The something soft looked like a bundle of clothes, something far too familiar from their other finds in other caves. Nothing she could do. She swept the light from side to side back up the slide. The strip where Moonshine had climbed out was narrow but widened as it went up. Maybe she could get a purchase on it.

"Can you bring it up?" The sheriff's voice.

"How can she do that an' climb, too?" Rosy's voice.

A low, rumbled conversation followed, but Nellie couldn't

hear any of it.

"Hey! I could wrap the rope around the . . . the thing, and you could keep pressure on it until I climb. Then I'd have something to hang on to." Nell didn't like that idea at all, but that was all she could come up with.

"All right."

"Nope. Let me come down and boost you up."

"No, Rosy! Don't come! We might never get you up. At least I'm light." She heard Moonie bark in the background. "Don't let Moonie back down either." Her voice was wearing out from shouting. "Hang on to the rope!" She pulled on it to get some slack, and then she squatted over the bundle and felt along it. Definitely a person. Almost frozen. She held her breath, pulled some more, and wrapped the rope around what felt like legs and then once again around the trunk. It wasn't easy, but the fact that it didn't move helped.

"I'm going to climb up where Moonie did. Keep the rope taut." She pulled on the rope and boosted herself to the narrow strip.

"You ain't that light, Nellie. Let us know when you're gonna pull!"

"I'm pulling from now on!" She couldn't do this with a flashlight in hand, so she stuck it down her sweater. Then she moved one hand at a time up the rope, taking little steps in the rocky strip. It wasn't rocky enough, and she slid several times. Her hands began to burn. Her gloves were in her camera pack—dumb to leave them there. "I have to rest!"

"All right. Let us know when you begin again." This time the sheriff's voice sounded much closer. Maybe she was making progress.

"Okay!" Nell began up again, and then her feet slid, but she managed to hold herself in place. Her arm muscles were trembling, and her hands ached. "Can you drop a glove towards me? I can't hang on without something for much longer."

"Can you wrap the rope around your waist?"

"It's fastened at both ends. How'm I going to do that?" She dug the flashlight out and looked around. Only parts of the slide were ice. There was another, wider dirt path if she could get over to it. The going might be easier than where she was.

"A glove's a'comin'."

A dark object slid toward her and then stopped out of reach. "Oh damn." She gripped as hard as she could and climbed up two steps and grabbed the cloth, steadied herself with one hand, and pulled it on. It was huge, but warm, and that helped.

"I'm going to try and swing some to the left—my left—and get on another patch of dirt. It looks wider and maybe not too steep. Hang on!" One, two, three, Nell counted to herself. She took a huge step to her left, and her foot at first skidded on ice, almost causing her to lose her grip. Then her boot stopped, and that foot was on dirt. Her gloved hand didn't slip at all. Her other foot caught up and helped her stabilize. Sweat trickled down her face and then her chin. Hard to think she was so hot in all the ice and cold. Once again, she stepped up. She could reach farther with the gloved hand, and she forced herself to ignore the burn on her other hand.

"All set?"

"Ye-es."

"Here comes another glove." This glove bounced and nearly slid past her, but she caught it, almost losing her balance in the process. Her other gloved hand saved her.

"Got it!" With two gloves on, Nellie made better progress and then could see Charlie's and Rosy's lights. "I'm almost there!"

"Hang on to me, Rosy. I'm going to reach down . . ." Charlie's hand appeared close to Nellie's head. She took another step and stretched as far as she could. He grabbed her wrist, and she grabbed his, and then he lifted her bodily into the air and out of the hole.

Nellie dropped to her knees, gasping for air. Rosy wrapped her up in his coat. "No, no. I'm too hot!"

"You won't be in two shakes." He kept the coat around her and helped her to stand up. "I'm gonna set you down over there, close to the lantern, while we drag up the . . . the thing you wrapped the rope around. Here's my canteen. Drink some."

In a moment, Nellie was thankful for the coat. The water in the canteen, smelling as usual of metal, tasted like ambrosia to her. She watched the two men pull on the bundle, hand over hand. "Do you want your gloves back, Rosy?" She could see his bare hands in the jumping light. She began to get up.

"You stay there, Cora Nell." This from the sheriff. "We almost have it. Do not get in the way."

Happy to stay seated on the flat rock Rosy had found for her, Nellie did as instructed. "Where's my camera? And Moonshine? And Tom?" She took the flashlight from her sweater and swept it around. Her camera leaned against the side of the cave. Tom and Moonshine weren't anywhere.

"Rosy, take Nell out of here, please. Round up Tom. Nell and Moonshine can wait in the light. The three of us can carry this . . . out where I can see."

"No, I want to help!"

"C'mon, Nellie. I'll carry your camera."

"No, I'll carry my own camera."

Rosy helped Nellie over the rough spots of ice and rock, and soon they returned to where light came through the hole in the dome. The area was empty, so Rosy and Nellie pushed on. She didn't care about another photograph at the moment. When they reached the stage, there was Mayor Tom, sitting with Moonshine, holding him with the leash.

"Need your help, Tom." Rosy turned to Nellie. "You wait

here. Keep Moonshine here, too." He patted her shoulder. "Dog saved you, y'know."

"Yes, I know." Nellie hugged Moonie and kissed him all over his face and ears. Moonshine cuddled up to her and folded his front legs in her lap. *Arp, arp.* "Let's go outside, Moonshine. Enough of this dark." Nellie stumbled from exhaustion but made it into the sunshine. Even the black lava fields were a welcome sight, but the blue skies and clouds were even more so. Clouds.

CHAPTER 10

Mrs. Bock held each boy by a hand and walked to the train station. "Here is where you arrived," she said. Neither boy said anything. "Now we'll walk to the school house." Ketchum was so small after the mines mostly closed there weren't many places to show the boys. The old mill down by Warm Springs was closed. The train still went to the mill, but she did not know if Guyer Hot Springs was still open in the fall. People from Boise and Idaho Falls and even farther away came through in the summer, either going to the hot springs or up and over Galena Pass to do campouts with the cowboys in the Stanley Basin. Nellie had described being at Fourth of July Lake and the camps there.

The school house sat large and empty on a Saturday. The huge gray stones added up to two stories, and a flag drooped from the flagpole in front. Stairs led to double wood doors. "This is where you will go to school, until your father can make arrangements for living and a job. You might move to Hailey. You came through Hailey on the train."

"I saw two boys playing outside the train. Are there any boys here?" Matt's yearning was apparent in the dark eyes he turned on her.

"I don't know, Matt. I don't know any, but there must be boys at school, and you will meet them on Monday." She hoped. Not many people left in town.

A man driving a paneled truck stopped near the three of

them. He opened the door and stepped out. "Are you Goldie Bock?"

"That's who I am. Who're you?" The man's dirty clothes contrasted with her sense of seemliness.

"Name's Max Adkins. I just come back from the lava fields. Trapper, here, was with me." He motioned to the other man in the truck. "We delivered a—uh . . . we made a delivery to the—to Hailey for the sheriff and Rosy. Rosy said to come tell you that he and the sheriff and that lady photographer are camping out tonight. They'll be back tomorrow but might be late. They's heading on to another section of the fields to see if they can find someone who's lost."

"What did you deliver?" She peered around him into the truck. The other man was just as dirty.

The man looked at the boys. "I'd rather not say, ma'am. They found what they was looking for, if you know what I mean."

"Was it lost?" Mrs. Bock released Matt's hand. He pulled away and stomped through a pile of leaves. "I thought they knew what they were getting."

"It was gone. But then they found it in another cave." Max moved to return to the truck, then stopped to talk a minute more. "Almost lost the camera lady is what I heard them say when they came back with . . . it."

Mrs. Bock shook her head. How Nellie got into so much trouble, she didn't know. "Thanks for telling me."

The trio walked back to the boarding house, and Mrs. Bock cranked up the telephone to call Guyer Hot Springs. She learned they were open on Saturday, and the group could come out to swim. The old shuttle train that used to carry ore to the smelter ran on weekends in the fall to the mill, and a carriage would pick them up. They could ride out, stay a while, and ride back later. Goldie asked Esther if she wanted to come with them, hoping Rosy's sister would say no.

"Yes, I would. I don't have a swimming dress along with me though."

"Well, neither do I, but we can figger out something to wear in the water. Do the boys have some short pants?"

Someone knocked at the front door. "Who d'you suppose that is? No one knocks." Mrs. Bock strode to the door and opened it. "This ain't a house . . ."

"Are you the owner here?" The tall stranger interrupted her and removed a huge Stetson to reveal thick pepper and salt hair when she opened the door. "I heard tell that Miss Burns lives here, the photographer, and she takes pictures of crimes. I want to report a crime and ask her to come and photograph it."

Mrs. Bock managed not to laugh. "I think the person you want is Sheriff Azgo. He's the crime solver around here. His reg'lar office is in Hailey, but he ain't there right now." It occurred to her then that she shouldn't say he was out of town. Maybe this man intended on committing a crime. "He's probably over in his Ketchum office right now. City Hall is around the corner and down the street." She pointed.

"I'll tell him soon enough. Meanwhile I need a picture."

"Can't help ya." Mrs. Bock rolled her eyes. "What sort of crime are you talkin' about?"

"Somebody abandoned a baby—right at the door of the church. I was visiting and found it with a note on it. Someone's gotta take care of it, and I want to be sure the basket and baby get looked at and seen just like it was when I found it." He fingered his Stetson by the rim so it moved up and down. "I don't want anyone accusing me of abandonment. The minister's gone, and no one's there except an old lady who talks all the time, and she'll throw it all away or my name isn't Peter Banks."

"Hello, Peter Banks. C'mon in." Goldie sighed. Weren't two boys enough? "You can telephone the sheriff's office from here.

Then I'll come back with you and see just what it is you're talkin' about. That'll have to do. Miss Burns is not here."

When Peter Banks and Mrs. Bock arrived at the church, Mrs. Henny Penny (as Goldie called her because she always swore the sky was falling in) sat on the church steps. " 'Bout time you got here. Where's that picture lady? I told this man we needed proof that this child was left and abandoned right here on the steps. I thought at first this man left it here, but upon reconsideration, I changed my mind. Where would a man get a baby, now I ask you." Her mouth closed for three seconds, and Goldie hastened to get her own two cents in.

"Now, Penelope, Nellie Burns ain't here. I'll take notes and give 'em to the sheriff. Just tell me what you found and how you found it."

"This man here—"

"I can tell my own tale," he interrupted. "I went into the church to say a prayer for my sister who has the cancer. When I came out, here was this pile of blankets right by the door. I could easily have stepped on it. I stepped over it and was going on my way, because I thought it was a bum of some sort. Then I heard a squall, so I leaned down and lifted up one corner of the filthy thing. And there was this baby."

Mrs. Henny Penny moved aside. Hidden by her skirt was a dirty sheet wrapped around and around a baby, whose head barely peeked out. "Newborn it is," Penelope said. "I can tell 'cause I seen lots of newborns around these towns, between all the Catholics and the Mormons. They're always havin' babies. We could fill up every town . . ."

Goldie swept up the sheet and baby. The cloth was so dirty, she didn't want it to get into the baby's mouth. "Where's the note? I'll take this little thing over to my boarding house and find someone who can take care of it." The bundle mewled like a tiny kitten. "Have you even fed it?"

"He told me not to touch anything or do anything! Or he'd have my hide!" Mrs. Henny Penny stood up and was about to hit the stranger, Peter Banks, with her purse. He fended her off.

"I told you. I didn't want anyone to accuse me of leaving this baby here." Peter Banks's voice rose.

And now why would they do that, Mrs. Bock wondered. How many men went around with babies in their company. "I have it now. I'll see it gets fed and cleaned up and find a nurse or someone to take care of it until we find out where it come from." She turned to the man. "You better come with me. You need to write down what you found and when. And where you live and how the sheriff can find you. And we need the note."

The baby was a girl. Goldie washed her in the sink and swaddled her with a wool blanket. She heated up some milk and fed her with the end of her finger. There was a scab, moist and scaly, where the umbilical cord had been cut away but not cleaned. She thought the little mite was lucky to be alive. It couldn't be more than several days old. Her mewl was so weak, she might not live yet. Then Goldie telephoned the hospital, if it could be called that, in Hailey and asked to speak to the head nurse—probably the only nurse. Mrs. Bock explained the circumstances and asked if there was anyone in town who just had a baby. This child needed breast milk and more care than Goldie could give. Meanwhile, Esther paced around, watching and complaining about the baby and whoever had left it. Civilized folk didn't do things like that. And who would take a strange baby under her care. She wouldn't.

Peter Banks sat at the dining room table and wrote out a long letter to the sheriff. "Here it is. And here is the note." It had been stuffed in his pocket and was crumpled.

"What does it say?" Goldie asked.

"It says something about here's a baby. Take care of it."

Goldie took the note. The writing was loopy and disheveled,

the same as the note. Goldie could barely make out the words. She read them aloud. "Take care of this little child. God says 'come unto me, you little children,' and so I am leaving her at this church." It was unsigned, of course.

"Humph. Well, I never." Esther left the room and went upstairs. The boys were outside, playing in the side yard, which was mostly dirt. They had raked up a stack of leaves and were jumping in it and shouting.

Goldie swaddled the baby. She had no clothes for her and wasn't sure where to find any. She wished Nellie would return but now didn't expect her until the next day. The baby nuzzled at her chest. "Nothin' there, little one. I'll feed you some more milk. Hope I hear back soon from Hailey."

CHAPTER 11

Sheriff Azgo spent time over the body outside in the light. He motioned to Nell to take photographs. The woman's face was scraped from her fall down the ice cave. The sheriff moved the clothes from her neck where red scratches marred it. Either Nell was getting used to the grisly details, or her experience in the ice herself had hardened her. She noticed a fragile chain had broken, maybe losing a pendant in the woman's clothes.

After the sheriff tucked the clothing back around the neck, he shifted his attention to the long, black skirt. "Help me with this. I want to see if there are any other wounds. I do not think her neck was scratched or her face marred when we first found her."

Nell was reluctant to touch the body's clothes, but she pulled up the skirt as the sheriff lifted the torso. "Oh! There's . . ." She held her hands up. They were covered in a light sheen of red. "It must be blood. Dried blood that the ice—" Nell drew away and then wiped her hands on her pants. "I can't."

"Never mind. We will bundle her up and send her to Hailey. The doctor there can find out where the blood came from." He laid her gently down again. "We will continue our search. We know there is one more person to find."

Nell released her camera from the tripod and put it away. Then the sheriff helped Max and Trapper and Tom load the body onto the stretcher, tied it around with a rope, and sent all three off to the road. He didn't ask Tom to come back as Rosy said he could help them find the tree molds and then find their way back to the road. Tom would meet them there in the afternoon and take the horse back to Arco. In the meantime, the sheriff, Nellie, and Rosy would use it to carry gear. Tom described where a water hole could be found near the Big Sink. Whether there was water in it, he didn't know. "Bein' it's fall, there might not be any. Still, the caves had ice."

"Let's get to the Big Sink and set up camp," Rosy said. "Then we can figger out about water. We got canteens for now." He helped load the horse and took its lead. "Good thing I don't have to carry moonshine on this trip."

Nellie was surprised at how much cheerier Rosy was without his once ever-present jar of hooch. She almost missed his contrariness and his honesty. Now, he seemed more like most people. He and Charlie were nigh onto friendly. And she sounded like a Westerner even in her thoughts. "Do those clouds worry anyone?"

"I have been watching them. We may get rain tonight, but that would be unusual. The tent is big enough for all three of us to lay out blankets and sleeping bags. The ground will be harder than it will be wet."

"Mite cozy, don't you think?" The horse was having some difficulty traveling. Even Moonshine appeared to be high-stepping over the rocky ground and all its clinkers where they traveled. "You two keep on straight." He pointed to the west. "See that steep hill with the rocky top, like two points? Keep headin' in that direction. You'll know the Big Sink when you get there." Rosy pulled the horse and called for Moonshine to follow him. Moonie looked at Nell. "Go on with Rosy. He'll find a better place for your paws." The small leather booties were wearing through.

The sheriff kept up a good pace, and Nellie found herself falling back. She still had her camera on her back. So far, there were not many places where a photograph would reflect the grotesque surface. Still, the clouds blossomed higher, and several had flat gray bottoms. She decided to set up her camera and see what she could see on the back screen. "I'd like to stop and take a photograph, Charlie. You keep going. I think I can see you when I start up again."

He sighed. "We do not have a lot of time to set up camp and prepare something to eat. I know you are tired, but the sooner we get to the Big Sink, the sooner you can rest. You can take photographs there."

"Then it might be too dark. Leave me your compass and point me where we are going. I'll follow as soon as I take a photograph here. The best light is coming from around those clouds." Even as she spoke, Nell glanced around, looking for a suitable spot for her tripod.

Another sigh. He pulled the compass from his pocket and handed it to Nellie, showing her how to sight on it and where she should keep the arrow in order to follow the same line he would be following. "Come no later than fifteen minutes from now."

Nellie nodded, put the compass into her camera bag as she pulled out the camera, and set up the tripod. By the time she had her camera and black cloth ready to cover her head, the sheriff had already disappeared in the distance. She wished now she hadn't been so stubborn about a photograph. The sky hung like a dark bell around her, and the deepening shadows seemed as if they muted all the sounds of even the quiet desert. There were no birds in sight, and not a lizard or a squirrel disturbed the immense silence. "All right," she told herself, just to hear a sound. "I'll hurry."

Once the black cloth was over her head and she focused on the long-distance scene of rocks and clouds, planning the photo as three-quarters sky and clouds and one-quarter land, she lost herself in finding the right angle. She might have one of her best ever photographs of this strange moonscape. After she pushed the shutter, she readied herself to follow the sheriff. She peered in every direction but could see nothing but lava rock and occasional grass.

When she opened the compass, she wasn't certain she remembered what the sheriff had told her. There was north. She was to travel south, but not due south. She studied the arrow, and, even as she watched it, it vibrated, as if pulled in the wrong direction. To travel south now looked as if it was at a different angle from where she had decided a few moments ago. Then the arrow swung ten to fifteen degrees back and forth. She held her breath, and it seemed to decide where to land, and it was not in the same place as it had been. What had Rosy said? Nell looked around again and saw the rocky-topped feature in the distance. That was where she was supposed to go. Something was wrong with the compass, and she couldn't depend on it.

With her pack on her back, Nell began her trek toward the rough top. It looked far away, and she knew already that distances were deceiving in this strange country. Walking toward it—stumbling would have been a better word—took her in what she hoped was the right direction. The sun sank lower, and the angle of light changed. A dusty, almost white, path appeared in the lava not far from her. She scrambled over to it. It ran roughly in the direction she thought she should be traveling.

Once again, she pulled out the compass. This time, the needle pointed north, almost directly behind her. It didn't swerve or swing or tremble. She was facing south. The dusty path veered off to the right. A rock cairn caught a late sunbeam. And then in the distance, she heard a series of howls. They made her skin crawl and the hair on the back of her neck rise. Whether this was an Indian trail or an animal trail, she didn't know, but, whatever it was, she would follow it. It seemed to aim in the general direction she should travel. Surely, the sheriff had seen it, too. Maybe he had built the cairn. The path was so much smoother than her earlier travel, she could hurry faster. The only bad thing was that it also seemed to be heading in the direction of the howls.

Nevertheless, Nell picked up her pace. It grew darker, and then she felt a raindrop, and two and more. The clouds sank almost to the ground. She still had a flashlight in her pack, so she dug it out, along with a rain poncho. The light barely shone. In the distance she saw what looked like a campfire. The howls had stopped with the lowering of the clouds. At last, she neared the fire. There was no tent, but a tarp had been strung up over the branch of a pine tree. A figure crouched near the fire while sitting under the edge of the tarp. This was not the sheriff or Rosy.

"Hello," Nell called.

A face, pale in the flames' reflection, turned toward her. The person watched her as she neared the fire. "Still out here, are you? You should be at home, cookin' dinner for a husband and kids. Not wanderin' in the lava fields."

It was Ben O'Donnell, the cowboy who said he herded cattle in the area. Nell relaxed. She really hadn't expected a ghost, but the eerie world of the craters seemed like it could conjure up anything, especially after two bodies had been found. "Hello, Mr. O'Donnell. Are your cattle close?"

The man gestured off to the darkness, growing blacker by the minute.

"I was following Sheriff Azgo and Rosy Kipling to a campsite by the Big Sink. Is it near here?" Nell took a step toward where the cowboy had gestured. "My compass stopped working."

"The Big Sink is that big hole in the ground. You ain't too far. Not sure you can find it now that it's dark." He patted the canvas cloth next to him. "Sit a while. Maybe your friends'll come lookin' for you." Then a person crept out from the back of the tarp. When the person looked out and up, Nellie started.

"What are you doing here?"

"Pearl! I could ask you the same question." Nellie moved closer. "You're a long way from home."

"No, I'm not. I work here with Ben now. I wasn't wanted in Stanley, and I wasn't going to stick around there, not after . . ." She looked at Ben and stopped.

In the firelight, Pearl's hair looked almost white. She grabbed Ben's shoulder and pulled herself up at the edge of the tarp. "How're you doing? Is your arm all healed up?"

Nellie was so surprised to find Pearl, her almost-friend from the summer and companion in the escapades around the mountains in the Stanley Basin, she didn't know what to say.

"No. Yes. My arm is fine. Are you really a wrangler, like Mr. O'Connell said? Was that you the other day?" No wonder the person on the horse had seemed familiar. She was.

"Ben here is the wrangler." She patted his shoulder. "I just ride along to help." A sly smile moved her mouth. "Don't I, Ben?" Pearl motioned to the fire. "Set a while. There ain't no moonshine here."

Nell stayed where she was, undecided. Her friends would be worried about her, and so would Moonie. There was still some light left, but not much.

"I think I'll keep going. My friends will worry." Her stomach grumbled then. She was sure Ben and Pearl could hear it. "I'll follow this path I've been on."

"That won't take you to where you want to go," Ben said. "It heads back to the blue lava—sacred grounds accordin' to the Indians. Who knows if their spirits are out there dancin' and whoopin' it up. For all I know, they sacrifice bodies here. Savages. I've heard strange sounds when I been campin' around these rocks."

"I'd go with you," Pearl offered, "but we can't leave the cattle in a storm." Ben made no motion to get up.

"You'll need to veer off to the left, over thattaway." Again, he gestured, but his pointing was so vague, it didn't provide any real direction at all. "You better set yourself down. We got a little dinner left. You can have it."

Pearl said nothing more. When Nellie demurred, she moved again to the back of the tarp. "Suit yourself."

Nell decided to trust her instincts and leave. "I'll find them. Thanks for the offer." She returned to her path and moved as fast as she could without actually running. When the fire was far behind her, she again looked at her compass and tried to re-orient herself. It wasn't bouncing around this time, and her flashlight had enough power to show its face. That path continued to go the way she wanted to go. Were Ben and Pearl trying to mix her up? Why were they so far from the cattle if a storm was coming? And Indians. She doubted if there were any in these lands anymore. The white people had made certain of that.

A gigantic spear of lighting flashed in front of her, followed immediately by the crash of thunder. It was so startling and bright, she jumped a foot and gasped. There were few trees around her, and she might be the tallest thing in the area. This time, she did run, but stumbled and nearly fell. The lightning sizzled again, and in the afterglow, she saw a figure off to her side, tall as a man, but bent forward, perhaps twenty or thirty feet away. This time, she screamed, but it was lost in another thunder crack.

"Charlie! Rosy! Where are you?"

CHAPTER 12

An animal leaped on her, and she wrapped her arm around her head, trying to protect herself. And then the animal licked her face. "Oh, Moonshine! I thought you were a wolf!" She held him, and the tears flowed and mixed in with the rain. "I'm lost."

"You are not lost, Nell." The sheriff strode up and put his arms around her and hugged her to him. "We have you." The sheriff's flashlight showed the way on the ground. It was in a different direction than Ben O'Donnell had pointed.

"Were you over there?" Nell pointed and held onto Charlie's arm. "I thought I saw a man when the lightning flashed."

"No. I am right here. No one else is here, except Rosy in the tent."

Nell knew she had seen someone—or something—but she didn't argue. She was safe. Moonshine stayed close to her. She could feel him nudge her leg and then her arm. If Moonshine had seen anyone, he would have barked. Maybe she imagined it. The rocks formed all kinds of strange constructions, especially when seen in the dark. She could investigate in the morning.

"Come along. Dinner is ready for you."

A fire lit the tent. Rosy stepped out and added another piece of wood. "Can't no one sneak up on these rocks." He, too, wrapped an arm around Nell. "What're you tryin' to do? Give this old man a heart attack?"

"You're not old, Rosy. The storm made it so dark, I thought I lost my way." She stood in front of the fire. The rain, light as it was, had chilled her. "I ran into Ben O'Donnell back there. And guess who was with him? Pearl from this summer." She turned to Charlie. "They had a fire going and Ben acted strange—he sat there and pointed me in the wrong direction." Nell rubbed her hands together. "Charlie mentioned food? I turned Ben and Pearl down, although they were courteous enough to offer me the remains of their dinner." There had been no sign of any food anywhere. What had they been up to?

"Got beans and biscuits—your favorite." Rosy filled up a plate. "You ain't never gonna want beans and biscuits again in your life!"

"I grew used to them this summer, although I usually had lamb to go with," she said. "And rosemary and wine."

"I got just the thing for you, then." Rosy sorted through his pack in the tent's doorway and pulled out a dark-green wine bottle. "The Basque make the best. Here's a cupful for you. This'll heat you up fast enough." He glanced at Charlie. "You want some, too? Might be good for what ails ya." He held up the bottle. "I won't tell nobody that you're breakin' the law."

A smile tugged at Charlie's mouth. He brought out a cup from his own pack and held it out. "These are special circumstances, I would say. Even for you."

The electrical storm had moved away, and the rain stopped. The three of them sat around the fire on a long dead branch Rosy had found. The night felt grim, and none of them said much. Then Nellie remembered about the compass. She told Charlie how it had jumped around.

"The lava must have been magnetic near where we were," he said. "I should have thought of that. I am sorry you were confused."

"Will that always happen out here?"

"No, only at certain places. If you move around, you should

be able find the spots where the compass will work—away from any magnetism."

Rosy retrieved a canteen from the horse, which he had tied loosely to a nearby tree. They could hear the animal munch on leaves or shrubs. Rosy poured water in a small bucket and gave it to the horse. Nell borrowed Charlie's flashlight and walked a short ways from camp to be private. When she returned, both men were in the tent, and Rosy was asleep, rolled in his blanket.

"You get the middle, Nell, so you will not wander off." Charlie had laid out her sleeping bag. She crawled in, thankful to be protected by two strong friends.

Morning brought sunshine again. No clouds marred the deep blue of the bell sky. When Nell realized both men were up and about, she pulled herself out of her bag and rolled it up as they had done with their bags and blankets.

Rosy stirred a pan of mush over the fire and served it out on the metal plates. There were a few biscuits left from the night before, so they ate and then tidied up. Being waited on agreed with Nellie.

They were perched at the bottom of a steep slope, black and red and bare. The few trees and shrubs around the base didn't extend up. "Where's the Big Sink?" Nellie asked.

"Take a hike up yonder. You'll see. Don't fall in." Rosy packed their gear on the horse.

Nellie climbed. And climbed until she reached a steep incline down the other way. Before her lay a giant crater, aptly named. It was hundreds of yards across and dry as a bone. At the inside base, a circular field of flat rock looked as if it could hold an army of tents and men. A movement caught at the corner of her eye. A short way around the arc, two marmots chased each other, their fur golden. One stopped and whistled, then disappeared into an animal tunnel or hole. She turned to watch

Charlie and Rosy far below. Camp had almost disappeared, and they were ready to begin the search again. Rosy whistled and gestured to her. "C'mon down!"

This day, Nell planned to stay close. Photographs be damned. As they marched along, she remembered she had hoped to investigate what she thought she saw the night before. Too late. A skein of wild geese flew over them, honking. Small birds flitted in swoops in front of them, as if leading the way. Nell kept looking around for more animals, hoping to catch sight of another lizard or chipmunk or marmot. The lava fields appeared alive this morning with animal and plant life. They strode alongside a field filled with the lava bombs. Some had cracked tops; others formed into spirals and other bizarre shapes. Crunchy cinders reflected light in prisms, tossing off millions of miniature rainbows. The brief spate of rain the night before made everyone happy, even their trio.

They continued south and slightly west. As the early morning passed, the heat began to gather. Soon, they were shedding coats. Nell tied a scarf around the top of her head. "Do you know where you're going, Rosy?" she called to him.

"Yup, I do. The tree molds should be turnin' up soon. They look like clay had been wrapped around trees, and then the trees—poof—disappeared. Burned up, I'd say. You might want to take some pitchers."

The trio entered an area with evergreens and shrubs, the latter either bare of leaves or with some orange and yellow remnants, soon to be gone, too. Along the ground were several trenches—tree molds. Bark imprinted on the encircling lava looked as Rosy described. Nellie squatted to touch the patterns. They felt like, and were, stone.

"Are you going to stay around this area? I'll take a few photos if you are. Otherwise, I'll stick close to you two."

"There's no caves right here," Rosy said. "We can scout for

footprints, but that rain last night mighta scoured everything clean. I'll go on up ahead, Charlie. You look around here."

The light wasn't right to get much definition on the tree molds. Nell tried, but eventually lost interest and turned her attention to the surrounding area. There was what looked like an island of trees, shrubs, even grass to the west, but she was reluctant to walk away. Charlie was in sight, but farther along a path, and Rosy was nowhere to be seen. The horse was once again tied to a stout shrub. Moonshine sat in the shade of one of the tree molds, licking at his front paw. The leather cover had dropped off.

While she was deciding what to do, Moonshine stood up and growled. The hair on the back of his neck stood straight up. "What's wrong, Moonie?" Nell glanced around but saw nothing unusual.

Her dog barked and then ran off in the direction where Rosy had walked away. "Moonie, come back!" Charlie tried to stop him, but the dog turned and ran toward the island, barking and growling. Then she saw what he had seen or heard—a huge cat. A mountain lion. "Oh no! Moonshine! Come here!" She began to run after him. Charlie caught up to her and grabbed her arm.

"You can't get in that fight," he said. He dashed forward himself and scooped up one of the smaller lava bombs. He threw it at the lion, narrowly missing its head. The animal stopped short, swung to look toward Charlie, who threw another, smaller missile, again just missing, but scuffing at its feet. Moonshine stopped, too.

Nell followed Charlie's lead and picked up a much smaller stone. Her aim was truer. It smacked the lion on its nose. Outnumbered by man, woman, and dog, the lion turned and ran back to the island, where it disappeared in the brush.

"Moonshine! You might have been hurt. Were you protecting

us?" Nell sank to her knees and pulled the dog to her. "And look at your sore paw. Sit still, and I'll tie a scarf around it." She pulled the scarf off her head and wrapped it securely around the front paw. The other leather pouches still held.

"I am going to that area with trees and brush. You stay here and wait for Rosy. He should be back soon. And then we will return to the road. The rain ruined any prints around here, if there were any at all." Charlie began to walk away. He turned back toward her. "Your rock did the trick."

Nell waited with Moonie until Rosy returned. "Nothin'." She told him where Charlie had gone and about the skirmish with the mountain lion. She wanted to get back to Ketchum to develop her photographs. There were so many, she might have to travel to Twin Falls to print them, using the dark room belonging to Jacob Levine, the photographer she first met the previous winter. She had not worked for him much during the summer and could use the extra money. Her own facilities were still so limited, although she had been searching for a place to set up a proper dark room with the right equipment. The money she had earned from her photos for the railroad would buy the most expensive piece of equipment, an enlarger. The trays, lights, and chemicals would be cheaper, and maybe Jacob would give her items he had discarded.

When Charlie returned he said he found a possible campsite, but he could not tell how old it was. There had been a fire round and some broken branches stacked for burning. It could have been there for months or for days. The storm had licked up any better signs of occupation. "Take us to the road, Rosy. We can always come back later, but I think we have found what we are going to find."

"There's one more cave—not too far from this side of the Big Sink—along the slope near the jagged top mountain, close to a smaller cinder mountain with a huge crack in it. Do you wanta check on it? It's been a long time since I was there. Mighta fallen in by now."

Nell thought the sheriff looked tired and discouraged. She knew that was how she felt. Two bodies. No obvious answers. A possible third one somewhere in these wild places, surely one of the women based on Mayor Tom's description of the people who disappeared.

"How far out of our way to return to the road?"

"Not so far. We gotta head kinda that way anyway."

The sheriff nodded. He picked up the lead on the horse and followed Rosy. Once again, Nell took up the rear. Moonie stayed with her, limping on his scarfed paw.

CHAPTER 13

Goldie didn't want Esther along at the hot springs but couldn't think of an excuse to keep her away. She wanted time alone with the boys. As it turned out, she didn't get time alone anyway. Goldie had forgotten, if she ever knew, that men and women bathed separately in different pools—women with clothes on and men buck-naked. Campbell wanted to stay with the women, and Matt didn't want to go alone with the men.

All four stood in a quandary while a clerk waited impatiently to pass out towels and shepherd the boys to the men's pool. Campbell held Goldie's hand.

"Let's just go back home," Esther said. "I don't want Matt going in there all alone. Who knows what goes on?" She huffed at the idea of "all those men" being naked. Goldie doubted there were many men at all. She asked the clerk.

"Just two or three," he offered and named two people Goldie knew. The third one was Peter Banks, the man who brought the orphan to her.

"Can I send in a note with Matt?" Goldie asked. When the clerk nodded, she wrote a short piece asking one of the men, Bert the butcher, to keep an eye on Matt and sent him off. "Campbell can come with us," she told the clerk in a tone that brooked no argument.

In the women's pool, where almost a dozen women enjoyed the heat, all wore costumes of various vintage: Some wore short dresses; some wore jersey union-type suits; some seemed to be dressed in men's swim suits with a form-fitting top and tight breeches to the knees. Several women floated lazily or sat on benches around the sides. Campbell wore short pants and played water games in the shallow end. One woman, less covered than anyone, floated close to the wall separating the sexes. She stopped from time to time and tried to peek through what looked like chinks in the wall. Esther stood and pointed her out to Goldie. "I swan. That woman is trying to look at the men!"

Goldie didn't care. She watched Campbell and from time to time tossed a ball back to him that he had thrown into the water. When she looked up, the woman, who must have heard Esther, moved away from her peeking with flushed cheeks. Goldie did not know her, which was a little unusual in itself. She had a nodding acquaintance with everyone else. On weekends in the fall, people usually came from Boise to take the waters, but this was a quiet Saturday. More would arrive in the late afternoon.

After an hour in the mineral baths, Goldie sent Campbell to fetch Matt, while she and Esther changed from their put-together swimming outfits into street clothes. Still no boys when they moved into the lobby area. After another while, Goldie asked the clerk to retrieve the boys. Again, the women waited. At last, Matt and Campbell came running out with Peter Banks. At the same time, the curious woman entered the lobby, dressed in a long, black dress. She walked up to Peter as he was greeting Goldie and latched onto his arm.

"I hope you haven't waited long." Her lips mouthed an air kiss, and she stood as close to him as she could get without devouring him.

"We had a great time! Mr. Banks played ball with us, and we raced from one end to the other! We chased it, pretending we were black Labs!" They play-acted their activities in the pool.

Peter smiled at the clinging vine but loosed his arm and

stepped away. "Mrs. Bock. Were you able to find assistance?" No mention of the baby.

"Yes." If he was going to be cryptic, so would she be.

"Assistance with what?" asked the vine. "My name is Euphemia. What's yours?" Her voice was high-pitched and sounded almost like a child's. Peter turned to look at the woman but said nothing.

"I'm Mrs. Bock." Goldie shushed the boys, glared at Esther, and turned to go. So, the man who found the baby was not alone and, even more, apparently had a wife, or maybe a sister. Maybe the child was hers, although her straight figure did not seem to have been enceinte recently. Hard to tell.

But Esther stayed to talk. "I'm Esther Kipling. Maybe you know my brother, Ross. Some people call him Rosy." She threw a glower in Goldie's direction. "We have recently moved from Chicago with my two nephews, Matt and Campbell." The boys joined her, then romped off to the front lawn of the Guyer Hotel. "Are you from here—you and your husband?"

"She's not—"

"Peter is not my husband, are you, dear. He's just a good friend. We came up from San Francisco to enjoy the waters. I have an arthritic condition, and the minerals are helping me."

"Are you staying here?" Esther wasn't bashful about her own curiosity. "I've never been to California."

"And I've never been to Chicago. Do you live in town here? It doesn't seem like much of a place to live. It looks abandoned, almost a ghost town—all except for this lovely lodge."

Mrs. Bock admired Esther for her blunt snooping but had work to do. "We're leaving, Esther. Are you coming with us?" She turned. "Boys. We're going home."

"Can Mr. Banks come too?" Matt called.

"No, your father should be home tomorrow. He can bring you out here again another day."

CHAPTER 14

Unlike the other caves, this one alongside the cracked mountain opened under a lip in a circle of rock that looked like a small crater. There was an opening on one end that didn't go anywhere. On the other side, like the other caves, a rock fall impeded their entrance, but the afternoon light coming from the west shone in much further. There was no warning that this one might be the cause of disaster, until, on the way down, the sheriff leaped from one unstable rock to another. As he landed, the stone surface split, and his fall tumbled him down into the tunnel.

"Charlie!" Nellie scrambled across the rock fall as fast as she dared. Rosy was already in front of her. Moonie was quickest and scooted down on his paws until he could stand next to the sheriff, who didn't move. Rosy reached the bottom and called back.

"Stay there! You'll cause other rocks to fall." He turned toward the sheriff.

Nell could see Rosy crouch down, touch the sheriff's head, then feel along his limbs. Moonie stood still, as if he knew any movement would cause trouble.

The shadows lengthened. When the sun dipped behind a nearby broken rock wall, a chill seeped across the face of the lava and flowed down to where they were, Nellie on top, the two men and dog in the darkest part.

"Is he all right?" Nellie's voice quavered. "What can I do?"

She wanted to scramble down, too, but that would only change the position of her helplessness.

"Got to keep Charlie warm," Rosy yelled up. "Get my blankets."

"All right." Nellie hurried back out of the cave, slipped herself, and slowed down. Two hurt people could be a catastrophe. At the horse, she untied Rosy's bedroll, grabbed a canteen, and looked for a flashlight. Her batteries were dead. Not there. Rosy and Charlie carried both. She did find matches in a saddlebag and grabbed a dead branch as she carried her load to the top of the hole.

"Is he awake yet?"

"Comin' 'round. Broken leg."

Oh no, Nellie thought. "I'm rolling your bed roll down. I have a canteen, too." The bedroll slipped a ways and stopped. Nellie prodded it with the branch, and it rolled close enough for Rosy to climb up and retrieve. "I'll throw the canteen. Watch yourself." She aimed it just short of Rosy and hit her target. He took a huge swig and held it up to Charlie's mouth.

"Do you have a flashlight?"

Rosy had taken off his pack and laid it aside. "Yup, if it still works."

"I can gather wood and build a fire up here—or come down and do it there."

"No room. Stay there. Gotta think what to do."

Charlie groaned.

Oh no, oh no. "We have a rope," she called. "I'll see if it's long enough to stretch from the horse." She picked her way out again. The light was leaving the cave area, and she had to be more careful than before. She untied the horse and brought it as close to the cave entrance as she could. There was a good-sized rock in the circle that might hold a rope. The other piece of luck was the loop still tied at the end of the rope. She placed it over the saddle horn, used the reins to link the horse to the rock, and then unrolled the rope as she stepped over one rock and another on her way back to the hole. There were three loops left, maybe just barely enough to reach Charlie.

"I'm not sure it's long enough." All her exertion brought Nellie to a cold sweat, and the rope length almost drove her to tears. "Wait. I'll see if I can get the horse in closer."

"Don't break its leg," Rosy shouted. "Then we'll really be in a pickle."

Back at the cave entrance, Moonie joined Nellie. She cleared a path as best she could so she could lead the horse closer to the hole. The horse did not want to go. Nellie held the horse's head and talked to it. "It's okay. You'll be okay. We need your help." She couldn't even remember the horse's name. Gradually, it took one step and then two. Moonie nudged the horse's front legs. Nellie pulled gently, wanting instead to jerk it ahead. Back again to Rosy and Charlie. "Is that any better?"

Rosy grunted and pulled Charlie up several feet inside of the hole, swearing and breathing hard. "All right now. I'm going to tie the rope around his chest. Then get the horse to pull back—slow as can be. Can you do that?"

I'll try, Nellie mouthed to herself. At the horse, Nellie kept a hand on the rope loop on the saddle horn. If the animal spooked, she would have to get it off as quickly as possible, or Charlie would be pulled across the rocks. She couldn't even imagine what damage that would do. The horse stepped back, stopped, stepped back, and stopped. Nelly hugged its neck lightly. She wanted to call to Rosy but didn't want to frighten the horse. Another three steps back. Then the horse seemed to stumble. Nellie pressed her face to its neck. "It's okay. It's okay. Hold still. I've got you. It's okay." The animal calmed, but a shudder ran through its head and down its neck. Nellie and the horse reached the crater's edge. Moonshine sat beside it as Nellie released the loop, tied the horse to another rock, and rushed back to the cave entrance. "Rosy? Are you up yet? I released the rope. Should I put it back?" She waited. "Rosy?"

"You'll bust my ears," he said, almost beside her. She jumped and then grabbed him for a hug. "Where's Charlie?"

"I've got him above the hole and propped up against a rock. Blankets are all tucked around him. Got to find a splint of some sort, so we can move him onto this flat crater area."

"Moonshine, go sit with Charlie." The dog left his perch beside the horse and trotted over to Charlie above the rocks at the cave entrance. "Keep him warm," she called. She looked around and so did Rosy. Other than the dead branch Nellie had carried in earlier, neither found a straight stick or tree limb. "I know. My tripod. We can use that." She hurried back to where she had left her camera and pack and opened the leather case. She pulled out the wood three-legged tripod and released one of the legs, feeling a twinge inside, briefly, and returned to Rosy. "You can tie this to his leg. Where is the break?"

"Lower leg, thank god. Upper woulda been real bad. This way, I think I can get him on the horse. I need another piece to tie to both sides of his leg. Without a good splint, he'll be in real trouble." Rosy's face sagged with lines of worry all over it.

"Get out tonight?" The sun had dropped out of sight and the evening dusk was dimming. "Can we see enough to find our way out?"

"Nope. It's been too long since I been here. We'll wait 'til mornin'. Maybe someone will figger out we're in trouble and bring some help." Rosy took the tripod leg. "I think this'll work. Bring a second one. Then you go about buildin' a fire while I fix Charlie up. He's some scratched up, but otherwise, I think he'll be all right. 'Cept the leg of course."

Nellie found enough pieces of dead branches and pine needles to pile near a circle she built with lava bombs and chunks of rock. It did not look to be a comfortable night for any of them. She secured the horse after giving it and Moonie water. There was more forage, so she didn't feel bad about the horse. She unloaded the packs and saddlebags and scrounged up what food she could—one sandwich, a slab of cheese, enough flour to make biscuits, no more beans, some bacon. She worried about their water supply.

"I need some help, Nell," Rosy called.

Nell scrambled over the rocks to Charlie. He stood with Rosy's help, but they appeared stuck right by the stone that split when the sheriff landed on it. She studied the men and then the rock. "You'll have to sit on it. We can lift your legs and move them to the other side. It'll hurt."

Charlie nodded and hobbled forward to sit on the edge. Rosy and Nell picked up his two legs and swung them as carefully as they could up and around, facing him toward the camp site, with his back to the cave. Then Nell got under one arm while Rosy supported Charlie's arm and back. Charlie grunted a couple times as he moved his splinted leg, but they managed to get him to the fire ring and to his bedroll that Nellie had spread out. So far, he hadn't said a word that she heard.

"Rosy, any wine left? That might help Charlie's pain, maybe put him to sleep."

"Look . . . in my pack," Charlie said, his voice stiff and un-natural. "A leather bag—it has wine. Take some yourself first." He sat against the dead branch with his legs outstretched. "We could use more water, Rosy. Any ideas?" His Stetson had fallen off along the way, and his thick black hair, tinged with gray in a few spots, was long and lank.

Rosy shook his head. "Nell, get the fire goin'. Can you make biscuits?"

"Not really, but I'll try." She tried to remember how she and Pearl had made biscuits in the summer.

"Fry up the bacon. That'll give you some grease. I'll prowl around for more wood. Doubt if there's any water." He disappeared in the gloom.

"I can instruct you how to make biscuits, Nell."

She heard a hint of a smile in his voice. "So I can act like a woman instead of a man?" Nell touched the sheriff's shoulder and then clung to Charlie's hand for a minute and squeezed. Unless she was mistaken, he squeezed back. "All right. Let me get the fire going first."

Between the two of them, they managed a fry pan of biscuits and bacon. When Rosy returned with more wood, they ate, sparingly, so they would have something in the morning. Rosy took one blanket and found a place away from the firelight and wrapped himself up. Soon Nell heard his deep breathing and a light snore. She helped Charlie lie flat on the ground and tucked his bedroll and the rest of the blankets around him. She rolled out her own sleeping bag. Moonie lay down between them, keeping them both warm.

At first light, Nell woke and stirred the fire. Dead cold. She scraped together pieces of half-burnt wood and more pine needles. Just as a trickle of smoke rose from the round, she heard scrambling and a horse. She looked over to the sound and saw a man with a horse some distance away. Moonie didn't growl but stood on guard.

"Hallooo?"

"Mayor Tom! Tom, we're here," Nellie called. "Charlie broke his leg!"

Boots stomped, and Mayor Tom's welcome face appeared. "That boarding house lady telephoned me early—woke me up. Said you must be lost. So I thought I better come look. You're a long ways from where you last were."

By then, Rosy was up and heating the rest of the biscuits.

"Got any water with you? Or food?"

"Couple canteens. Figgered you'd be thirsty. Some beans." They all groaned. "Storm coming. We better eat some and head out. I see you still have the horse." He knelt next to Charlie. "How ya doin'? Can you ride?"

Charlie's face looked pinched. "I can do whatever I need to do, but you will have to help get me on the horse. Thanks for coming, Tom. I know Rosy and Nell will appreciate the help. I will, too."

After gulping down food and water, Rosy and Tom helped Charlie onto the horse. Only one moan escaped his lips. They made their way in a cross-wise fashion across the lava, seeking out non-rocky ground or only small cinders where they could. Nell rode the second horse partway and walked partway. Moonie kept up, limping on one paw, and then raced ahead when they neared the automobile and a truck.

Tom helped Rosy and Nell place Charlie in the auto and across the back seat. His face was white with the effort. "I'll get the horses back to Arco—one at a time, I guess," Tom said, "but let me know how you do, Sheriff."

"When you can, Tom, bring the bags those people left to my office in Hailey," Charlie said. "I can at least investigate those."

"We didn't find any more traces of anyone except a cold camp, used maybe a week or so ago," Nellie said.

"Guess any more searchin' is goin' to have to wait a bit," Rosy said. He turned to Tom. "If you hear about anyone or anythin' in these rocks, let us know."

CHAPTER 15

Goldie took charge when Nellie arrived back at the boarding house with Rosy and the story of Charlie's accident. Charlie had been left with a doctor in Hailey to place a cast on the broken leg. The doctor said he would keep Charlie there for another night. Both Nell and Rosy were so frazzled, they could hardly talk.

"What will we do, Mrs. Bock? Charlie can't work. He can't stay alone. I have all these photos . . ." She had trouble keeping herself from sinking with frustration.

"Now, Nellie. We'll figger this out." She pulled out bread and meat and slapped together some sandwiches. "Here. Eat." She puttered around to make tea and coffee, then placed a tea cup in front of Nellie and coffee in front of Rosy.

"Here's what we can do. Rosy, you take the boys and your sister and move into that little house of Charlie's there in Hailey. The boys can start school there." She wiped her hands on a towel and sat in a third chair.

Rosy opened his mouth. "I don't . . ."

"Wait. There's more. Charlie can move in here until he can get around good. Shouldn't take more than a week or two. Gives you time to find a diff'rent place."

Rosy took a bite of his sandwich.

"Nell, you head off to Twin Falls on the next train. Stay there a couple days and get your photos all done up. I can keep an eye on Charlie."

Both Nell and Rosy sat like two lumps on a stone.

"When you get back, you can confab with Charlie about the two bodies. He may have some ideas about getting a deputy to do some investigatin'. Maybe that Tom fellow from Arco. Nothin' much is goin' on around Ketchum or Hailey—just a few moonshiners and a drunk or two—and an abandoned baby. I already took care of that." Goldie stood up and put her hands on the back of Nellie's chair. "Well, I gotta get dinner ready. Esther and the boys will be back from that play they went to in Hailey. I had Henry take them in when I got your telephone call from the doctor's office."

Nellie felt like Mrs. Bock had just slapped her back and told her to sit up straight or she would get rounded shoulders and they'd freeze that way. Her plan sounded so simple.

"What do you think?"

Nellie glanced at Rosy. "What do you think?" She definitely liked the idea of Charlie staying at the boarding house.

"I may take to drink again," Rosy said. "I lived with Esther for nigh onto six months. Guess I could do it again, if'n I can find a job and be outta the house all day." He looked up at Goldie. "You know where Charlie's house is? I hate to be beholden to him like that."

"You want to move in with that ornery sheep rancher Gwynn Campbell in Twin?"

"Gawd no. Then I'd be sure to fall off the wagon."

Goldie opened her ice box and took out a dozen chops to fry up. "Nellie, could you peel a mess of potatoes for me? Busy hands will let your mind think on this." She turned to Rosy. "I could use some firewood if you ain't too tired."

By Tuesday evening, Goldie's plans were all executed. Sheriff Azgo was installed temporarily in the parlor cum studio, because he couldn't get up the stairs. Rosy's family was all moved after the boys oohed and aahed about the plaster cast and asked a hundred questions each. Esther hummed while she packed up and moved out of the boarding house, although she had declared Charlie's house a mess, but acceptable. For now.

Nell took the train on Wednesday and had made arrangements by telephone with Jacob Levine to use his darkroom most of the day on Thursday. Mayor Tom had been asked to bring the bags left by the Craters of the Moon visitors to Charlie in Ketchum. Rosy was knee-deep in plans to hunt for a job.

Reports came to Charlie by messenger about the two bodies. The man died from the blows to his head. The woman had borne a baby and bled out, whether from the birth or the stalactite, the doctor couldn't be sure.

Nell rode the train to Twin Falls. A woman Nellie had never seen before entered the train with her but sat at the far end of the passenger car. She was taller than Nell and wore a cloche hat and well-made clothes, her skirt almost up to her knees in the newest, somewhat embarrassing, style.

Nell didn't sit near her, as she wished to mull over what she and the sheriff had found in the desert. The two new facts they had learned from Goldie were strange and added to the mystery of the whole situation: a lost and found baby and a newly birthed baby in a cave. Were they one and the same? When the travelers arrived in Twin Falls, Nell noticed the stylish woman entered the station but left it soon afterward in a motor carrier. Maybe the woman lived in Twin.

After Nellie checked in with Mrs. Olsen at the Clarion Inn, she walked to Jacob Levine's studio. It had become familiar to her over the months since she first developed film and printed photos in his darkroom.

Jacob met her at the door and escorted her to his wide oak desk. "Nell Burns! I am so pleased to see you!" Behind him were the portraits of his customers—a talented display of Idaho characters.

"I see you have more superb photographs on your wall. Even I recognize some of your rogues' gallery." She stood to look at several. "There's Gwynn Campbell. You have certainly captured his split personality, ornery and kind at the same time."

Jacob smiled, obviously pleased with her comment.

"Oh my. There is Cable O'Donnell from Stanley. I'm not sure his criminal disposition shows, but there is a certain evil slant to his eyebrows and smirk to his mouth. Those cold eyes look almost white." She felt a shiver.

"You must have met him. I recall some set-to between you and the cowboys up in the Basin." Jacob plucked O'Donnell's framed photo off the wall and handed it to Nell.

"Set-to. Yes, that is a good description." Just thinking of the summer in the mountains caused her arm to ache. "When and how did he come to you? I would have thought he wouldn't leave the safety of Custer County."

"He comes to town regularly," Jacob said. "I believe he has a wife here. Do you know his son, Ben?"

"I thought he had a wife in Stanley," Nell said. "I met Ben recently. I've been with Sheriff Azgo investigating a murder, we think maybe two, at Craters of the Moon. That's why I'm here." She stretched her hand with the frame to Jacob. She didn't care to be associated with O'Donnell, even his photo. "Ben O'Donnell was herding cattle nearby. Apparently, the O'Donnell cattle empire extends far south of Stanley."

As Jacob moved to take the frame, Nell kept hold of it and peered at it more closely. "What is that on O'Donnell's lapel? It is a strange pin of some sort." She looked at the photo more closely. "It almost looks like an ankh—an Egyptian symbol. Is he a traveler?"

Jacob, too, studied the photo more closely.

"Hmm. I saw it while I was photographing him. I didn't want it to reflect light so I moved it slightly. I didn't ask about it, though. I think it might symbolize one of those religious off-shoots here in southern Idaho and in Utah. You may have heard of them."

She thought of Mayor Tom's comment about the people who wanted to go into the Craters, the people she and the sheriff had found.

"They left the Mormon religion because they disagreed with changes in policy—most of all the forbidding of polygamy." Jacob shrugged. "They didn't want to give up their extra wives, I gathered." His mouth drooped slightly. Nell wondered why that would make him sad.

Jacob re-hung the photo. "So, your transition from artistic and commercial photography for the railroad to crime photography is complete." He smiled, almost friendly in contrast to his formality when they first met. "Do you want to go to work now?"

"No, I'll wait until tomorrow for my work. I thought I might help you if you have any orders waiting to be printed." She continued standing and decided to venture a question. "And how is Emmaline?" Jacob's fiancée had been quite frosty to Nell.

Jacob's even deeper frown told Nell more than his words. "She decided to visit her parents in Boston. She wanted me to go, but I am too busy."

"I didn't remember she was from Boston." That would explain her haughty attitude and her old-fashioned dress. Such a contrast to the woman on the train. "You must miss her."

Jacob waved his hand but didn't say what it implied: not so much. Nell felt her spirits lift. "Come with me to the darkroom," he said. "I always have work. You can begin on a wedding project. Unfortunately, I can't join you. I have already been around the chemicals too much today. I do have a client coming in as well and another one tomorrow. I need to prepare my portrait studio."

After two hours in the darkroom, Nellie stopped work and stepped outside, closing the door behind her. Jacob sat at his desk, sorting through proof sheets. He looked up. "You must be tired."

"I am, but I finished your project. Do you want to join me at the inn for supper? I'm sure Mrs. Olsen won't care."

"Yes, I would like that."

The two talked about photography over their food. Jacob had seen Nell's photos from the Stanley Basin and knew of her success with the San Francisco gallery. He had news to share as well. A photography magazine published in Washington, D.C., had accepted his portrait spread of Wild West characters, and it would be released in November. Their conversation veered to technical aspects of black and white photography and the differences they perceived between portrait and landscape photos, sometimes agreeing and sometimes disagreeing. When they continued on to questions such as *What is art?* and *Where is the West?*, Nellie stifled a yawn.

"Time for me to say goodnight, Jacob. It has been a treat to talk shop with you. No one else I know understands the joy and difficulties of photography."

"I enjoyed it, too, for the same reasons, although Emmaline does try." He stood and Nellie accompanied him to the door. "Or did." Nell wasn't sure she heard his coda and so said nothing. They shook hands, agreeing to meet at the studio in the morning.

Nellie arrived early the next day. She began to develop the film from the scenes of the bodies first and printed out proof sheets. Over a sandwich prepared by the inn cook, she tried to study the proofs to decide which to print for the sheriff. She could hardly stand to study the gruesome photos of the dead man but forced herself to view them as unrelated to a living person. The two photos in the cave with the woman looked like a posted tableau. Jacob's reference to a rebel group raised the idea again of a religious cult.

Finally, she was able to turn to developing the film of her efforts at landscape art. She would review them the next day. Nell wanted to see if Franklin, the inn's proprietor, would take her to see Gwynn Campbell, the sheep rancher with whom she shared summer adventures and trials. She hadn't seen him since July, and she didn't think he knew that Lily's children—his grandsons—had returned. In the flurry of everyone settling down in either Ketchum or Hailey, she had not thought to ask Rosy.

When Nell left the darkroom, she stepped into the studio. Jacob was posing a striking woman with a parasol on a bench with a lattice of flowers behind her. It struck such a false note on a gray, fall day, Nell didn't look at the woman at first. When she did, she saw that it was the woman from the train.

"Nellie, this is Euphemia Thorpe. Miss Thorpe, this is Miss Burns, a photographer from Ketchum." Jacob moved the parasol one way and then another. His frown expressed dissatisfaction, either with the woman or the parasol, or maybe the whole effect.

"Hello. Didn't I see you ride the train from Ketchum yesterday?" Nell felt as if she had seen the woman before. "Do you live in Twin Falls?"

"Oh, no. I mean yes—sometimes I do." She twitched the parasol, too.

Jacob moved back to the camera and instructed: "Hold still, Effie."

That name caused Nell to pause a moment, but then she slipped out the front door. Soon, she and Franklin Olsen motored their way to the Campbell home on the edge of town. "Didn't I hear Ross Kipling and his two boys were back in Ketchum?" No secrets in this town, or any other in Idaho, Nellie thought. If Franklin knew, Gwynn did.

"Let me see if Mr. Campbell can bring me back, Franklin. Then you could go." Gwynn could, so Nellie waved good-bye.

As soon as Gwynn and Nell settled in the parlor with hot tea and biscuits and Gwynn with a small glass of sherry, he said: "Do you know that damned miner is back with my grandsons?"

Nellie laughed. "How are you, Gwynn? I've missed you. I am well, not that you asked." She sipped her tea as he apologized. Gwynn's face seemed to have aged more since summer.

"Yes, the boys and Rosy, their father, are back and staying in Hailey where the boys are now going to school. They're all healthy, and Rosy's sister, Esther, came with them, so they're getting a maternal touch." Of a sort, Nell continued to herself. The parlor chairs had the look of never being used. No maternal touch there, she concluded. The sheep rancher must be lonely, having outlived both his wife and his daughter Lily.

"I'll go up to see them tomorrow! Where are they?" Gwynn looked ready to leap up and head north right then.

"Perhaps you should wait for the weekend. And telephone Rosy to let him know, or even ask him to come here with the boys. They are darlings." They would be good company for him, she thought.

Gwynn spluttered and swallowed all of his sherry. He stood up and poured a brown liquid into the sherry glass. "Hmmph."

"I have been out in the lava fields with Charlie Azgo, photographing. Three people disappeared there, and we found two of them dead."

Gwynn sat down again and sipped his new drink. "You attract dead people like coyotes to sheep, Lassie. Why don't you settle down and act like a woman for a change. You ain't getting any younger, you know."

"How gallant of you to remind me, Gwynn." Nell placed her cup in the saucer. "What do you know about a group of polygamists?" She stood up and moved to the couch next to Gwynn. "And is Cable O'Donnell one of them?"

"They're crazy people. Who would want more than one wife for god's sake? One's a handful in the best of times." He stared at Nell. "Why? Are these bodies part of that mess?"

"I don't know. What we found is indeed strange, and I can't get it out of my head." She described the scene and what they learned. "One of them is still missing—the other woman. No sign of her so far."

"What does that varmint O'Donnell have to do with this?"

"Jacob, Mr. Levine, has a photograph of him with an unusual pin in his lapel that seems to identify him as a member of the cult, I guess you'd call it. He also said O'Donnell has a wife in town. Doesn't he have one at the ranch in Stanley? Did you meet her when you were looking for me?"

"Gol-darn. I don't remember. I was so worried about you, I didn't take no notice of anything except whether he was hiding you somewhere." He paused and rubbed his hand over his thick, white hair. "There was a woman, but she mighta been a servant or something. No one said anything about a wife or introduced her. I mighta been a tad mad at everybody."

Nellie reached to touch the old sheep rancher's arm. "Don't worry. And thank you again for your help in finding me! I could not have made it without you."

"Damn near died myself up there, what with all the scalliwags and chasing around." He put his hand on Nellie's. "Glad to help."

"I need to get back to the inn and look at the negatives of the photos I took at the lava fields. Could we go now? And is there any possibility you might take me up to Ketchum tomorrow after I print some of them? Otherwise, I need to work tonight and early tomorrow so I can catch the train." She stood, but paused. "Still, you better telephone Goldie and see how to reach Rosy and the boys. I could use the time tomorrow to print photos and help Jacob. Then we could drive to Hailey when the boys are getting out of school."

Gwynn grinned at her. "Jacob, huh? Now, he'd be a catch. Got his own business. Does darned well with it, is my guess. Even took my picture."

"Yes, I saw it. Very handsome."

Gwynn beamed.

"There is one more thing, Gwynn. You must promise not to cause trouble with Rosy over the boys. This was all settled last winter, and you agreed. No fights over where they live."

His beam disappeared.

"Promise? Otherwise, I'll take the train home, and you won't know where they are."

He opened and closed his mouth and finally nodded. "All right. A deal's a deal."

"They are staying at Charlie Azgo's house in Hailey. Charlie broke his leg and is at Goldie's in Ketchum until he can get around again." This was the other reason she wanted to get back to her studio.

Nell looked through the negatives, still sick at heart when she held them up to the light and saw the tableau in the cave. Both appeared to have taken, although one had a blurry spot past the head, that lovely Madonna-like face. It was probably an icy patch farther back in the cave. She would print both. She spent the day printing most of the photos from the two bodies and then worked on several of hers that seemed worth her while. After a rest, she printed a project—another wedding—for Jacob.

As she worked, she thought again about Matt and Campbell.

Those two boys needed love and support in a strange town, a new school, different living quarters—not tension and name-calling. She wondered how she could help Goldie with Charlie. She doubted he was an easy patient. Still, she had the prints to show him. Together, they might piece together what might have happened. She and Jacob had pored over the prints with a magnifying glass. They disagreed on what they saw, but, because Charlie had been there, he might have a better sense of what that blur was. Nell also realized why the poseur Effie looked familiar. The face in the cave bore a striking resemblance to Effie, quite strange unless they were related. Again, Jacob didn't agree, but he allowed Nell to take one of the prints from his own photo session.

Next day, Nell waited for Gwynn with her bag and camera at Jacob's studio. While she waited, a tall, older man came through the door, hat in hand, and dressed to the cowboy nines, complete with large silver belt buckle. A woman, much smaller and drab compared to his fancy duds, followed.

"Is Jacob Levine here?" And then Cable O'Donnell recognized her. "What are you doing here?" His eyes, blue and cold as they had been when she met him in the Stanley Basin, searched her from face to shoes and back up, but not all the way.

"Hello, Mr. O'Donnell." Nell shifted so her traveling cloak covered her front. His glance lifted back to her face. "I'm waiting for Mr. Campbell to take me home. Why are you here?"

Gwynn Campbell motored up to the studio. Nellie didn't wait for an answer. She studied, briefly, the woman with O'Donnell, but then hurried to join her ride. As she climbed into the auto, she turned back to see the woman enter the studio, but O'Donnell remained at the door and stared at her. If the dagger in his eyes could kill, she would have dropped on the spot. After their set-to in the Galena Lodge in the summer, she wondered if she had the same look in her eyes.

CHAPTER 16

Nell only knew the address of Charlie Azgo's house. She had never been there. Even though Charlie wasn't there—he was still Goldie's patient—she felt nervous as she and Gwynn arrived at the front door. It was a small house, clapboard with a white picket fence around it. The yard was covered with aspen and maple leaves, all yellow, as if paved in gold. Curtains hung in the windows. Who takes care of this for him, she wondered, feeling a stab of jealousy. Don't be silly, Nell, she told herself. Taking care of a home for a man represented all she fought against.

"Damn small. Can everyone fit in there?" Gwynn asked. Nell wondered the same question. Maybe it was bigger in back.

"Guess we'll find out." She stepped out of the auto as two boys slammed out the front door and Moonshine followed them. Moonie ran up to her and almost jumped up, but she stopped him. "No, Moonshine. Where are your manners?"

The boys stopped, too, as if she were scolding them. "Matt and Campbell, this is your grandfather." She swept her arm toward Gwynn. The boys turned shy and stuck to her side. "At least shake hands," she said. Each raised his little hand to be engulfed in Gwynn's large one. Then, in a file, boys and dog ran back to the house, and Nell and Gwynn followed.

Inside, it was small and gloomy with dark furniture, a wood stove, and cramped kitchen. Esther stood at the stove, stirring something that smelled like venison stew. Rosy wasn't there.

One bathroom, Nell noted as she wandered around, and three small bedrooms, one with bunks in it. Someone had worked fast to accommodate the boys. Probably Goldie.

Gwynn stood in the kitchen doorway, looking big and uncomfortable, his Stetson in his hand as Nell introduced Esther and the rancher.

"Let's give the boys a ride to Ketchum with us," Nell suggested. "Is that all right, Miss Kipling? Gwynn can bring them home again after he drops me off. After all, he is their grandfather."

Esther sniffed. "I never met him before. Rosy didn't say anything about him."

Nell didn't think that was true but said nothing. Esther assented when the boys begged and pleaded to go for a ride in the automobile. Nellie thought they might have had peach pie on their minds. "I'll see they mind," Nell promised.

And off they went, peppering Nellie with questions for the next ten miles. "Did you find any more dead bodies?" "Did any ghosts show up?" "Can we see the pictures you took?" "Where are all the sheep?" Nell was relieved when they turned their attention to Gwynn.

"What shall we call him?" Matt whispered in Nell's ear.

"How about Granddad? What do you think, Gwynn?" She laughed at his squirming. He wanted his grandsons, but not the title. He threw up a hand. "Guess so."

"Granddad it is, boys."

Moonie sat in the well by Nellie's legs and rested his head in her lap. He seemed worn out and soon slept with her hand on his head. Maybe Rosy would have to get the boys a dog. She wasn't going to give up hers.

In Ketchum, all four plus the dog entered the kitchen door, where Goldie also cooked. She gathered up the boys and gave them a big hug. She declined to shake Gwynn's hand, using her floured hands as an excuse, and ignored Moonshine, who circled by the wood stove and onto his piece of carpet. "Looks like a group for peach pie!" To the accompaniment of whoops, Goldie set out filled plates of pie made from her preserved fruit and glasses of milk. Nellie just raised her eyebrows at Goldie, who motioned to the parlor.

Nellie walked softly, thinking Charlie might be asleep. She was wrong. He sat on a couch that had been used for group photographs, and he was writing in a notebook. Nellie had never seen him do that before. She realized she had only seen him in action, especially last summer, when he helped the sheepherder, arrested her, and raided a moonshine camp, and then in the caves, climbing in and out, directing others in removing bodies, setting up camp. Now, he was taking enforced rest.

"Writing?" Nellie walked over to Charlie and peered down to see his handwriting. It was neat, slanted and clearly read, not unlike the man himself, although maybe he wasn't so transparent as she sometimes thought.

"Yes, trying to figure out where we are on this case. Two dead bodies, both moved. One eaten by animals, the other speared with a stalactite, then found at the bottom of a hole. And now these packages Mayor Tom had delivered to me." The sheriff waved to several boxes lined up near the couch.

Nellie moved into the room and sat on the gossip chair facing Charlie. The gossip chair had two seats, one facing one way, and the other facing another, in the form of an *S*. It belonged to Goldie, who couldn't remember where it came from, maybe from the big old house itself. It was upholstered in maroon velvet and was Nellie's favorite piece of furniture. When she was tired, she sat in one seat and then moved to the other, hoping a change in perspective would help her with her photographic processes. Looking at any question from two different sides always taught her something.

"What's in the packages?" She glanced toward them, hoping she could open at least one.

"I do not know. I needed you to open and sort through. I did not want to ask Goldie to help, and no one else has been around." He shifted on the couch to face Nell directly. "You, at least, are officially on my staff as a photographer. Can you help now?"

Standing taller than Charlie's head was an unusual experience for Nell. Mostly, she looked up to him, both literally and figuratively. "Gwynn just brought me from Twin Falls, and he is here now with the boys. Until they leave, I should help Goldie. Do you want to see Gwynn? Or the boys? You probably can't do one without the other."

Charlie pulled his hand through his black hair. His expression was one of puzzlement. "I do not know. I would rather see them when I am able to stand on my own two feet."

Nellie nodded. She left the room and returned to the kitchen. Gwynn, Matt, and Campbell were all eating. "I am going to my room to rest, so I will say my good-byes now." When Gwynn glanced up, a fork full of pie near his mouth, Nell could see his consternation. "When you're all finished with pie, Gwynn, why don't you take the boys back to Hailey? If you wanted to stay around for the weekend, you could get a room at the Hailey Hotel, or even out at the hot springs in Croy. Then you and the boys and Rosy could plan an outing of some sort. I know the sheriff has a telephone at his house, so I will give you a call if I can join you." She turned to leave but looked back. "Thank you for bringing me home," she said and paused. Then said, "Granddad." What was the expression she had heard Goldie use— butter wouldn't melt in her mouth? No, that didn't make sense.

When Nellie heard the automobile leave with the boys fighting about who would get to sit in the front seat, she skipped back down the stairs. The sheriff was still writing on a pad of paper, one that looked like an accounting sheet. "This was all Goldie could find for me," he said.

"Do you want to look at the photos first or open the packages first." She carried a thick envelope in her hand.

Charlie looked from the boxes to Nellie and back again. "Let us go over the photographs first. Did you notice anything unusual in them?"

"Yes, but I will tell you after we go through them."

Nellie dragged an ottoman over to the couch for Charlie to put his leg with the cast on it, so she could sit next to him. This wasn't as close to Charlie as riding behind him on a horse, but it was closer than they usually were. He smelled of liniment and his hair of soap, Ivory soap. She wondered how Goldie had accomplished that but decided not to ask. His nails were clean, and the black hairs on the backs of his hands looked like silk, tempting her to stroke one to see. Instead, she opened the large manila envelope and pulled out almost two dozen photographs.

"Here are the first ones of the man after we took him out of the cave." Nellie placed them in Charlie's hands.

Sorting through them one at a time, Charlie stopped at one with a view of the man from the feet up. "It is apparent he was dragged, but that might have just been Mayor Tom and I getting him out of the tunnel." He tapped his finger. "All black clothes. Do you think he was a preacher of some sort?"

Nellie had a small bag with her and drew out a magnifying glass. It was an extra that Jacob owned and had lent to her. "You might want to use this to study his clothes, maybe his hands . . . or his head." Both Nellie and Jacob had done so and found a small rip in the man's jacket lapel. She wanted to see if the sheriff could see the same flaw.

After a few minutes, he pointed to the jacket lapel. "It looks like this was torn, maybe on the way in or the way out. Still, that would be a strange place to be ripped."

"That's what we thought. It might just be a flaw in the material, but it almost looks as if something was torn away. Maybe it was flung away, too, but finding something black with something else on it would be almost impossible in all that dark lava. It could still be in the cave or any number of cracks and holes outside. I do have a theory, though."

"Yes, I guessed you might." He held up the photo and magnifying glass.

"One of the photos on Jacob's wall . . . um, Mr. Levine's wall . . . was that of Cable O'Donnell—you remember him from this summer?"

"I should smile—or maybe frown—I do."

"He had a small pin on in the photograph—a kind of cartouche, an Egyptian—"

"Yes, I know what a cartouche is."

"How does everyone know that?"

"I read. Do you?"

"Yes, of course," Nell said but felt her face get hot. She hadn't been reading much in the past six months. Just photographing.

"Anyway, Mr. Levine thought it symbolized a sort of cult—those who left the main church when the polygamy laws were passed for Utah to get statehood. He even thought that Cable O'Donnell might be a polygamist—with a wife there in Twin Falls and another one at the ranch in Stanley."

"Sounds like a lot of gossip to me," Charlie said. He rubbed his face, which needed a shave. The sound was like sandpaper. Maybe that was what his hand hairs felt like, too. "Still," he said and shrugged, "maybe there is something to it. I doubt if any prosecutor would bring a charge for polygamy against anyone in this area. Getting a jury might be difficult." He turned to Nell. "Sounds like you and Jacob Levine are on friendly terms."

"I do work for him, Charlie. Just like I work for you."

Charlie sighed. There was no other word for it. "You do when I can get back to work." He tapped on the cast. "This piece of plaster is certainly keeping me from doing anything. Let's get back to the photos."

One by one, they studied each photo, which, after the dead man, were of the cave where he had been and then the place where they camped and the cave where the woman had been found and the two photos from inside. Once again, Charlie picked up the magnifying glass and studied the figure at length. "Tom said those ice spears are mostly calcified with limestone. That is why one could be passed through a human body. There is little frozen water left after a period of time. When we went back to retrieve her and she was gone, it did not occur to me to see if the stalactite was still around, or maybe broken and thrown away, again there in the cave. She seemed so stuck to the ground, I do not see how anyone moved her, when Tom and I could not."

"I think her clothes were wet with blood and then froze to the ground. Even if the stalactite killed her, I don't think it could have pierced the stone under her, do you? Maybe if we had had something to pry her loose with, we could have done it, although I certainly wasn't much help."

Charlie studied Nell and nodded. "You may be right. And if the blood dried, she might have been easier to move." He paused, then continued. "But where would one get a lever of any kind out there in that desolate place?"

"Maybe a jack from an automobile. Maybe a crank." She had thought of something else. "Mayor Tom knew that a lever was needed. I hate to think it, but could he have circled around and then removed her before we had a really good chance to see her?"

Charlie nodded his head. He looked through the magnifying glass again and pointed to the white blur. "Any idea what this is?" He moved it closer to his face. "It could be ice behind her."

"I don't know. I saw it when I was printing the negative." She took the glass, and she, too, studied the white patch, then shook her head. "A ghost."

The sheriff laughed. "That would have been the place for one." He gestured toward both photos. "These give us a good picture of her. She was beautiful."

"That's what I wanted to tell you. While at Jacob's studio, I met a woman posing for a photo. Her name was Euphemia. Jacob called her 'Effie,' the name Tom mentioned. She was not as beautiful as this woman, but when I printed this photograph, I realized they resemble each other—strongly. I think they might be related." She knew this was all speculation, but the words tumbled out of her. "If so, maybe they are sisters, and that takes care of the third person in the trio. No one has been left out there in the lava fields. And, if she is related, then she escaped—before or after her sister was murdered. Or died."

"That presents another puzzle, then." Charlie held his head in one hand. "I need to get back out there." He slammed his hand on the cast. It didn't break, but his hand might have.

"What about crutches?"

Another sigh. "I cannot even imagine trying to get across those lava fields on crutches."

"A horse?"

He thought. "Yes, I could do that." He shifted and turned toward the packages. "But first, let us go through those. I have not opened them yet. They do not look as if they have been opened since Tom found them in the deserted auto. The brown tape has not been disturbed as near as I can tell."

Nellie walked to the first—there were three. She lifted the package by the twine wrapped around it and brought it to the couch next to the sheriff. "I'll get some scissors and a knife." When she returned the sheriff had managed to get the twine off with a pocketknife and was working on the paper tape, which easily broke apart. Charlie lifted the flaps on what was a cardboard box and whistled.

"Well, that is a surprise," Nellie said. Lying in the box were packets of money, dozens of them. "Are they real?"

"Huh. I do not know." Charlie riffled through the stacks and pulled out one packet of ten-dollar bills. "There must be around a thousand dollars in here." He pulled one out and used the magnifying glass to study it closely. "Looks real to me. I would have to have a banker inspect them to be certain. I know counterfeiting is a fairly common crime in the East, maybe in Chicago, but we have seen few phony bills around here, or even in Idaho, as far as I know."

"Let's look at the others." Nellie moved the first package and brought the second one again to Charlie. It was smaller but wrapped in the same manner—twine and paper tape.

The sheriff opened it with little trouble, and, once again, there were stacks of bills filling the entire package. He shook his head. "Why would those three leave money sitting in a parked automobile near the lava fields? Anyone could have stopped by and stolen it. Clearly, they intended to return, but still—several thousand dollars, I would guess." He glanced at the last, smaller, package.

Goldie appeared in the door. "Are you two hungry? What is all that money for?"

Nellie's inclination was to cover the opened box, but Goldie had already seen it. "We don't know. These were found in the automobile by the road, apparently belonging to people who went into the lava fields."

The sheriff must have had the same idea, because he folded one of the flaps over and then stopped. "There is one more box. Come in, and you can guess with us."

This one Nellie opened. There was no money, but instead

baby clothes, including a blanket, a knitted hat, and a small sweater and pants, all in blue, and wool nappies. "This seems to confirm a baby was expected." She rubbed her hand over the items. "These almost make me cry. They were hand knit, I think."

Charlie studied the money and the baby things. "Was the money to be traded for the child?"

"And where would a religious cult get that kind of money?" Nellie said. "I shudder to think what went on in the lava fields before we arrived. It must have been terrible."

Goldie so far had said nothing, unusual for her. "Of course they were hand knit," she said. "I used to do baby things like that myself. Easy as pie. 'Course, I didn't do them for any child of mine, having had none. All those religious people get together in sewing bees and knitting bees, like the quilters do. Could have been knitted up by any one of a hundred people." She strode to the box and lifted them out. "Humph. Not a practiced hand, I'd say. Probably a learner." She laid them back down. "And as to money? That sect out in the desert by Idaho Falls makes people pay to join 'em. And the men take a dowry from the girls that are sent out there. There's enough people who want to get rid of extras in their households, so they sell 'em off, especially if they ain't pretty and can't get a man on their own."

"You've never talked about them to me," Nellie said.

"Ain't been no reason to. Shameful practices. So far as I know, no one around here has had anythin' to do with them."

"Do you think that baby came from them?" the sheriff asked.

"Doubt it. They want to keep all them girl babies. If it had been a boy, I might have thought that. Those dirty old men don't want boys around. They sell them off, too, to farmers in the area as workers."

The sheriff nodded his head. "I will make enquiries of the

town in southeast Idaho where they are supposed to live—Utah City. Maybe there is a sheriff or some kind of law there, although I suspect not. 'God's work,' the man said, so God's law may be the only kind they follow, or at least their interpretation of it."

CHAPTER 17

After much wheedling, Nellie had been able to get crutches from the small clinic in Hailey. She brought them back to the sheriff, using the automobile belonging to Henry, one of Goldie's boarders. She had driven an auto all summer when she traveled back and forth to the Stanley Basin, after she spent time at the Basque sheepherder's camp. It took a few minutes to get used to driving again, but then she felt at home. She even missed the upholstery smell of old cigarette smoke and that hint of moonshine—the liquid kind.

Charlie struggled with the wood supports, but, after a few adjustments in their height and several practice rounds of the boarding house and up and down part of the stairs, he said he was ready to try them out in town. He drove a county automobile and allowed Nell to drive it while he sat in the passenger seat. Charlie said little as they headed to Hailey, except a few gasps and grabs of the hand hold in the door. His left leg jammed the floor several times. Nell tried her best to be careful and not to cause any of the aforementioned reactions from Charlie. Having a passenger was not her preferred situation, and having the sheriff was definitely to be avoided in the future.

In Hailey, they parked near the butcher shop. There was no snow yet, which was a grace, and together the butcher and Nellie managed to get the sheriff into the ice room. The butcher asked several times when the bodies could be removed. He needed the space for venison and elk that hunters were bringing down from the back country. The coroner, a man named Jack Sharp, met them.

"The doc looked over them two," Jack Sharp said. "I couldn't even guess how that lady died. Although she had a big puncture wound in her stomach." He glanced at Nell and then away. "Doc said she bled out from having a baby, but he needed to do an autopsy to make a final determination. Was there a baby with the body?" When both the sheriff and Nell said no, he continued. "The man's end was pretty clear. See those dents on the back of his head? Probably spewed brain all over." He shuffled his feet and, to Nell's thinking, avoided looking at her. She was just as happy. She stayed as far back as she could.

The sheriff peered closely at both bodies. He picked up the man's lapel and poked his finger through the rip he and Nell had seen in the photograph. At the woman's side, he fingered her dress material, felt along her body, including her arms, turned her head one way and then another. The ice upon which she lay was tinged pink. Her skirt was still stiff with dried blood, and it had leached onto what appeared to Nell to be a pedestal. She no longer resembled a Madonna, however. The skin on her face had shrunk, and the bones of her head looked as if they would eventually rid themselves of the skin cover. Nellie grasped her arms around herself and bit her lip.

"Contact the doctor, please, and ask him to do the autopsies. If we cannot find relatives by then, I will authorize their burial," the sheriff said. He motioned to Nell to leave, and he hobbled after her on the crutches, narrowly missing a hanging slab of raw venison. It still had legs on the bottom half. She couldn't get out of there fast enough. Jack Sharp closed off the cold room.

The butcher met them at the front counter. "Thank you for the use of your cold room. One of these years, the county might build a morgue that is more convenient for everyone," the sheriff said.

"Always glad to help the law."

"I searched their clothes for identification when we found them but might have missed something. The circumstances were not optimal. Did you find anything when they arrived here?"

"Dunno. Didn't look myself. I don't know about the fellows who brought them here. Maybe talk with them?"

The sheriff nodded, and he and Nell went back to the county auto. "Now where?" Nell asked. "Are you tired?"

"Yes, but I think we should try to find the fellows and see if they did any searching on their own." He climbed into the passenger seat, so Nell circled the auto to drive. "The problem is, I do not know who they were. Mayor Tom found them. Could you go back and ask the butcher for their names? Maybe he knew them."

Nell did as asked and returned. "He didn't know them. He thought they might have come from the Basque boarding house. Were they familiar to you?"

"It has been a long time since I did any sheep herding," the sheriff retorted. "I already said I did not know them."

Nell climbed again into the driver's seat. "Close the door." She started up the auto and did a U-turn to head back to Ketchum. So much for being helpful. "Max and Trapper were the names of the men who took the woman out." She glanced at the sheriff and back at the road. "Maybe Goldie knows them. She knows everyone else in the valley."

They drove the ten miles without talking to each other. At the boarding house, Nell realized the sheriff had dozed off. She touched him gently on the shoulder, and he opened his eyes. They stared at each other, and Charlie took her hand. "Thank you." His face was drawn, and he half stumbled when she helped him place the crutches under his armpits. "I can do it."

After Charlie was settled again in the parlor, Nellie sat in the kitchen with Goldie. "It was gruesome, looking at the bodies," she said. "Charlie didn't know the names of the men who helped Mayor Tom bring in the man. The other two were Max and Trapper. Do you know those names?"

"Trapper used to work at the Triumph mine. When they cut back, he was let go. I don't think he does anything now except sit in a beer—uh, soda parlor. Max—hmmm. That would be Max Adkins. He's the one who told me you two were staying out at the lava fields. He works in a warehouse there in Hailey—maybe one connected to the railroad. I think they pal around with each other. Not sure how Tom would know them. Rosy might. Probably does. They all had the same affliction."

"Do you think they would have searched a dead woman's clothes?"

Goldie shrugged. "They might, looking for a few coins. Doubt if they'd take anything but money though." She paused and thought a moment longer. "Jewelry maybe. Did you notice if she had any? A necklace or bracelet or ring or something?"

Nellie tried to visualize the body in the icy cave. "Yes! There was a necklace. I don't know if it was still on her when Rosy and Charlie brought . . . her up from the hole in the cave where I—" She stopped. No one had mentioned that Nell had fallen, along with Moonie, and had to be brought up by rope. And, so did the body.

To avoid Goldie's sharp look, Nell turned the subject to the man. "The man might have worn a ring. Certainly, he was there with me alone long enough. You'd think I would have noticed something then." Again, she tried to picture him with his face covered and his cloak wrapped around him. No, she didn't think his hands were visible. Ben O'Donnell had approached him, but she was sure he didn't touch the body. "He was covered up, I guess. I'll ask Charlie if he noticed anything. He and Mayor Tom carried him quite a ways."

"What hole? What happened?" Goldie was not to be diverted.

"I slipped down a hole when we were in one of the caves." Nell told Goldie the whole story.

"Lands' sakes. You get out of my sight, and there you go—gettin' in trouble again." She shook her head and stood up. "I don't think this work for the sheriff is a good thing. I have a mind to give him a piece of mine!"

"No, Goldie. I have to be like a man—be strong and steady. Otherwise, he won't hire me. I need the money, and I like the work. It is one of the few things I can do and still be a photographer. Besides, here you are running a boarding house. I doubt if you think a man should be the one to do that." Nell stood as well and reached for Goldie's hand. "How would you like it if you were told this wasn't a job for a woman. Look at Franklin in Twin Falls. Mrs. Olsen helps, but mostly, she does the cooking. You do the whole thing. And a good job of it, too. So do I."

"Hmmph." Goldie took Nell's hand in both of hers. "I just don't want you gettin' hurt or killed yourself. You ain't no policeman."

"No, I'm not. And I am careful. It's just that sometimes—"

"I get to thinkin' you are a big part of my life, Missie. Don't leave it."

Tears sprang to Nellie's eyes. "You're a big part of mine, too." She felt awkward, but she put her arms around Goldie, who was warm and smelled like flour and butter and cinnamon. Nellie missed her mother but wouldn't trade Idaho for Chicago now for any reason.

Charlie insisted on going to his office in Ketchum where he could use a telephone without being on a party line. Nell insisted that he talk to the doctor who molded the plaster cast to his leg before he did any more work. She had seen how exhausted he was when they returned from the morgue trip to Hailey. The doctor would see him the next day, so Nellie said she could take him in the county automobile again, and she would ask Goldie to locate Max or Trapper to talk to. The doctor might have finished the autopsy, and they could learn of any results as well.

Once again, they embarked—the sheriff on crutches and Nellie in the driver's seat. She tried her best not to grind gears, but, when she did, Charlie said nothing. She was not even sure he heard, as he simply watched out the window and was in a brown study. The cottonwoods along the river flashed lemon yellow in the sunlight, and a few orange-yellow aspen varied the texture. All the grasses beside the road shone gold and amber. It was another blue sky day, an Indian summer after a week of cold, not unusual for October.

"I have been thinking about what you said—money in exchange for a baby. Why would anyone do that? Even if the mother was dead, wouldn't the sister have wanted to keep the child? Or maybe it died, too. There were a myriad of crannies and holes in the lava where it could have been hidden or buried."

The sheriff seemed to wake out of his thoughts. "I have thought again, too, of that idea. Goldie said the baby left at the church was only a couple, three days old, and, although it was hungry, it was not starving."

"She," Nell said.

"Yes, she. And why would a sister leave it at the church? Maybe the sister wanted a boy baby, not a girl. Or the mother wanted a boy. Would the mother have been the one to knit the clothes?"

"Heavens, I don't know. I've never been around mothers and babies. Grannies and aunties might have been the knitters. And, for some strange reason, nearly all fathers want a boy, so that might be why the clothes were all blue. Pink is for girls."

"I never see you in pink," Charlie said.

"I'm not a girl. I'm a woman, and I don't like pink."

He laughed.

At the doctor's office, the doctor sawed off the plaster cast. Nellie couldn't help wincing with the noise. She was afraid the saw would cut into the sheriff's leg. However, the doctor said he thought the leg was healing nicely, and he put on another, much smaller, cast. When he talked about the dead woman, his cheeks sagged, and his eyes almost teared up. "The ice spear is what killed her. She would have died anyway, but, when she was stabbed, the wound bled. She had already lost a lot of blood from the birth of a child, judging by her clothes. Her lower limbs were swollen with eclampsia. She should have been in bed, not wandering around the lava fields. What were her companions thinking, I wonder? Lots of women die in childbirth, and so do babies." He shrugged. "She might have been one of those women, even without being on the ground in a cave."

"Did you see the baby that was left at the church?" Nellie asked.

"No, but I did find a nursing mother to feed her. From all reports, she is doing fine, although the wet nurse would like someone else to take the baby. She has a child of her own to tend to."

Charlie and Nellie looked at each other. Goldie was not a good answer. She had her hands full with roomers and with Rosy and the boys on the weekends. Nellie didn't like to think her landlady was too old, but she certainly couldn't nurse a child. "Can a baby have a bottle instead of mother's milk?" She felt herself blush. She wasn't used to discussing such private affairs as breast feeding out loud and to men.

"Lots of children do," the doctor said. "There was a woman lost her baby about six months ago. She might agree to take this one, but I don't want to do it if there is a chance someone from the family would retrieve her." Nellie had speculated with the doctor about the possible aunt. "That wouldn't be fair."

Neither had mentioned the money. "Let us try to find family or the aunt, then. Will the wet nurse keep her for a while longer?"

"I think I can persuade her to do so," the doctor said. "She is my daughter."

Outside the office, Nellie turned to the sheriff. "What a nice man that doctor is. All the doctors I ever met were crusty and often arrogant. This man wasn't at all."

"Small town doc," Charlie said. "Makes a difference." He could walk better on the crutches with a lighter cast and the practice he had. "Let us go to my office. You can read reports from the doctor and the coroner. A coroner's jury is set for this afternoon."

"What is that?"

"It has to decide how the people were killed and whether murder was involved. Mostly, the verdicts come back 'death by misadventure by person or persons unknown.' It is the law when someone doesn't die of natural causes or an accident."

"What about Max and Trapper? Goldie found Max at the rail warehouse. Do you want me to go talk to him?"

"No, I think I should be doing the police work. You are the photographer, and I do not have any photographs for you to take now. After I contact that little town in the southeast, if I can find anyone to talk to, we can go to the warehouse. You can come with me, but I want to ask the questions."

Nellie thought the sheriff sounded a little huffy. "All right."

The town was named Utah City and had a population of around five hundred, hardly a city. There was no sheriff's office, but there was a town mayor. He said there were no reports of missing persons, but that he knew two people who had left town in the last two weeks, Elder Joshua and Sister Faith, his wife. The mayor didn't know where they went or what their plans were or even whether they were expected to return. No, he didn't know how old they were, but Elder Joshua was maybe in his fifties and Sister Faith was perhaps twenty, and, yes, she was a beautiful young woman. When the sheriff asked about multiple marriages, the mayor said he couldn't comment on that and hung up.

The sheriff called the mayor back, and the woman who answered the telephone said he wasn't there and wasn't expected back for several days. Nellie took the telephone and said she was looking for relatives of Sister Faith, and did the person on the other end of the line know of any and could they be reached. The woman seemed more inclined to talk to Nell than to the sheriff, and she said no, that Sister Faith had come from out of town about six months ago. However, she did know that Elder Joshua had relatives—his wife of twenty years. Then she stopped herself, and she, too, hung up. When Nell tried to call back, the telephone rang and rang, and the operator said no one was at that number.

"Guess we better find Max and see if he remembers any jewelry or whether he or Trapper searched Sister Faith's body."

"We may get the same reaction from them," Nell said. "Why don't you go alone? I will read the reports you said you had."

Charlie just stood there. "On my crutches?"

"Oh, I forgot. Better yet, why don't we ask Rosy to go. He knows these men and probably sat next to them in one of the bars from time to time. He is much more likely to get information from them than one of us is."

Charlie sat down again. "I think you are right. Maybe Rosy is the person I should name deputy while I am bound up in this plaster cast."

CHAPTER 18

Goldie knocked on Nellie's door in the boarding house. "I took the boys out to the hot springs two Saturdays ago. I'm going again today with them. Do you want to come? A good dose of mineral waters might do you good."

Her first inclination was to say no. She wanted to spend the time with the sheriff, going over what they knew, what they didn't know. On the other hand, it would be good to spend time with the boys. Taking them would keep them out of both Rosy's and Charlie's hair. Maybe the two men would sit down and talk. It was way past time.

"All right. I do have a bathing dress. I'm not even sure why I brought it, except I thought if I went to California, I could go to the beach." She made a face, and Goldie laughed.

"People come in all sorts of costumes to the springs. Some of them have those new-fangled bathing outfits. They look like men's undershirts on top and men's shorts on the bottom. Indecent is what I call 'em." She looked almost startled. "That isn't what you have, is it?" Her face flushed.

"No, I am definitely not new-fangled. I think my dress dates back to before the war. I'll be lucky if it even fits me!"

"Nobody won't care. All the women swim together, and all the men swim nekked in another pool. Campbell will stay with us, and Matt has to go with the men, unless I can change the steward's mind." Goldie left the room with a determined look on her face.

Henry's automobile was available again, so Nellie, Goldie, and the two boys drove from the boarding house, past the shut-down smelter out the Warm Springs Road to Guyer Hot Springs, the roadway following an arch of burnished gold trees. Goldie insisted the boys stay with them in the women's pool, at least at the outset. Matt begged to go to the men's pool in case Peter Banks was there, and she relented.

Nellie played ball with Campbell, both of them laughing and soaking each other as it splashed down around them. Goldie sat around the edge and beamed. When the ball flew out of Campbell's hand and landed across the pool, one of the women it splashed turned to frown and scold the boy. She opened her mouth and then shut it again and turned away. In that moment, Nellie recognized the woman in Jacob's studio, Effie.

"Let's stop now, Campbell. Go sit with Goldie and maybe paddle with her back and forth," Nellie said. She waded chest deep over to the woman.

"Hello again. Didn't I meet you at Jacob Levine's studio in Twin Falls?" Nell held out her hand.

Effie looked at Nell's hand but didn't raise her own. "Yes, I think we did. What are you doing here? I thought perhaps you lived near the studio."

"No, I live in Ketchum. I was there to do some photographic work. Jacob's is the nearest photography studio." Nellie let her hand drop. "Don't you live in Twin Falls? I could ask the same thing." She smiled to seem friendly, although really, she just wanted information, lots of it.

"I have to go now." The woman waded over to the stairs, climbed out, and disappeared into the dressing room. Her bathing costume was new-fangled, as Goldie called it. That didn't surprise Nellie. Effie's prompt disappearance did.

After a moment's hesitation, she, too, headed for the dressing room, not sure what she would say, but wanting more information. As she neared the door, she heard a man and woman talk-ing behind the screen that marked both the men's and women's entrance.

"I don't want to go yet," the man said.

"We have to. That snoopy woman I told you about in Twin Falls is here."

"You go to the room, then. I'll meet you later."

"Why are you so anxious to stay? I don't want to go alone."

"The mineral water helps my aching bones. Climbing around in those caves didn't do me any good you know. I can't help it if I'm not as young as you are."

Nell thought she heard skin against skin behind the screen but couldn't see the two. She didn't want to interrupt them.

"All right. But remember, we are going for a late-night swim. You promised."

Almost as if she could see it, Nell was certain the man grinned. A late-night swim—in the hot springs. Anyplace else would have been too cold. She'd have to ask Goldie if the springs were open at night. Even if they weren't, two people could probably sneak down from rooms at the inn and jump in, especially into the men's side, as it was less exposed to the guests at the inn or to people arriving. And who would arrive at night?

Nell decided she would. These two people knew something about what happened at the lava fields, and she was determined to find out.

Once again when Goldie had Matt called out of the men's pool, he appeared with Peter Banks. Peter introduced himself to Nellie and added: "Ah, the famous photographer. You're so young and attractive." He stood straighter and sucked in his stomach. Nellie wasn't sure what to say. She liked the compli-ment but stepped back so he wouldn't touch her. Usually, she would hold out her hand to shake but avoided doing so here.

He preened at Goldie, too. He even asked about the baby. "I tried to get you to take a photograph of the child," Peter said to Nellie. "I wanted proof that I found it at the church, but Goldie here will vouch for me, won't you?" Without waiting to hear Goldie's answer, as if it were a foregone conclusion, he continued. "I hear you're a crime photographer, Miss Burns."

"Oh, who told you that?"

He hemmed and hawed but didn't name anyone. "Word gets around in such a small town. Have you been out photographing crimes?" He leaned toward her, as if sharing a secret.

"As a matter of fact, I have," Nellie said. "Maybe you've heard about what happened at the lava fields?"

Peter's face turned scarlet, and he began coughing. Matt slapped his back. "Are you okay?"

"Must have swallowed wrong," the man said. "Thanks, mate. I'm okay now." He patted Matt on the head and turned to go. "Nice to meet you, Miss Burns. Don't take any wooden nickels." He waved and turned tail. And ran, Nellie thought.

"Swallowed what? My eye," Goldie said. "He didn't stay long enough to hear what happened, did he?" She rested an arm on Matt's shoulder, as if reclaiming him.

"I noticed that, too." Something about Peter Banks made Nellie feel slimy. She was glad he was gone.

"Why? What happened?" Matt asked.

"Did he say he was staying here?" Nellie asked Matt, not wanting to discuss her photos. They were too gruesome for a child.

"He never said much at all," Matt said. "I asked him, but he didn't hear me, I guess. It was noisy on the men's side today."

Nell drove out to Guyer Hot Springs in the dark. She parked down the road so no one would notice a strange automobile driving up to the front door. Goldie insisted she take Moonshine for protection, although Nell resisted. Moonie wasn't always silent, especially when Nell needed him to be so. Nevertheless, she agreed and brought a leash for him.

The dark was almost complete except for two or three lighted windows at the inn and a small porch light. Nellie wished she had explored in the daylight, so she knew where to go. Twice she stumbled over rocks and then almost fell over a log marking a parking area where there were no automobiles. "I'm going to tie you up here, Moonshine. Lie down and be quiet." Moonie circled the spot where he was tied, sank down, and placed his head on his paws. Nell sat next to him on the log and listened. She could hear water bubbling in the pools, a door shutting with a bang inside the inn, and a breeze rattling the dead aspen leaves nearby. A slight smell of sulfur, like rotten eggs, spoiled the image of paradise that the hotel encouraged. She crept around the outside of the two pool areas.

No one was in either pool, she decided. This probably was a wasted trip. She waited a while longer and was ready to untie Moonshine and walk back to the borrowed automobile. Neither Rosy nor Charlie knew she was out. She had sworn Goldie to secrecy. And then she heard bare feet padding near the changing rooms. A giggle, followed by quiet splashing and someone or some two moving around in the men's pool, the farthest pool. Nellie sneaked as quietly as she could below the women's pool and tried to find a spot where she could peer into the men's pool. Grasses, shrubs, and some sagebrush tangled her feet and sounded like an announcement of her presence. Again, she stopped and listened. Two voices, a man's and a woman's. It must be Effie and the man she spoke with earlier. So far, Nellie couldn't hear what they said to each other, and why, she thought, would they even be talking about the lava fields? This clearly was a romantic tryst, not something she felt she should eavesdrop on, but she was curious. Who was the man? She assumed it was Peter Banks, but it didn't have to be.

A moon slid out from behind clouds and acted as a spotlight, reflecting off the water and lightening up the area where Nell sat, exposing her by casting a shadow onto the women's pool. She ducked down and waited. No exclamations from the other pool. Just as she decided her trip was a bust and she should leave, the voices in the pool ceased being quiet and their pitch raised so she could hear the words. What had begun as a tryst was turning into an argument, a loud one.

"Don't you touch me. You're a two-timing devil." A woman, obviously unhappy.

"Don't get high and mighty with me, Miss Screechy. You're no better." A man's lower rumble, but still audible.

"Greedy and selfish. You're only out for yourself."

Nellie wasn't sure who they were, as she didn't recognize the voices. Perhaps the man was Peter Banks trying to keep his voice low. The woman certainly wasn't quiet. Where was Effie? She bushwhacked back to the front of the hotel as a fancy automobile pulled up and a man stepped out. Moonshine was still tied near the front steps and had stood when the door opened, but he didn't bark. The hotel was not a structure he was supposed to guard.

When the porch light fell on the man's face, Nellie recognized Cable O'Donnell. And then she saw Effie on the porch, apparently waiting for him. This was such an interesting development, Nellie decided to stay a while longer to see if she would learn something more about both of them. Now, if only Moonie didn't give her away. She crept close, still hidden by shrubbery, to eavesdrop.

O'Donnell seemed to ask questions, and Effie answered, clearly upset. He was whispering, and she was not. He sat on the porch, and Effie walked back and forth, her voice coming and going. Then she stopped, half turned to her inquisitor.

"After I gave Elder Joshua the money, he said I had to go with him while he sought redemption for Hattie. It was the only way I could see to help her. She . . . she was going to have that baby any minute it seemed. Elder said Hattie had to pay for her sin, but that he would ask for God's forgiveness."

A low question came from O'Donnell. Nellie couldn't hear the words, but Effie's answer told her what it was.

"She wouldn't say who the father was. At that point, it didn't matter, did it?" Effie turned and paced again. "That place! It was all monstrous shapes, and we ruined our shoes on the cutting lava. It was all I could do to keep Hattie upright. And then the caves . . ." The sounds Effie made told Nellie the woman was crying. Another whispered comment from O'Donnell. Effie stopped, her back to the man. "It was getting dark, so I insisted we stop and find a place to sleep. I refused to go into any of those caves at night. Anything could have been in them." She turned. "Elder wanted me to be his wife. He even grabbed at my chest, as if he already owned me!" Her anger seemed to dissipate her tears. "Elder left us. He wanted to sleep in a cave. He wasn't around in the morning but showed up before we could leave and said, 'I've found an altar to God. Bring Hattie, and we will deliver her from her sin.' I didn't argue. I thought if Hattie were 'cleansed' according to Elder, we could return to the auto and get Hattie to a hospital."

For a while both O'Donnell and Effie didn't talk. Maybe O'Donnell was saying something, and Nellie couldn't hear. She wanted to crawl closer but was afraid of exposing herself to them.

"I tried. He wouldn't let me. We went into the cave he found. He brought a torch and the firelight reflected off ice all around, and rainbow colors flashed like a kaleidoscope. It was wondrous and terrible at the same time. Elder insisted that Hattie would have her baby right there. He had dreamed it. 'The ice will cleanse her,' he said. He looked half crazy—his hair on end, fire reflection turning his skin red. He was filthy." Effie lifted her hands to her ears. "Hattie screamed. I found a flat place she could lie down. I wrapped my cloak over her, lifted up her skirts and pulled her underclothes away. I raised her legs to my shoulders. And there the baby was, between Hattie's legs!" Effie turned away from O'Donnell. Her shoulders shook. "I took my cloak off Hattie and wrapped the little thing in it. I needed to cut the cord, so I asked Elder for his knife."

Again, Effie stopped her story. O'Donnell said something. Effie lifted her face from her hands and shouted, "Elder had a sword in his hands, and he plunged it into Hattie, right through her stomach! He wouldn't stop. I screamed at him again and again!"

Nellie was stunned by the cruelty of what she heard. She wanted to run up the stairs to Effie and hold her close. O'Donnell apparently had no such urge.

"Then Elder said he wanted the child, a wee baby. That the baby was the 'spawn of the devil,' and he would kill it, too. I was frantic. That sword must have cut the cord, because the baby was loose. I had to find my way out, get away from him. He was the devil himself!" Effie fell onto her knees. "I managed to get to the entrance, and then, thank God, there was—" O'Donnell stood up and put his arm around Effie, and he looked straight at Nellie in the bushes. Even as he stared at her, he said to Effie, "Elder owes me that money. I want it back. You need to get it for me, Euphemia." Coldhearted as ever.

It was then the two swimmers appeared on the porch on their way back into the hotel. Nellie didn't know the woman, who wore a robe around her swimming dress. But Peter was recognizable. He appeared to be chasing the woman, dragging a robe behind him. "Wait, darling . . ." His muscled arms and chest gleamed in the porch light.

Nellie almost laughed out loud. The expressions on everyone's faces might have stepped off the stage of a romantic comedy: Effie's chin dropped, Peter looked frantically around, perhaps looking for an escape, O'Donnell stood there open-mouthed, as if he were a cuckolded husband, and the young woman briefly glanced at all three and slipped through the front door and disappeared.

Effie recovered first. "Peter! Who was that? What . . . ? I don't believe . . . !" She was in tears again.

O'Donnell hurried off the porch and strode around to where Nellie was trying to get back to her automobile. She loosened Moonshine from his tie-up. The man grabbed Nellie's arm, and Moonie snarled and prepared to leap on him. "Stop, Moonshine." She attempted to pull her arm away, but it was the arm that had been wounded during the summer, and she couldn't. "Let go!"

"What in hell are you doing here? You damned busybody, snooping . . . girl! Didn't you cause enough trouble last summer?" He had come off the porch without his hat. His hair was disarrayed, and his hairline seemed to be receding, something she had not noticed before. It changed his appearance. At first Nellie could say nothing.

She floundered. "I—I wanted to see Effie, learn what I could about her sister." Nellie stood as tall as she could.

"I am tempted to kill that dog of yours. Serve you right."

Fear struck Nellie. This man seemed smaller than she remembered from meeting him at the saloon in Stanley when she was with Gwynn Campbell and again in Twin Falls, but meaner. His voice held more animation than the night they shared a dinner. She remembered it as flat and icy, like his eyes. She looked at his lapel to see if that strange symbol was still pinned. It was too dark to tell.

"You're such a meddling hussy. I don't wonder you are

snooping around. Trying to see if your precious sheriff is here with another woman?"

Effie was beating Peter on his arm, and he kept backing away. He managed to escape through the front door as well. She followed him.

"I know where he is. Do you know where your wife is?" Maybe she should say "wives," if he indeed was part of the polygamist group. Even in the dark, she knew her words hit some kind of target. "Or maybe one of your wives isn't as precious as the other."

Nell ducked to avoid his arm trying to knock her over. Moonshine growled and prepared to leap again. "No." She put her hand on her dog's head. "I work for the sheriff now, taking photographs of crime scenes. We just spent several days out at Craters of the Moon, where we found two bodies. Do you know anything about that?"

O'Donnell sat on a stump. "Why would I?" He looked worn out. Maybe Effie's story had affected him as much as it had Nellie.

"We think one of them is connected to a group of religious people, and that you might be, too." It was definitely a stab in the dark.

"What does that have to do with your being here?"

"One of the people we believe was with the two who are dead is here at Guyer—Effie, the woman you were just talking to. I wanted to see who was with Effie."

"So did I," he offered. "I wanted to find Elder Joshua. He owes me money." Curious that he didn't say anything about Hattie, after Effie's horrible story.

"She is not with Elder Joshua. He is dead." She took another small step backward. She decided not to mention Peter Banks; that was Effie's business.

"Where is my money? Did you and the sheriff steal it from him?"

"Why does he owe you money?" He seemed not to have noticed that she had retreated a few steps.

"None of your damned business." The man's face was turned so no light fell on it. Clouds covered the moon again.

"The money might still be at the lava fields." Then she said something she hoped she wouldn't regret. "I could show you where the bodies were found. Maybe the money is there."

"I already—" He cut himself short. He faked a cough but didn't resume.

So, he had been out there. Maybe he was there when Nellie, the sheriff, and Mayor Tom had been there, or even when Rosy had joined them.

"There was a farther cave, near the tree molds. We tried to get into it but couldn't. Maybe the man you mention—Elder Joshua—put the money there. There was no money on him when we found him." She took two more steps, this time off to the man's side. "I am leaving now. I'm expected at home, and, if I don't show up soon, a whole bunch of people will be looking for me." Goldie wasn't exactly "a whole bunch of people," but, knowing her, she would round up a search party if Nell didn't return as planned. "I saw your son, by the way. Did he know you were out there?"

"I will come by that boarding house where you live and pick you up tomorrow. Can you find that last cave again?"

"Maybe. I can get someone to come with us who knows for certain how to get there." Nell wondered how O'Donnell knew where she lived. Maybe he wasn't so surprised to see her in Ketchum.

"No! Just you."

"Do you have a compass? I can try. Moonshine has to come with us. And Effie. I have no reason to trust you, on any count."

"I will be there by 9:00. See that you are there, too."

"Bring Effie," Nell repeated. She knew she was getting herself in too deep, but it was all she could think of on the spur of the moment. When she retreated to her automobile with Moonie, she realized Effie knew the money had been in the automobile. And a long drive with Cable O'Donnell was the last thing she wanted to do. He couldn't be trusted at all. She was left with the questions of whether O'Donnell had killed the man in the cave, and why did Elder Joshua owe O'Donnell money?

CHAPTER 19

"You can't go out there alone with that varmint!" Goldie turned to Charlie. "Don't let her go! I just shake my head at how foolhardy you are sometimes, Nell!"

"Effie will be with us, too. If O'Donnell wanted to hurt her, he could have done it last night." Nell knew her arguments were weak. "O'Donnell knows I have you, the sheriff, and others behind me. He'll know that you know I'm with him. I might get him to admit he killed Elder Joshua, and, even so, he might have done it because Elder killed Hattie." Nell had recounted the overheard conversation to both Goldie and Charlie. "Or, I might find out why the dead man owes O'Donnell this money." Nellie swept her hand toward the boxes under the window in the parlor. "Maybe I could take a small part and put it in a cranny somewhere, and he could find it."

"No! I won't have it. Let's get Rosy to go with you, or that Mayor Tom."

Charlie had said nothing about Nell's explanation of the night before or her plan to go back to the lava fields with O'Donnell and Effie. He sighed. "Keeping Nellie from doing something foolhardy is like stopping a waterfall, Goldie. If she does not go, now that she offered, O'Donnell will think she learned something more about the whole situation, something that implicates him. If she does go, she is in danger." He stared at Nellie, as if to ask why she was the way she was. He pointed to his leg, still in the cast. "Clearly, I cannot go out onto the lava fields, but I could be in an automobile." He turned back to Goldie. "If we can get Rosy to be somewhere in the vicinity, then at least we have a back-up position for Nell if something goes wrong." He looked back at her. "As it always does."

"Moonshine is coming with me. I insisted on that."

Charlie rolled his eyes. "There is that." He gathered himself up to his crutches. "I will telephone Rosy and explain what we need. You two stay here."

As soon as he was out of the room, his crutches pocking on the floor, Nellie motioned to Goldie. "Help me. I'll take some of this money and hide it in my camera pack. I do plan to take photos while I am out there. I can stuff a bunch of bills in one of the crevices or holes that we come across and then pretend to find it." Or, better yet, she thought, go into that last cave by herself before O'Donnell does and place a bag of money in there. "Get me one of your small shopping bags. I'll use that."

"You will not." Goldie sniffed, but hovered over the bills. "You'll need a sack so no one could tell where the bills come from." She hurried out of the room and returned with a waxy bag, like the kind grocery stores gave out for big loads. "Here, dump some of those bills in here. Then close it up so Charlie won't notice."

When Charlie returned, both Goldie and Nell sat on the couch. "You two look like you are up to something." He looked from them to the boxes with the money. Both were shut up tight. "Rosy will leave at 9:00 and be there at the wagon road before you. If he is there, it would be difficult for O'Donnell to ignore him. Even if he did, Rosy could follow you. And, since he knows the territory, it makes sense that he stick close and direct you to the correct caves."

"Thank you, Sheriff."

"Do only as you said, Nell. Nothing more. And take this." He handed her his gun. "I won't need it here. And don't forget water and food."

Although Goldie watched Nell nod her head and look exasperated, Goldie didn't think Nellie knew what the words "nothing more" meant. She wished she could go with her roomer. She left to go to the kitchen and prepare at least a sandwich. "Where's the canteen?" she called. Nell brought it and filled it. "Don't worry, Goldie. I'll be fine."

Next morning, when a large automobile pulled up to the front of the boarding house and Nell waved and left, Goldie turned to Charlie. "I have a bad feeling about this."

Charlie's face was a pocket of frowns. He looked his age, which wasn't all that old, and older. Getting his leg broken had set him back more than almost anything else that had happened to him.

"What did you tell Rosy?"

"Just the circumstances and asked if he would go in my place."

"You were gone quite a while." Goldie knew Charlie didn't like her prying, but she knew both men well, better than they knew themselves, she sometimes surmised. "Do you and Rosy ever talk about Lily?" Now, that was prying.

"You and Nell must operate on the same set of assumptions about Rosy and me."

"We are both women," Goldie said. "Mebbe the better question is, do you and Rosy ever talk?"

"About what?"

Goldie flew her hands up. "Boys. Last Chance Ranch. Drinking. Craters of the Moon. I could list half a dozen things you could talk about. Nell."

Charlie smiled. "Yes, we have talked about Nell. We did just now. He did not want her to go out to the lava fields with O'Donnell either. You both had the same reaction."

"Does Rosy have a gun?"

"What do you think?"

Goldie pondered. "I know he didn't when he was drinkin' so much. Mebbe he does now."

"I told him where to find one in the house. He now has one."

"That makes me breathe a little easier. Does he know how to use one?"

Charlie leaned his head back. "Rosy has done his share of hunting, Goldie. Every man in this country has. He also herded sheep for a while and knew how to kill a coyote." He closed his eyes. Goldie knew he wouldn't answer anything more.

Worry didn't keep Goldie from preparing dinner for her boarders. She missed having the young boys there and wondered if Esther could cook or did, in fact, cook. Maybe Rosy had to do it all. If he was gone, his sister would have to do it. "I'm just a jealous old woman," Goldie said to herself. Talking aloud had long been a habit when she was alone nearly all day. Having Nell in the house with her portrait studio created a new situation. Although she had complained to herself at first, she had grown to like having the younger woman around. "I wonder if Nellie's mother misses her. I bet she does." She finished a chicken pot pie and put it in the icebox until time to cook in the oven.

Chapter 20

Nellie placed her camera pack in the back of the car alongside her tripod, canteen, and lunch. Moonshine occupied the well around her feet. She turned around. "Where's Effie?"

"Damned woman." O'Donnell never spared himself any swear words. "She took off early with a man in his car. They both stayed at that hot springs. That's what the clerk said."

Nellie wanted to back out, but she felt she was committed to go. Maybe they would come across Effie and, she assumed, Peter, at the fields.

"After my money, I figure." O'Donnell pressed on the accelerator. The two of them had little to say to each other. The automobile was a newer model than Nellie had ever ridden in, even in Chicago. She enjoyed the space and the luxury of extra-padded seats. Sheepskins covered the seats and almost curled around her backside.

Nell sought to get information, if she could, from the rancher. "I saw Pearl the other day. Tending cattle seemed to agree with her." She watched O'Donnell closely to see his reaction to the mention of Pearl.

"She always was a good rider." He stared straight ahead. "That's better for her than working in a saloon in Stanley, even if—"

"Why did that churchman owe you money?"

"None of your business. And he isn't, or wasn't, a churchman. He left the church, not agreeing with some of the tenets of that religion."

"You mean he wanted more than one wife?"

"The Lord said to be fruitful and multiply. The church caved in to blackmail." O'Donnell looked over at Nellie. "Seems like you forgot that, too. A single woman like you is an abomination."

To whom, Nellie wondered. Men who wanted more than one wife? She studied the landscape outside the automobile window. She felt as if she were treading familiar ground, not only the sagebrush and wrinkled foothills, but the old argument about not getting married. If she thought being a wife was akin to slavery, she figured being one of several wives to one husband must actually *be* slavery. Did O'Donnell buy the dead woman from Elder Joshua? And so, no wife, no money due?

"Is Effie related to you? And Hattie?" Nell asked.

"No," he said. "Not really."

Nell wondered what that meant. Either she was or she wasn't. He already refused to talk about the money, so Nell rode in silence, watching the scenery.

O'Donnell slowed the automobile and swung off the road onto a narrow strip bordering sharp cascades of black lava. It was as if the lava had hardened just the day before, the piles of broken flows looked so fresh. "Why are we stopping?" she asked.

"We'll enter the fields near here. There's an old Indian trail we can follow past the worst of this, and then we'll find our way to the caves. Besides, if Effie is here, they must have gone on to the wagon road. This way, we'll get to the last cave first. I searched the others."

"I don't know this way. I can't lead you anywhere in this . . . this tortured moonscape." And, Rosy would be waiting at the wagon road farther along the craters. He wouldn't see or hear them this far away. If Effie were there, wouldn't she tell him about O'Donnell? And, what if she did? Charlie already had warned Rosy. A cluster of anxiety threatened Nell. Maybe this hadn't been such a good idea. "Moonshine can't walk across these shards. If he can't go, I won't go either."

"Your damned dog be hanged. Come or not, but you'll have to hitchhike back to town." O'Donnell exited the automobile and opened the boot. He pulled out a pack and a rifle. "The trail leads off the roadway about a quarter mile. If you decide to come, follow it." And, then he tramped along the road and soon headed down into the cinders.

Nell waited until she could no longer see O'Donnell, and then she climbed out of the automobile as well. Maybe she could get a message to Rosy, if only another auto would come along the road. She hadn't seen any all the way to the lava fields. Soon, though, a Model T came chugging along. She flagged it down. An old man drove, and he looked angry at being stopped. "Whatcha want in that fancy carriage there?"

"I have a friend up the road a ways. Could you stop and tell him that the photographer and the driver are hiking into the craters from here?"

He grumped and half-nodded his head and took off again. Nell wondered if he would do anything. Should she wait for another? No, she decided. She loaded up her pack and tripod and canteen and called for Moonshine. Up the road she found where O'Donnell had left it, and she followed his track. It was narrow, but had been used for a long time, maybe by the Indians. Moonie followed. Nellie had taken care to place pads on his feet. As she walked, she realized this wasn't too far from where Charlie, Rosy, and she had left the craters from their last sojourn, a couple of weeks ago, when Charlie broke his leg. Perhaps, this was where Effie escaped from the Craters of the Moon with someone and motored on to Ketchum, carrying a baby with her.

Nellie passed stacks of lava resembling square houses. She

decided to stop and take a photograph. This topography was different than the area she had traveled before, much rougher. If she didn't get anything out of O'Donnell, then she could at least take photos, build up her portfolio of Idaho landscapes. These stacks almost looked like planned structures—ancient houses built from lava rocks. In the sunlight, their color verged into red. Bright green lichen speckled the cinders, creating almost a cheerful mood. When she finished, she packed up her camera again, squeezing it in beside the bag of money and Charlie's gun, and studied the ground around her. In the distance, she could see cattle and wondered if the herd belonged to O'Donnell and was being tended by Pearl and Ben. Ben reminded her a little of Ned Tanner, the cowboy she'd met in the Stanley Basin, the one Pearl had seemed keen on. If this area became a national monument, as Mayor Tom had suggested, would those cattle have to be moved? They made the area seem more pastoral than it really was.

The thought of losing grazing rights must enrage the cattlemen. Mayor Tom had said as much. Dead tourists would not help the cause of those who wanted a monument. People in Arco would benefit from more tourism. And, the lava fields were a strange sight to see, even if forbidding in many ways.

It was quiet. She hadn't seen a squirrel or a bird or any other animal. Maybe they were hiding from her, thinking she was a hunter, even though she didn't carry a rifle, and her gun was hidden in her camera pack. Maybe she should have it handier, she thought, and decided to carry the gun in her waistband in the back where it would be covered by her jacket. She couldn't shoot anything far away, but, it was when an animal, or man, was up close that was dangerous anyway—a lesson she had learned in the summer. Before she began trekking deeper into the craters, she looked back and studied the path, hoping to see Rosy hiking along it. Nothing. She sighed and hefted her pack.

"Come, Moonshine. We should keep going, although I am not sure why anymore. Maybe to find Effie if she is even here. Maybe she and Peter eloped."

The sun rose high, and the day grew hot. A shot rang out, closer than she would have expected. Moonie barked and began to run ahead of her. "Stop, Moonshine!" He did but kept looking back at her, wanting to go ahead. She didn't want him to be the target for O'Donnell or anyone else. And she didn't want to be one, either.

The path petered out ahead of her. She stopped and crouched down against a dead tree trunk, so she wouldn't be in the skyline and could look ahead. The tall cinder mound lay slightly to the east. And, then she knew where she was—on the way to the tree molds. The craggy mountain was directly ahead, and the cave was around to the other side. That was where she wanted to plant the money sack. She had no idea if O'Donnell were already there, but probably not, assuming he was the one who fired his rifle.

When Nell walked around the hill with the jagged top and the long fissure, she knew she was near the last cave, where Charlie had broken his leg. Again, no one was in sight. Nor had she seen a dead or wounded animal that would explain the gunshot. She wouldn't even consider that the bullet had been meant for a person.

The approach to the cave was as she remembered—a pile of rubble—broken pieces of lava and chunks of stone fronted by a flat slab of rock. Orange lichen covered many of the surfaces. Nellie dug out the flashlight she had brought and climbed with care down the rock slide and ducked under the lip entrance. A metallic smell met her nose, with overtones of dust and even water. Nothing rotting that she could tell.

"Stay close, Moonie." The tube, or cave, like the others, opened into a large area. Nellie tried to hug one wall, but the scattered rocks and uneven surface—a *pahoehoe* look-alike in the beam of her flashlight—made it more difficult, and she lost her touch until she realized by swinging the light around that she was in the middle of the room-sized cave. She stopped and stepped back to the wall again, trying to orient herself to the exit. Her camera pack wasn't heavy, but it caused her to sway when she balanced on one booted foot. "Where shall I hide the money?"

Without her flashlight, she would have been in stygian darkness. Even with it, she felt surrounded by a starless night with not much more than a candle to find a likely spot. She almost fell into a niche her light had failed to illuminate, and she stumbled trying to stay upright. "Ah, this is the place. If I couldn't see it even with my flashlight, then maybe O'Donnell didn't see it either, if he really was here before." Moonshine didn't answer her. She lowered her pack and pulled out the waxy bag to place it at the base of the niche, hiding it behind two chunks of lava. "Let's get out of here, Moonie." She swung her pack over her shoulders. But which way? Was it her left hand or her right that had last felt a wall's surface? She decided to turn off the flashlight to see if she could see a glimmer from the entrance. Nothing. With the light back on, she said to her dog: "Take me out, Moonie. You can find the way, can't you?" She looped a finger in his collar. "Go." He made a sound but stayed still.

"Took you long enough to get here." A light turned on and pointed at her.

"Aaa!" Nellie was so startled she lost hold of Moonshine and about dropped her flashlight. She couldn't see the person behind his light, but she recognized the voice. She moved her own light back and forth, and there, not ten feet from her, stood Cable O'Donnell, the rifle in the crook of his arm.

"Where did you come from?" She tried to keep the quaver

out of her voice. Had he seen her put the bag in the niche?

"Back there." He gestured with his head. "You have company."

"Company? What do you mean?" Nellie could feel the hairs on her neck stand up. This man had no scruples.

"Take that dog with you, and go find out."

"No." She wanted to grab Moonie again. "Who is it?" She didn't want to give Rosy's name away, just in case it was he. It could be someone else.

"Weren't you looking for someone?" He chuckled, a sound without an ounce of humor in it. He moved the rifle and pointed it in the direction beyond him. "Now you can be a hero."

The man stepped closer, so Nell moved back and felt Moonshine against her leg. "Did you find the money you were after?"

"There's no money here. The sheriff has it. You must know that, too."

"If he does, he didn't tell me," Nellie lied and took another cautious step back, Moonshine moving with her. "Who said so?"

"Give me your flashlight," the rancher said.

"No!"

"Give it to me, or I'll kill your dog." O'Donnell raised his rifle and pointed it at Moonshine.

Nellie could only hand over her light. "Why do you want it? You have one." O'Donnell stretched forward to grab it and then stepped back.

"I want whatever you stashed in the niche behind you," he said. "And, then I'll leave you to figure out how to get out of here without it. I have some business to take care of out there. I don't want you along. You might get hurt." Again, that humorless chuckle.

"What did you do with whoever is back there?" She gestured

with her hand, not knowing in what direction "back there" might be.

O'Donnell stepped around Nellie to the wall. He took his eyes off her, but not long enough for her to do anything. He reached down and grabbed the waxed sack she had stowed. He glanced into it briefly, smiled, and moved beyond Nell. Moonshine followed him. O'Donnell raised his rifle and struck Moonie on the head. The dog sagged to the ground.

"No!" Nell rushed toward her dog, tripped, and fell, landing so hard, she hit her head. The rancher disappeared from the cave, leaving dog and mistress in utter darkness. Nellie couldn't tell if her eyes were open or closed. Her fingers could feel rock— smooth and wrinkled. It was black, so black she couldn't see her hand. With care, she moved her arm around her, close at first, then wider. Only the ground was firm. The rest was black air.

She struck canvas. Her pack. She pulled her pack closer and hugged it. She rested her head, feeling the scratchy canvas, the leather straps, even finding the small metal buckles comforting and familiar. She could feel her gorge rising but swallowed convulsively. She wished she had water. Then she felt her coat front and found the canteen strap and the canteen and shook it. The welcome sound of water sloshing greeted her, so she unscrewed the cap and drank deeply.

Now what? Calling out wouldn't help. Again, she wondered what or who the "company" was, what O'Donnell had meant. She shivered and grabbed her pack again and held it to herself like a shield, then opened it. Her camera box lay where it should. Her tripod, reassembled after the legs were removed from Charlie's broken leg, was still attached. No gun. Then she remembered it was in her back belt. She wished she had pulled it out when O'Donnell was threatening her. Too late. She felt into an inner side pocket, not expecting to feel anything. But she did—the folded flash powder holder. Flash powder. She had brought a packet with her. And matches.

With shaking hands, Nellie felt for the matches. She had grabbed a handful from Goldie's kitchen box and wrapped them in a paper and put them in the bottom of the pack. Eight matches. She must use them carefully and first think about how to use them.

Arp. Arp. Moonshine! Where was he? She had not reached her dog before she fell and O'Donnell hurried out of the cave. "Moonie! Come here, boy." One match for Moonshine. She pulled one out of the wrapping and struck it across the rock she was sitting on. No fire. She felt around to be sure the rock wasn't wet and rasped it again. A flame burst and then settled into an unwavering light. She saw the walls and, five or six feet from her, her sweet dog.

"Oh, Moonie!" Nellie crawled to him. Her light burnt her fingers, and she dropped the match. She retrieved her pack and felt for her dog, and then the suffocating black took over again. By feel, Nellie examined Moonie. He seemed all right but kept making the strange sound, like he had around the opium last winter. He licked at Nellie, covering her face and hands with saliva.

Nellie would use another match. If only the little flame could give her an inkling of which direction was out. Again, the light burst up and then steadied—no wind at all. "Ow!" Nellie dropped the match. The wood burned a little longer so Nellie looked Moonshine over again. He still lay down. She pressed her hands along his side and back and down each leg. *Arp.* She pressed his head to her chest, and she felt a lump behind his ear. She would get even. Hitting her would have been one thing, but smacking her dog's head was unforgivable.

"All right, Moonie. Let's see if we can get out of here and get some help. I'm not going to try and search for the 'company'

without a flashlight and preferably company of my own choosing—like Rosy." Don't let it *be* Rosy back there, she continued
to herself. If necessary, she could go back to the road and hitchhike to Arco to find Mayor Tom.

Moonshine pulled himself to his feet, and Nellie's match
went out. She thought she heard a moan. A chill ran down her
spine. She listened for another sound. Nothing. No drip, no
scraping. Nothing. Whoever was "company" in the cave was not
moving.

What if it were Rosy?

CHAPTER 21

Gwynn showed up with Matt and Campbell again. He didn't seem to know what to do with them besides bring them to see Goldie and eat pie. This time, when they had eaten their fill, she said, "I'm coming back with you to Hailey."

"Why? How will you get back?" Gwynn turned from Goldie and shooed the boys out the door.

Goldie figured Gwynn had something up his sleeve, and she wanted to keep an eye on him. He had been particularly pleased to learn that Charlie wasn't at the boarding house and in fact had managed to get a ride to the lava fields. Goldie had tried to stop him, but he wouldn't be swayed. He and Mayor Tom had cooked up a plan.

"I have something to talk over with Esther, Rosy's sister. And, the boys need clothes. I can take them shopping." There was precious little for boys even in Hailey, but a Sears catalog might be available at the one clothing company.

"You can do that over the telephone."

"No, I can't. I don't want everyone knowing my business—or yours either, as far as that goes." Goldie pulled on a sweater and grabbed up her purse—a large satchel. "Besides, I want to ride in that fancy automobile of yours. I can catch a ride back easy." She bit her lip. She certainly didn't want to get stuck with Esther.

Gwynn sighed but bowed to the inevitable, it seemed. Goldie

told the boys to sit in back, and she sat in the front passenger seat.

The ride south was filled with yellow cottonwood leaves, sheep in the flat meadows, at least one green and white sheep camp, the sparkling Big Wood River where it curved near the roadway, and skeins of geese overhead. Goldie felt her chest open up to the late fall day. Even if Gwynn caused trouble, it was worth it to see the slant of the sunlight and the enormous bloom of white fall clouds. She hadn't been outside in days, except at Guyer Hot Springs.

"Where is Rosy today?" Gwynn kept his eyes on the road as if he didn't really care one way or another.

"The sheriff made him a deputy and sent him off to do a job." Goldie didn't think she should tell Gwynn about the lava fields and Nell's journey.

"Is that his job now?"

"I don't know. As long as Charlie is laid up with the broken leg, he needs the extra help. We'll need more people in our towns to keep two officers busy though."

Gwynn said nothing.

"The federal marshal has called on Charlie more than once, you know. The federals seem to think Charlie is the real goods." She decided to lay it on a little more. "I wouldn't be surprised if they offered him a full-time job in Boise. He's a good man." She couldn't help the last dig.

"You can thank me for that," Gwynn said. "If I hadn't thrown him out of town, he would never have amounted to a sack of horseshoes."

Goldie decided not to rise to that bait. "Rosy is being a real help."

When they arrived at Charlie's house, the boys jumped out of the auto and ran around the house, whooping and hollering. Gwynn climbed out and let Goldie fend for herself. They arrived at the door stoop at the same time. Esther, her face a series of frowns from her forehead to her chin, opened the door. She stared at Gwynn. "You can't let those boys run around like Indians. They have homework to do." She sniffed and turned away from Goldie as she moved to step into the house.

"That's Mr. Campbell's fault. I just came along for the ride."

Gwynn stepped in, too. "I am going to take the boys out to my ranch, Miss Kipling. Can you pack up a few things for them? They can take their books and homework with them."

Esther stopped and glared at him. "Who says so?"

"I do. I'm their grandfather. This place isn't suitable for them. It's nothing more than a cracker box."

"And, what does their father—my brother—say about that?" Her folded arms conveyed her own thoughts about Gwynn's idea.

"I know Rosy will agree. He's working for the sheriff and not likely to be around much. The boys will have horses and a better place to live."

"Since when are fathers ever around very much?" Esther drew herself up. Goldie thought she looked like a formidable opponent to Gwynn. He once was a big man, but age had dwindled not only his size, but his presence. "I'm here to take care of the boys while Rosy works," Esther continued. "And that is what I'm going to do!"

"You could—" Gwynn stopped. Goldie wondered if he had thought of inviting Esther to the ranch and then realized that might not be such a good idea. "I have a housekeeper who will help with the boys—do cooking and such. They'll have a grand time."

"And, what about school?" Goldie asked. "They are all settled into the school here in Hailey. Besides, you promised."

"I won't hear of it," Esther said. "They aren't going to another new school. As for this house," she said and gestured around, "it's fine for now. We'll find another place as soon as Rosy finds the right job—"

"And, he might have one already," Goldie said, interrupting. "I told you, he is working for the sheriff right now."

Gwynn looked from one to the other. "Then I at least want them to come out on weekends when they aren't in school. I'll come get 'em and bring 'em home."

Esther said what Goldie was thinking. "Ha! Why should I trust you to do the right thing? They'll stay here. If Ross says they can come for the weekend, then I'll come with them."

Goldie could hardly suppress a smile. "She's right, Gwynn. Rosy has to approve any arrangements."

Esther glared at her, too. "You stay out of this. This is my and Ross's business."

"Well, I am taking the boys over to the store to get them some clothes. They look like sissies in those short pants, and they need winter pants and boots." Goldie swept out the front door and called, "Matt! Campbell! We're going shopping!" How was she going to get back? She'd worry about that later.

As Goldie and the boys walked down the street to turn toward Main at the corner, she heard Gwynn's automobile start up and shift into gear. He didn't pass her, so she figured he didn't want to talk to her again. She might have laughed at him—done in by two women—so it was just as well.

CHAPTER 22

Nell decided she had to check the back of the cave, even though all she wanted was to get outside to breathe fresh air and look at the sky. "Can you walk?" Moonie pressed against her side and seemed steady enough on his feet. "Let's go." Nell swung her pack to her back, hugged her dog, and then, not so steady herself, took small steps to the far wall and headed in what she thought was the right direction to go deeper into the cave. A pile of broken slabs made her pause, but she circled as best she could, using one hand on the rocks to keep her balance. Bright lichen—yellow, green, orange—lit up under her match. She continued on, soon finding herself in what felt like a different space. Her flame flickered out. She lit another match, but the light only extended a few feet. More rocks. More broken slabs. No, a bundle at the far end of her light. It couldn't be Rosy— too small.

She could turn around and leave. No one would be the wiser. But she couldn't. She was the sheriff's envoy so must do what he would do, and that was check out the bundle. She wished Charlie were with her. Or Rosy.

As if her thoughts conjured the men, Nellie heard voices, this time coming from the direction of the cave area she had left. But who was out there? Maybe O'Donnell with companions, maybe his son. Whoever it was could mean more danger for her. She scrambled back to the pile of broken rocks she had circled and squatted down, blowing out her light and pulling

Moonie next to her. Soon she saw a faint glow, which grew.

"She ain't here," came Rosy's voice. "I'll look a little farther on. You stay where you are." His light appeared at the connecting of the two spaces.

Nellie stood, waved her hand, and placed her finger on her lips, trying to signal to Rosy to say nothing about her presence until she knew who was with him. She shook her head and then ducked down again, hoping he understood.

"She ain't here either," Rosy said. "Looks like the cave ends at the back of this room. I'm comin' back." He flicked his light two times and then disappeared.

Nell could hear the other voice. "Now what?" The large room distorted it, so she didn't recognize him. Both voices faded away, and, once again, Nell was in the dark.

With the men out of hearing, Nellie scratched another match and sidled toward the bundle, Moonie mimicking her motion. The pile looked to be all clothes, but she put out her hand to lift at least part of them up. The bundle moved, and Nellie gasped and fell back. Moonie *arp*ed. "Help me," it said. "Please help me."

"Are you hurt?"

"Yes. No. Help me."

Nell felt around the bundle to find a shoulder, an arm, or a leg. She found what felt like an arm and moved the person around. The voice was definitely female. "What happened to you?"

The person sat up, and the match's flame lit her face. Effie. "What are you doing in here? Can you stand up?"

Effie shook her head. "I don't think so. My legs don't seem to work."

Nellie groped along one leg bone and then the other.

"Owwww!"

Oh, oh. Just like Charlie. Maybe her leg was broken.

"My head hurts." The woman sagged against Nellie and then slipped back to the ground. "I can't."

"Oh, yes, you can, or I am going to leave you here while I get help." The flame was growing dimmer and then out. "And soon. Tell me what you can do."

The woman's hands scrabbled on the scratchy lava, and she tried to push herself up. Nellie stood, too, and reached down to wrap her arm around Effie's waist. "All right, together. One. Two. Three." And both were standing, Effie leaning hard against Nellie. Then Nellie realized she had to light another match. She had only three left. "Can you stand alone?"

"I don't think so," she said. "It's too dark." But then she moved one leg and then another. Not broken.

"One more." Nell lit another match. She re-circled Effie's waist, and they began to walk, moving like a two-sided crab back to the rock slabs and then around them.

"I can't!"

"Yes, you can. You're doing it." Calling her a sissy wouldn't help anyone, but Nell was beginning to get tired herself, with most of the weight of Effie on her side. Her clothes had hidden the fact that she was not slender, but her bathing outfit at the Guyer pool had shown she was not a thin woman. Nell's pack weighed on her, and her hand holding the match was losing its grip.

They struggled and strained and made enough noise to alert anyone who might be outside. Still, Nellie made her burden sit down near the entrance where they could see the light. "I need to see who or what is out there."

"Don't let that horrible man see me!"

Nell didn't stop to ask which horrible man. There were several candidates. She hoped all she found was Rosy—and she did. He appeared to be alone, but Nellie couldn't see above and behind the entrance. She tossed a small rock toward him, where he sat with his eyes closed. One eye and then another opened. He looked toward her and shook his head with a bare movement. Someone else must have been nearby. She dropped back in and whispered into Effie's ear. "Wait. Someone is out there."

The woman began to cry, and Nellie shook her shoulder. "Be quiet!" she said, right into Effie's ear. "Or the horrible man will see you!" Nellie remembered her canteen and opened it to give Effie a sip. The woman grabbed at it, and it fell with a metallic *clunk, clunk, clunk.* Water gurgled out before Nell could rescue it.

"What was that?" a man called, his voice coming from right above Nellie's head.

"Just my flashlight. I dropped it when I dozed off," Rosy said. "How long we gonna wait here for—"

"I don't know what happened. I'll head back down that Indian trail and see where they are."

It was the man from the pool—Peter Banks. Effie had come out to the lava with him. How did they get separated? And, how did he and Rosy get together? And, where was O'Donnell? Who were they waiting for? Maybe it was O'Donnell. Or, maybe Ben and Pearl, the only "theys" she could think of. Or, Mayor Tom and help?

After a silence of a quarter hour or so, Rosy's boot and then his face appeared in the entrance. "Are you all right? Scared me to death. Who's that?"

"That's Effie, the third person who came into the lava fields. The only one alive at the moment."

Effie struggled to get up. "I heard Peter! Where is he?" Her leg seemed to move much better. More play-acting? Nellie wondered.

Rosy stepped down several rocks and helped Effie up and then gave Nellie a hand. She hugged her rescuer as she, too, climbed out of the cave. "How did you know I was here? That old man in the Model T must have stopped and given you my message." She sank down onto one of the larger lava pieces. "Oh, Rosy. This was such a stupid thing to do."

He snorted. "You're all right now, Nell."

"Don't tell Charlie. He'll never let me go off by myself again!"

"He'd be right, too." Rosy patted Nellie's shoulder. "With any luck, he'll be comin' 'round that mountain soon—on a horse. When I got your message from that old guy, I sent him on with another to Mayor Tom to call Charlie and get both of them out here."

Nell nodded toward Effie. "How did Peter Banks get mixed up in this?" Effie hadn't moved from the ground, where she hugged a large rock. Her breathing sounded ragged, but she no longer cried.

Rosy shrugged. "He said he was lookin' for a missin' woman, just like me. So we joined up. I found him lost on the Indian trail on the other side of the rocky mountaintop there."

"I heard some of Elder's money was out here, and I persuaded Peter to bring me," Effie said. She put her hand to her forehead. "That money belongs to me. It was for my sister." Her tears began again, a silent crying from a face as still as the stone she grasped.

Nell stepped over to Effie and wrapped her arms around her shoulders. "I am so sorry we didn't get here in time."

Effie shrugged her off. "It is all those horrible men—wanting to make slaves of every woman they meet." Her tears stopped, and her eyes narrowed, her mouth a slash of red in her dirty face. "Well, they won't make Hattie a slave anymore." She sat up. "Peter was here? Where is he?"

"I sent him off to look for help." Rosy stood and climbed a slight rise. "Don't know where he went."

"I told him about the money," Effie said. "That is what he's after—not me." She slumped again and closed her eyes.

Well, Nellie thought. That money is of interest to a lot more people than she suspected. Who else? Maybe the money was the reason for the two killings—and the attempts on Effie and on her. If she made public the money was at Goldie's, there would probably be attacks there. She and Rosy could talk it over when Effie wasn't present to overhear.

"They're coming!" Peter clambered over the edge of the nearby hillside.

"Who?" Three voices asked the same question. Effie stood up, again her face a contrast of feelings. Her eyes widened. Her mouth stayed open. She hugged herself and stepped over to Nellie, almost hiding behind her. Peter didn't seem to notice her.

Rosy chuckled. "A treeful of owls."

"Mayor Tom and the sheriff. At least I guess that's who the second man is. They're riding horses." Peter turned and stared at Nellie and Effie. "What are these two doing here? Where did they come from?"

The two horses clopped on the smoother lava. Mayor Tom led, and the sheriff looked uncomfortable. When they pulled up to the group near the cave entrance, Mayor Tom dismounted. Sheriff Azgo stayed where he was. He searched the group and found Nellie. She walked over to him, leaving Effie in the open.

"I am glad to see you," she said. She wrapped her hand around his good leg.

"I could say the same thing," he said, his voice as quiet as hers. She nodded and rubbed the bump on her head from her fall with her other hand. She doubted he could see it.

For a moment, no one said anything. A magpie's croak filled the silence. Then Nell did. "Effie has been hurt. She needs to go back to Hailey to see a doctor." She turned to Mayor Tom. "Can you take her on your horse?"

The sheriff surprised her by interrupting. "I can take her. She can ride behind me." He motioned to his saddle. "Nell, you can ride with Mayor Tom. Rosy, you and Banks will have to walk back. Rosy's auto is at the wagon trail. There's another auto near the lava fields down the hill from there. Whose is that?"

Peter said, "That's mine. I came looking for Effie. She was out here, searching for money." He frowned her way and said nothing about being the person who brought her. "I can take her, if you'll let me borrow your horse, Tom. I could leave it at the edge of the road."

"No," the sheriff said. "If I take her, I know she's safe."

Those words prompted Effie to walk over to the sheriff and stand by his horse. "I'll go with him."

Nellie wanted to go with the sheriff. She didn't want to ride with Mayor Tom, and she couldn't walk all the way back to the road. She sat down on the ledge leading to the cave. Rosy watched her. "I'll help Nell get back. You two—" he said and motioned to Peter and the mayor. "You two can do what you please. Go back into that there cave for all I care. I don't think you'll find any money there. Now."

The sheriff studied the two men. "The money that was in the abandoned automobile is now in the bank in Hailey. It will go to the person to whom it was intended, once we find that out."

"It's mine," Effie said. "It's the ransom for my sister. If you give it to anyone else," she said, emphasizing *anyone*, "it will be adding another crime to her death." She spoke to the sheriff, but when she said "anyone," she looked directly at Peter. "How do I get on this horse?"

Rosy gave her a leg up. Nellie felt a stab of jealousy. She remembered another occasion when she rode behind Charlie with her arms around him to hold on.

"All right, Missy, you get behind Mayor Tom. That will be better than me trying to lug you across these blamed lava fields." Rosy motioned for Nellie to mount up.

"I think I'll stay here for a while. You and Peter Banks go on. I have something to talk about with Mayor Tom."

Everyone turned to stare at Nellie, including Mayor Tom. The sheriff opened his mouth but said nothing. Rosy said, "I'll wait."

"No, you better lead the sheriff out." She didn't want to say anything about his broken leg, although Mayor Tom must have helped him get on the horse. How he got pants on over the plaster was something she would have liked to see. "Take Mr. Banks with you, too."

Tom had not remounted, so he tied the horse's reins to a nearby tree and joined Nellie near the cave entrance. "What can I do for you, little lady?"

She wanted to say, I am not a little lady. I am a crime photographer. But she didn't say anything until the others were gone. Charlie didn't so much as look at her.

"Tom, did you look in those packages before you delivered them to the sheriff?"

A rosy flush filled Tom's face. He knelt down so his head was on her level. "Why would I do that?"

"Then why did you tell Mr. O'Donnell that the money was with the sheriff?"

He stood again, his face a scowl. "I didn't tell O'Donnell anything."

Nellie continued to study the mayor. As friendly as he had been, and as cheerful about helping the sheriff and her with the exploring and moving of bodies, she thought there was something about him that didn't quite fit the whole story. He had taken them directly to the first body and, after a few side trips, to the second body, as if he knew right where they were.

"Do you know Mr. O'Donnell?"

"Sure I do. He's the big cattleman around here. I know his son, Ben, too. But I don't see them in a month of Sundays."

Mayor Tom moved over to the cave entrance and then back again. "I did look in the boxes, but not the little package. When I saw it was money, I figured I better get it to the sheriff. I thought I might find something about the identity of those three people." He stooped and picked up something from the ground. "This here's a cigarette butt. Do you smoke?"

"I didn't smoke here." Nellie walked over to Tom and inspected the butt. "Who else smokes? Do you know?"

"I could make a guess. Maybe Effie." He threw it to the ground again. "I told her what was in the boxes, but she already knew. Or, at least she said she did." He looked at Nellie. "She came by asking for 'em. I told her I had to turn 'em over to the sheriff." He scratched his head and craned his neck around. "She wasn't happy about that."

"When did she stop by your station? Was she driving herself?"

"I think it was one of the days you was out here. After we found the two bodies. I guess after Rosy took my place."

Nell wanted to scream at him, and it took some effort to keep her voice down and not raise her arms. "Didn't you think that was information we should know?" She turned away.

"Maybe it was after you were gone from the area. I got busy at my gasoline station and kind of forgot about it."

"Was anyone with her?" Nell turned again and held her arms around herself. All she could think was that he was either stupid or lying. She studied him. He was flushed again.

"She was in a big automobile, and someone else was driving, but she got out by herself and came into the station. She didn't ask for no gasoline, so I didn't go out. When I told her no, she couldn't have the parcels, she yelled at me and then ran out, sayin' she'd remember how unhelpful I was." His face screwed up. "I told her I'd helped the sheriff and you for days to find those dead friends of hers." He paced back and forth and half stumbled on one of the lava rolls.

"What else haven't you told us?" She tried to keep her voice neutral and her hands still, although she felt like shaking him.

Tom heaved a huge sigh. "She left me a note after she copied the map. It was folded up with the paper, and I didn't see it for days, just before I called the federal marshal in Boise. It fell out. How'd I know she'd asked for help? It was all folded up in the map!"

"A note? What did it say? Where is it?"

"She wrote to follow them out to Craters of the Moon if they didn't come back in two days." He wrung his hands together. "I threw the note away, after I called the federals."

The silence between them lengthened. A chitting sound rang out from behind several trees. Nell took a deep breath. The air smelled of dead leaves and hot rocks. "I don't know what to say to you, Mayor Tom. I have to think about this. You may as well leave here with your horse. I'll catch up." Nellie didn't say she couldn't stand his company for another minute, let alone ride behind him. "Walk, don't ride." She left him and walked in the opposite direction of the trail out. "If you catch up with the sheriff, tell him what you've told me, but please, please, do not do so in front of Effie." She heard Mayor Tom pick up the reins and begin to walk away. "And try to remember any details about the auto that Effie came in."

Nellie unpacked her camera and took a photograph of the cigarette butt. It looked like the self-rolled kind. Maybe Effie waited at the cave entrance for O'Donnell or Banks, or someone else. It probably wouldn't help any but gave her something to do. Moonshine had rested quietly the whole time she and Tom were talking but joined her when she took the photo. Tom didn't know about the money, then he did know about the money. Effie left a note, but he didn't find it. Effie stopped by and wanted the money and left yelling at him. Whoever was with her obviously knew about the money, too. Mayor Tom spun tales in a web of deceit or incompetence or both.

CHAPTER 23

Nellie decided to head toward the tree molds. On that trail, she could see if cattle were being grazed in the west. She wanted to find Ben O'Donnell and Pearl and see what she could find out about Cable O'Donnell. She found it strange that his auto was no longer at the western end of the lava fields. Maybe she had been in the cave much longer than she thought, and he did have time to return to his auto and leave the area. Would he really have left her and Effie to die in the cave? As much as she disliked him, abandoning them didn't seem like something he would do. But how would she know? Certainly, last summer didn't speak well for his character.

After a short rest, she called Moonshine, who was curled up under one of the bushes shedding leaves into a red and orange pile. He came to her side, and she gave him some water from her canteen. "Uh-oh." She needed more water. She hoped it wouldn't take too long to find Ben and Pearl.

The track to the tree molds was familiar by now. Cattle grazed in the distance where the lava didn't extend. There were no trails in that direction, but she could see the animals, so she cut through cinders and over *pahoehoe* in a broken path. Throughout her walk, she had the sense that she was being followed and turned around several times. No one was in sight. Moonshine looked with her, but he didn't bark, growl, or bristle. The bump on his head might have deadened his senses. The breeze blew from west to east. As was usual, the smell of cattle thickened the air as they moved closer to the grazing area.

It wasn't too long before she spotted a rider and waved her scarf. She wished she had something larger. Still, the rider turned her way and eventually came close enough so she could tell it was Pearl.

"I need a ride," Nellie said. "Can you take me to your camp? I want to talk to you and Ben."

"What about?"

Nell remembered that Pearl was always suspicious of her, especially with regard to the men in Pearl's life.

"Not about Ben. His father was near here and now is gone. I wondered if either of you had seen him."

"Why do you care?"

Nellie felt like rolling her eyes. "I thought Ben might care." She tied her scarf around her neck again. "I am pretty sure you don't."

"You got that right. He's a double-crossing, two-timin' four-flusher. He can go to hell and roast there for all I care." Pearl extended her arm. "C'mon. I'll try to pull you up behind me. You look like you tangled with a tiger." She moved her foot from the stirrup, so Nell could use it. Pearl's strong arm propelled Nellie to a seat behind her. "I haven't seen him, but I've been out checking on the cattle—ridin' around the edges to make sure the coyotes don't set somethin' off."

The saddle rim offered itself as a handle for Nellie so she wouldn't fall off. Pearl didn't look big enough to hold onto, although her saloon girl dress had been exchanged for Levis and boots. The cowgirl made a *chic chic* sound with her mouth, and they all started off at a fast walk. "Follow us, Moonie!"

"Where's that sheriff of yours?"

"He's not mine, and, at the moment, he is escorting someone back to the road on the back of his horse."

"Girl?"

"Yes." Nell clamped her mouth shut. She didn't want to have this conversation, and she especially didn't want to give Pearl something to crow about.

"Worried?"

"No, of course not. Why would I be worried?" Nell shifted as the horse began to move a little faster. "I work for Sheriff Azgo now. I am his photographer."

"Mmmm." Pearl looked over her shoulder. "That sounds cozy. Does he pay you?" She giggled. The saloon girl was still inside somewhere. Nellie compared Pearl's blonde-ness with her own dark hair and brunette-ness. Her photographer's eye wished for a photograph of the two of them.

"I earn money with my photography, yes. Mostly I take photos of automobile accidents, suspects, dead bodies, broken guns—"

"Dead bodies? Any of those lately? I do recall you took photos all around that sheep camp last summer."

"Yes." No need to keep it secret. Half the county knew there were two bodies on ice at the meat packer's place of business. "There were some visitors to the lava fields whom we found in the caves. Have you heard about them?" Maybe Pearl's penchant for gossip would give Nellie information she couldn't get elsewhere. Nellie strained around to look behind her. Moonshine was keeping up well with the horse, and she saw no one around the tree molds or the trail she had followed. She thought of Rosy. Maybe he had followed her. That would be like him, to be sure she was safe. And Mayor Tom had his horse. Surely, she would have seen or heard a large animal. Still, she felt uncomfortable.

"Have you heard from Ned?"

A question out of the blue, Nell thought, about the cowboy from last summer. "No. Have you?"

"Yes, we write back and forth. I'm thinkin' of goin' to Oregon to meet up with him. Dick's no good for me anymore. As you know." Pearl turned her head to scowl at Nellie. They approached a ramshackle shed with a small porch and railing outside. A tent was set up nearby. "Here we are. I don't think Ben has returned, and it don't look like anyone else has visited either." Pearl slid off the horse and helped Nellie down.

"Do you have any water here? I'm thirsty and so is Moonshine."

"That dog," Pearl complained. "Come inside. I'll fix you up."

Inside, there was a sagging bunk, a rickety table, a couple of chairs, and a plank sideboard with a big bucket of water. Nellie filled up her canteen, found a metal dish, and put water in it for Moonie. She took the water outside, as the shed smelled like old meat, sweaty men, and burnt coffee. "Do you mind if I wait here for Ben?"

Pearl shrugged. "He should come round about mealtime. He expects me to cook for him. I sometimes do and most often don't. He knows how." She had tied her horse to the rail and sat on the stairs to the shed. "Take a seat. You need a rest."

Nellie sat on a nearby stump, placed close to a fire ring. "I do. I have a sandwich in my pack. Do you care if I eat it? Want a little of it?"

"No. I ate a while ago. Those people you found? Ben saw them back near those caves one morning. He rode over. They were a strange bunch. An old man and two young women, one of 'em probably pregnant, was what Ben thought, she was so round. They were kneeled down, praying. And then the man hit the round one and knocked her over. Ben was shocked. He asked her if she wanted to come with him. That old man threatened Ben, but he's big and strong. I guess you saw that when he ambled over to where you were."

"What did the woman say?" Nell was shocked, too. But then, the woman was now dead.

"She said no. She wanted to stay with the other woman."

Maybe "the other woman" killed her, Nellie thought. Somebody did. What a tragic end—abuse and then murder.

Pearl stood up. "Ben's coming. That's his trail of dust out there." Nell joined her. "He looks in an all-fired hurry, don't he?" Pearl said.

Before long, Ben pulled up to the shed and dropped off his horse. "What're you two doin' here? Pearl, you should be out checkin' on the cattle." He tied the reins around the rail. "Haven't seen you in a while, Miss . . . Burns. Are you takin' photo-graphs here at my shed?"

"No, I came to ask you about your father. Have you seen him?"

Ben wrinkled his face. "Not for a week or so. He comes around to see if I've kilt any cows." He laughed, and his face lit up, making him a handsome man. He took off his hat and slapped it against his legs, and a cloud of dust poufed out. "Why? I thought you two was enemies."

"I suppose we are. However, I think he might be missing. Have you seen his automobile? I came with him early this morning to visit one of the caves. I saw him there, and then he was just gone. His auto, too." She scratched Moonie's ear, and she could still feel the bump on his head. That made her aware of her bump. "Do you know Peter Banks or Mayor Tom?"

"I know 'em both. I go into Arco for supplies every week or so and visit with Tom. He's a good ole boy. Banks?" He shrugged his shoulders. "He hangs around the lava fields every now and then. He was with that group that explored it a year or so ago. Seems like he's not quit of the craters yet."

"Does your father know Banks?" Nellie wondered if Peter Banks was part of the group that wore the funny symbol on their clothes. She looked around for a stick, found one, and began drawing the ankh in the dust by the stairs. "Do you know what this means?"

Ben looked at Pearl and then away. "Yeah. Some of those old-time polygamists wear it to show they're from the lost tribes."

"Lost tribes?"

The cowboy shrugged his shoulders. "Part of their religion. Except the ones who wear that symbol because their church outlawed more than one wife. Most of 'em already had more than one." He climbed the stairs and entered the shed. Conversation finished, he seemed to be saying.

Pearl leaned over and whispered in Nell's ear. "His pa is one of them—more than one wife. He wanted me for a third!" Her voice squeaked up at the end. "Not me, I told 'im. Go find some other dumb dora." And maybe he did, Nell thought and was tempted to say but decided to keep her mouth shut this time. "Could you give me a ride back toward the tree molds? I'm supposed to be heading out to the road." Even she heard the tiredness in her voice. Walking all that way back wasn't appealing at all. She didn't think she could do it. Maybe the sheriff would come find her after he delivered Effie to—to where? He'd have to wait for Rosy and then send her back to Hailey if he wanted to assure her safety. He must think Mayor Tom and Peter Banks weren't trustworthy, either. But, then why did he leave her to talk to Mayor Tom alone?

Nell and Pearl rode in comfortable silence for a short while. "Pearl, why wouldn't you sign a statement against Cable O'Donnell last summer?"

Pearl continued to ride without speaking but then turned her head around toward Nell. "I thought he might marry me, and then I wouldn't be poor anymore. I didn't know he was already married—twice, it seems!" She pressed her legs to the horse, and it moved along faster. "I knew what he'd been up to because of that sad sack Dick Goodlight."

"Were you ever married to Dick?"

"No, and I won't marry him when he gets out of jail, either."

"How about Ben? He seems a nice man. And handsome, too."

"Ben had a girl. She's gone, but he can't seem to bounce back. We're just cowpokes together. Nothing else."

"Are you sure you're gonna be all right?" Pearl asked.

Nell had slid off her seat on the horse behind Pearl. "No." That was not the answer Pearl was looking for, she knew. "Yes. I'll be fine. I may just find a cozy spot in some of those limber pines and settle in for the night. It's getting late, and I have Moonshine to protect me." The sun cast a mellow glow over the lava, the trees, the dust, the shrubs. Golden tones comforted her, although she knew the country could be dangerous. A while ago, she had moved the gun Charlie gave her back into her pack. Before she started out toward the north, she would find it and stick it in her pants again—just in case—after Pearl left. "Keep an eye out for O'Donnell, will you? He might be in danger." Especially now that he had some of the money with him.

"He can take care of himself. He always has," Pearl said, her voice laden with disgust.

Nell had forgotten to see if Pearl still wore the lovely pearl ring, but her gloves covered her hands anyway. "Did he give you that ring?"

A blush colored Pearl's usually pale face. "Yes. I gave it back to him." She turned her horse around. "I wished I'd a kept it. It was the only pretty thing I had."

Nell patted Pearl's leg. "No, you have a pretty face and figure. Maybe you should go to Ned Tanner soon." She waved as Pearl rode off to the west, just like in the cowboy movies.

Nell trudged past the tree molds, wondering if she was brave enough to stay out all night and travel back to the road in the morning. She remembered her sense of someone following her earlier. "What do you think, Moonshine? Would you protect me if some wild animals—two-legged or four-legged—attacked me?"

He gave a short bark and looked up at her, his mouth open and seeming to smile. "Yes, I thought you would." Maybe that is what she should do. Once it was dark, she wouldn't be able to follow any trail at all. She turned in a circle. No clouds. Not even much wind—a nice change. If she cuddled with Moonie, they would both stay warm.

Only then did she hear what sounded like a horse coming along the trail, alternating between clops on dirt and rings on stone. She jumped off the trail and scooted to a clump of lodge-pole pine trees, hoping they would conceal her.

It was a man, tall in the saddle. The sinking sun was full on his head, but his face was mostly hidden by his Stetson. And, then she recognized the taut Levis, the heavy jacket. "Charlie!" Nellie tumbled out of the trees, right into his path. "Charlie!" She held onto his non-plastered leg.

He put his hand on her head. "When you and Mayor Tom didn't show up, I knew something was either wrong or you decided to do some scouting on your own." He waited until she had gathered up her dignity. "I figured the scouting part, so I sent Effie off with Rosy. He'll come back for us."

Nell reluctantly let go of Charlie's leg. She reminded herself she was an independent woman. "Did Mayor Tom tell you his news?"

"Tom? No. He never showed up. That was when I thought you might be in trouble. The other man—Peter Banks—split off to go to his automobile fairly soon after we left you. Rosy thought he knew the way. It seems we know some of the only people in the area who have spent time here. And you are becoming an old hand." He smiled at her, a warm smile.

192

"Thanks to you. I'm not so certain I'm any good at this crime detecting. I did go to Ben O'Donnell's camp and gleaned a little information. Mayor Tom gave up even more. I have a lot to tell you."

"Then, let us get you up on this saddle and head back to the wagon road. You can tell me as we ride along. The sun is setting, so we have only an hour or two before it is completely dark. Rosy will go wild if we do not show up." He extended his arm to Nell. She put her foot in the stirrup, and he swung her up, much more easily than Pearl had, but with the same motion. This time, she put her arms around Charlie to keep from falling off. No saddle rim with him.

Nell filled the sheriff in regarding her own adventures—letting O'Donnell go off on his own. Finding the cave, cache-ing the money . . .

"What money?"

Ooops, he didn't know about that; only Goldie did. So Nell had to admit her sneaking some of the money into her camera pack. "I'm sorry I didn't tell you." She was silent, waiting for him to tell her it was all right. No response. "If I hadn't done it, I would never have found out how greedy everyone—and I mean everyone—is about that money. It's a good thing you deposited the rest."

"I did not deposit the money. I wanted to get out here to find you. It still sits in the parlor at Goldie's. We better telephone as soon as we get to Carey and tell her to hide it somewhere. She might be in danger. Unless all who were here believed me."

Nell felt a cold shudder. A premonition? She hoped not.

"O'Donnell, or at least I assume it was him, fired a shot, but I didn't see him or what he was shooting at. In the cave, he snuck up on me and almost gave me a heart attack. He said someone was in the back cave. I was afraid it was Rosy. O'Donnell took my flashlight and the money. Then he hit

Moonie on the head. I fell as I ran to Moonshine and hit my head, too. O'Donnell was gone. And, I had no light but found matches in my pack." Nellie couldn't help going over the scene in the cave once again. "Speaking of Moonshine . . . where is he?"

"He is following us. He keeps running from side to side, smelling things. I have an eye on him. He will not let you out of his sight."

The way grew rockier, and the horse and its riders stepped back onto lava. Nell tightened her grip around Charlie's waist. He felt substantial, strong, a protector. Even with his plastered leg, he rode easily. "I could see that you were shaken up, but it looked like the other woman was in worse condition and needed to get out of there. It turns out, she had a wound in her leg, so it must have been O'Donnell who shot her, whether accidentally or on purpose, we may never know. Unless we catch up with him again. She would not name him as her attacker, however."

"I found her in the next room in the cave. She appeared almost dead, but then she woke up. Maybe O'Donnell was tending to her there or trying to finish the job. Her leg didn't work very well, but once I found out it wasn't broken, like yours, I helped her up and out. I wonder why she wouldn't name who shot her. It must have been the one I heard."

Nell continued her tale with the information Mayor Tom had finally admitted. He had looked in the boxes and also found a note. "That was when he called the marshal, he said." Nell and Charlie traveled to the west side of a tall cone, to keep the sun on their left. Nell didn't remember coming that way any of the times she had been in the fields. "What are those?" She pointed to what looked to her like miniature volcanoes—a series of them.

"Rosy called them 'spatter cones.' Lava came spurting out of them hundreds or thousands of years ago. They did not grow up to be full blown volcanoes." He pulled the horse to a stop. "I can't get down and back up again. Would you look around? Moonshine appears to be tracking something himself. See what you can see in this light. It is low enough now that shadows may show up."

Indeed, Moonie scooted along with his nose to the ground. If the lava hurt his feet, he gave no sign of it. Nellie slid off the horse, trying not to fall over as her camera shifted in her pack on her back. She just wanted to go home. Still, Moonie's activity piqued her curiosity. What was he finding? She crouched to her knees and grasped the lava to see if she, too, could find tracks to follow. The cinders hurt her hands, but she did see where something had been dragged from the trail and toward one of the spatter cones. It could have been anything—a large animal dragging a smaller one, a groove from an eruption eons ago. And, then she found a coin. And another.

"Someone dropped some coins along this groove," she called to Charlie. She pointed toward one of the smaller spatter cones. "Whoever or whatever it was, it went there."

Charlie pushed his Stetson back. He reined the horse to follow Nell and the dog. He took care to stay to the side of where Nellie crawled. Finally, she stood up and followed Moonshine. He seemed to have either the scent or could see the track better than she could. She left the coins, so she could return and re-start if necessary. Just two of them, and then another near the cone. Perhaps they had been dropped like crumbs from the children in the Hansel and Gretel story—an attempt to lay a signal—or, she thought, like a spider leading its prey to its web. The cool air caused her to shiver. Either that, or her thoughts.

"Is your flashlight handy?"

Charlie reached back to his pannier and pulled out the metal instrument. "I am not certain how much battery is left." He turned it on, and the light burst forth but then dimmed.

Nellie set down her pack. "I am going to climb this cone and see if there is anything in it. It looks like a hole near the top side."

"I am sorry I cannot help. Please be careful."

Nellie saw that the sheriff had lifted his rifle from its scabbard and held it pointed to the ground. The assurance of his back-up settled her nerves. Although it didn't appear anyone else was around, who knew in this landscape? Someone could hide behind any rock, any crevice, any swale, and neither she nor Charlie would be able to see him or her. Still, Moonie would give warning, she hoped. She thought of Pearl. Could Pearl have dragged something here with her horse? Or Effie with the help of one of the men? From her search that afternoon, she was afraid of what she would find. Moonshine followed Nell at first and then climbed ahead of her.

The cone was steeper and more difficult to climb than she expected. It was like climbing a stack of plates. The lava rocks and slabs kept slipping and sliding and cascading in little landslides. Her hands could hardly sustain her balance and were getting bloodied. "Moonshine, stay behind me. You're making rocks fall." She reached the hole and looked in. The hole was blacker than black and big enough to hold a body. Indeed, it did.

CHAPTER 24

Cable O'Donnell lay head down, face sideways, hatless, his hair covered with dried blood. His head must have caught on a small ledge, or maybe his extravagant belt buckle had stopped his slide into the pit. Whoever stuffed him there didn't wait to see if he kept falling. Nellie was afraid to touch even the man's boot, for fear it would cause the rancher to disappear down the hole. Moonshine tried to nose it, but Nell pulled him back. "Go down to the sheriff, Moonie. You're just in the way up here."

"I need a rope," she called. "It's O'Donnell. He met his just end." The man was so much smaller in death than in life, as if he had shrunk from losing his bluster and meanness. Still, she felt little sympathy, unlike what she had felt for the two earlier bodies they found, even though she knew this man and the others had been strangers to her. She squeezed out a spoonful of empathy for Ben, who seemed so unlike his father.

Charlie secured his rope to his saddle horn and then looped the end. "The best way for me to get the rope to you is to lasso you." Even in the gathering gloom, Nellie could see the sheriff's teeth in a rare smile. And he did lasso her. The lariat fell over her head and shoulders. Fortunately, he didn't pull the rope and tighten it around her. Nell could hardly suppress a giggle as she thought about the metaphoric possibilities—"roped her in," "rounded her up," "tied her to him." She must be getting silly from being tired. She pulled the loop up and over her head and then studied how to circle at least one of O'Donnell's legs

197

without disturbing how he lay. Really, she needed to get both legs together, but that would take more strength than she had and risk his continuing to slide into the hole. Nellie knew she couldn't prevent the man from sliding once he started.

She climbed with care over the upper ledge and set her foot on what looked like a stable rock, although she tested it first. No movement. She brought the loop with her and settled the top part on his leg. Inch by inch, she pushed the lower part under O'Donnell's boot by pulling out first one rock and then another and another. She thought she felt the body shift slightly, so she stopped. Then she continued until the rope circled the boot. Nellie called, "Tighten it!"

From her huddled position, Nellie clambered back over the ledge. "I think you'll have to pull very slowly or the rope will pull the boot off. I'll try to guide the leg up and over." Even as she helped secure the loop higher on the leg, she realized she had lost her squeamishness around this dead body.

"Nell," the sheriff called. "Can you take a photograph of him, now that we have a rope on his boot?"

Nell stared at the sheriff. How could she have forgotten to even suggest taking a photo? "Yes, of course." Maybe, she said to herself. She climbed down, secured her camera, several sheets of film, and the black cloth from her pack, then climbed back up. No sense in bringing up the tripod, as there was no place to put it. She would have to steady the camera on the lava ledge itself. She pressed the buttons on top, opening the mechanism and then pulling out the bellows both front and back. She had to stop and think about how to go about focusing on the dead man and stabilizing the camera. There were plenty of rocks to hold the camera in place, but she had to aim it down. His legs would look gigantic and his head too small. There was no help for it. Some cameras could be maneuvered to at least take into account the perspective, but hers could not.

"Can you do it?"

Nell didn't answer. She was trying to do it. Maybe the best she could do was balance the camera on his legs and boots and take it from there. She shuddered as her squeamishness returned. He had left her without any light in the cave and hit Moonshine. She would keep that thought in mind and view this as some form of retribution. She pulled the black cloth over her head so she could see through the ground glass, focused as best she could, and released the shutter. One more angle. She swung one leg over the top of the cone, resettled herself and camera, and took one more.

"All right. I did what I could." Nellie replaced the bellows in the box and closed it up. "Wait. I need to return the camera to my pack." By the time she reached O'Donnell again, she was "plain tuckered out," as Rosy might have said.

Now, their aim was to get the body up and out of the cone without losing it. Once Charlie had pulled enough to get the bulk of O'Donnell—everything except his arms and head—over the ledge and headed downhill again, Nellie picked up a rock the size of a bread loaf and dropped it in. She waited but never heard it hit bottom. This dead man would have disappeared forever if Moonshine hadn't stumbled on the trail and she and Charlie on the coins. She wondered if O'Donnell had dropped the coins on purpose or they had simply fallen out of his pocket as he was dragged along. She hoped the latter. Even she wasn't steeled enough to hope he died a slow death. His face was scratched and rubbed almost raw; all the blood seemed to be from his head.

Nellie climbed back down the cone, helping to move the body without scraping his head off. She had wrapped his head in his jacket, so she thought it might be intact. At Charlie's horse, she held onto the sheriff's good leg, again. "Now what?" She answered herself: "I should take another photo up close. I know we scraped him some as he came down, but . . ."

"Yes, that would be good."

Nellie unwrapped O'Donnell's head and went to work. His hair stuck to his skull. The blood, although mostly dry, still seemed sticky in spots. On the side she had not seen as he lay in the hole, the blood was much thicker and goopier. "Look, Charlie. It looks like he was either bludgeoned or maybe shot. You explore. I can't." She took the photo and then backed away. "I'll help you off the horse."

"It can wait, Nell. First, we—meaning you—have to build a fire. We are going to have to stay here for the night. I do not want to drag the body clear back to the road. There would not be much left of it." Charlie held onto Nellie's shoulder. "You are a strong woman, Nell." He unlooped the lasso from around the saddlehorn. "I can check the body in the morning." He turned in the saddle to look back toward the lava fields. "Maybe Rosy will see the fire and come this way." He turned back. "We can return to the path and leave O'Donnell here for the night. If we are close by, the animals should stay away. Having Moonshine will help. He will warn us if a critter comes creeping. I will stay awake. You can sleep. You need it. First, you have to help me down when we get to the trail."

Nellie followed instructions. Not having to think was a bonus after her long day, filled with fright, determination, confrontation, and now photographing another dead person. She trekked back along the path toward the tree molds, as there was little wood near the cones. She wondered if the lava fields were what hell looked like, if one believed in hell. She gathered dead branches and one larger gray piece in a stack about half way between where O'Donnell lay and the path. Charlie had extracted a canvas cloth from his own pack and handed it to her to cover up the lifeless man. He watched her comings and goings but also moved the horse around to find a place to dismount and one as comfortable as possible given the terrain.

When Nellie found a branch about the size of a crutch, she took it to Charlie. "Time to dismount. You can use this to hobble on." She hoped. She had tested her own weight on it, but that wasn't a good test for a man like Charlie. They found a level rock plate, and Nell tried to help relieve the weight on the sheriff's good leg as he lifted the leg with the cast over the horse. He took the branch and used it in place of his bad leg until he could get his balance. "I found a possible camp site over there." He nodded with his head. Nellie helped him hobble until they reached a spot with large stones, still warm from the sun, and a sheltered area without rough lava and few signs of any lava, except around the edges, an anomaly. From there, they could also see the fire, which Nellie had lit, using one of her matches and dried grass to get it going. Nell spread Charlie's coat on the ground with her own and helped him to a sitting position with his bad leg straight out in its cast. His grunts revealed his pain.

"Build the fire as high as you can. Then come back here and try to sleep, Nell."

When she returned, Charlie had built up a pillow with the rope and covered it with yet another piece of canvas. His panniers, which she had lifted from the horse and left near him, seemed a never-ending treasure trove of useful things. She lay down next to him, and he put his arm around her. "It will grow cold. Stay as close as possible." Moonshine eased up to her other side and curled around to sleep, too.

As Nellie drifted off to sleep, she wondered if it really would be cold or Charlie only wanted to hold her. Either way, the situation suited her just fine.

Nell shivered awake. It was still dark, and Charlie was not next to her. Neither was Moonie. "Charlie!" Nell tried to keep her voice down until she knew where he was and what was happening.

"Over here," he called in a normal voice from near the fire. "A coyote came creeping. Moonshine growled, so I decided to move and keep the fire stoked." He stood in an awkward position and laid several more branches, and the flames leaped up.

"Why didn't you wake me?" Nell jumped to her feet and joined him. "I can do this."

"So this is where you two ended up!" Rosy's voice made Nellie start. "I been lookin' all over for you. I got to thinkin' you found another cave to search and got lost." He joined them at the fire. "I saw this fire and figgered no coyote, except maybe the two-legged kind, had set it."

Nellie turned and hugged Rosy. "Did you get Effie delivered?"

"Yup. She dang near talked my head off the whole way back. I tried to leave her at the hotel, but she wouldn't have none of that. Said she was afraid she'd get killed, like the other two. So, I left her with Esther. Sorry 'bout using your house as a way station, Charlie. Goldie was there with the boys, too. Passel of women to take care of 'em, so we can take our time gettin' back."

"What did Effie say?" Nellie asked.

"What didn't she say makes more sense." Rosy dropped the pack off his back. "You two hungry?"

"I should smile," Charlie said. "At least I am. It's been a long day and an even longer night."

"Where's your horse?"

"Back over there, tied to a rock. Nell gathered all this wood, and I suspect she could eat a horse."

"Where's Moonshine?"

"Oh my heavens! I completely forgot about Moonie. He slept next to me for a while." Nellie hurried back to the trail and called. "Moonie! Moonie! Where are you?" She hoped he hadn't found another porcupine. She hurried to the horse and then back to the nest Charlie had built. Moonshine lifted his head from behind the rope pillow. "Oh, thank heavens!" She crouched down and held her dog in a body hug.

Rosy had followed Nell. "Just sleepin'. He was clobbered, Effie said. She could talk the tail off a coyote. I didn't always know what she was jabberin' about, but I did get a few things. One was that you were abandoned in the cave and then helped her out. Saved her life, she said."

"Did she say anything about Cable O'Donnell?"

"Plenty. C'mon back to the fire, and I'll tell you both. Charlie said O'Donnell is over there, deader'n this here lava rock."

All three of them and Moonshine gathered around the fire. "Nell, I did not know what a time you had in that cave. I could have sent Rosy back with Effie," the sheriff said. "Rosy, maybe you should take Nell to the automobile instead of staying here. You could take the horse and then bring it back."

The sheriff still leaned on the branch, but Nell thought he looked as if he could fall over at any moment. Carrying that cast around probably sapped his strength. "And what would you do? And what would we do with O'Donnell there?" Nell came to Charlie's side. "We all go, or we all stay until morning. Then we can decide what to do."

Neither man responded.

"That settles that." Nellie folded herself down near the fire.

Rosy helped the sheriff sit down and found a rock for his leg to rest on. Then he sat down himself and pulled wrapped sandwiches and cookies from his pack. "Goldie knew food was wanted," he said, chuckling. "While you two eat, I'll tell you about Effie." He tossed a few pieces of jerky to Moonshine, who gobbled them up. He was as hungry as the other two.

Effie was the dead girl's sister. Her name was Hattie. Elder found her in a train station in Pocatello, trying to buy a ticket

East, but she had little money and even less baggage. He took her to Utah City and planned on her being his wife, until he found out she was pregnant. Elder was furious because he thought he had a virgin in hand, apparently a scarce commodity. He said he was taking her to a crystal cave to have her baby, and it would be dedicated to God. Hattie was able to telephone Effie to meet them in Idaho Falls and help her. Effie contacted O'Donnell, because she knew he was part of the same group of polygamists that Elder belonged to. O'Donnell said he would pay enough money to Elder for the return of Hattie, who had run from Twin Falls. Effie took it with her and handed it over to Elder, but the old man still wanted to proceed with his plan. After the baby was born, Hattie could go to O'Donnell.

"Effie didn't have no choice but to stay with Hattie and hope she could save her. Hattie was terrified. She never did say who the pa was, although Effie said she thought she knew, but she wasn't tellin' either."

"Did Effie tell you what happened in the caves?"

"No, she just kept crying about her sister and the lost money. She says she has to pay it to O'Donnell, who was tryin' to save her sister. She did say somethin' strange, though. That O'Donnell said he'd get the money back from Elder, one way or t'other. Maybe O'Donnell had strings he could pull at Utah City. Effie thinks he helps support the place and may provide a bride or two or three. She don't like O'Donnell at all." Rosy wound down.

Nellie and the sheriff stared into the fire. She was too tired to go over what she had heard Effie tell O'Donnell, and she did not want to speculate out loud, but she had her own opinion about O'Donnell. Still, if he had tried to save Hattie, and even put up the money to do it, he must not have been all bad. And, why would a young woman as pretty as Hattie have had anything to do with the rancher? He was so much older. Maybe his money was the lure. Certainly, Hattie would not have been the first to succumb to the possibility of riches, especially if she wanted to escape from a background of poverty or abuse. Pearl seemed to have done the same thing. Nell hugged Moonshine closer. The next thing she knew, the sun had brightened the sky before topping the hills to the east.

Rosy stirred up the fire, pulled out a fry pan, and made biscuits and bacon. Charlie hobbled to the body, and, using his flashlight as another crutch, he lowered himself near the head and inspected the head, neck, and the rest of the man. He managed to stand up again and joined the others at the fire. He replaced his items in the pannier or around the saddle horn of his horse as it stood closer to the group.

"We been talkin', Nell," said Rosy. "I'm goin' to take you and that body there back to the automobile. We'll take it into Arco and arrange to get it moved to Hailey to the morgue. Charlie here will wait 'til I come back and get him."

"I'm not going to ride that horse with the body on it! Why don't you two take it back, and I'll wait here. Moonshine can keep me company. I can take photographs and keep myself busy. With O'Donnell dead, I don't think there is anyone else out here who would harm me." She stood up to sound firmer. "And, I have a gun."

Rosy looked at Charlie. "Told you she wasn't goin' to go along with it. Stubbornest female I ever did know." Nellie heard the postscript in her head and wondered if Charlie did: "just like Lily."

"I have examined O'Donnell as carefully as I could. I didn't want to roll him over as I might scratch him up even more. You were right, Nell. Either someone hit him with a sharp rock or maybe he was shot. I think there is something more to see. I want to get him to the coroner as soon as possible. He was stiff last night, but rigor mortis is about gone. He can be carried slung over the back of the horse. You and Rosy can walk. I can wait here until Rosy comes back to get me."

"You'll be out here for hours! That doesn't make sense at all." Nell wrapped her arms in front of her. "You ride. The body rides. Rosy and I will walk. Then no one waits here." As if it was all decided, she began to pack up her coat and camera. The two men shrugged at each other, and they, too, began to pack up. Moonshine herded them back and forth, more energetic than the day before.

When Rosy and Nellie reached Charlie at the automobile, both wanted nothing more than to stop and nap. Charlie had managed to dismount the horse and waited, his leg extended, by the side of the wagon road on a tuft of bunch grass, turned gold. The dead O'Donnell remained slung over the horse. Nellie wanted him out of her sight.

"Now what?" Nellie gestured to the dead man. "He won't fit well into the boot of the auto."

"Guess I better drive to Arco and get Mayor Tom's help," Rosy said. "He'll need to pick up this horse, too."

Charlie sat, his face a stone image. Nellie thought he could easily meld into the rock of the craters, except his color wasn't as dark. Moonshine looked from one to the other, also silent. He was probably as tired as they all were, but he at least had slept most of the night.

The sheriff's shoulders sagged. "If it were not for my carelessness . . ." He slapped the leg in the cast. He straightened and nodded. "All right, Rosy. I cannot think of another solution. We will wait here. If you can, telephone Goldie about the cash, but do not let Tom or anyone else hear you. Better not to call than to alert someone that the money is still at the boarding house."

"D'you think Tom is involved in all this?"

"He might be," Nell answered. "He certainly hasn't been honest about his actions, even if he has been helpful out here."

Helpful or scheming, she wondered. She had told the sheriff and Rosy about her conversation with Tom. He was so thoughtful about Moonie, it was hard to think of him as a murderer or even as an accessory of some kind. "He certainly wants this area to be declared a national monument, and he probably could use the money to wage some kind of effort." She faced Rosy. "Does it cost money to get a national monument?"

Rosy shrugged. "Probably takes money one way or t'other. To be or not to be." He grinned at Nellie. "I'll be back as soon as I can."

When Rosy had driven off to the east, Nellie approached Charlie. "Can I get you anything? Water? Food?" Her canteen still felt almost full. She found a rock out-cropping and called Moonie before she tipped some out for him. Charlie shook his head.

"I think it was one of O'Donnell, Peter Banks, or Tom who was in the cave with . . . Hattie at the same time we were there. That white spot on your photograph was one of them."

"It couldn't have been Tom. He was with us," Nell said.

"True. Then O'Donnell or Peter Banks. What do we know about him?"

"He goes swimming at Guyer Hot Springs. He seems to be . . . maybe intimate with Effie. Maybe even a ladies' man, first Effie and then that other woman. He tried to smooth talk me, too. He might be the person who delivered the baby to the church, probably with Effie's help. We don't know much. We know O'Donnell gave the money to Effie, who delivered it to Elder. Or, at least we know Effie said she did."

"That spot could have been her," Charlie said.

"Or, Ben O'Donnell or Pearl." Nellie tossed a pebble into the wagon road rut. "I doubt it was Pearl. She may be the only person out here not connected with this group in any way." She took a sip from her canteen and offered it to Charlie. "Ben seems removed, too, except for his father. Or, maybe the son was the father of Hattie's child. That might explain Cable O'Donnell's interest in getting Hattie out of the clutches of that religion. Ben would have had the same interest, or need."

The sun was warm where they sat, but it was a fall warmth, a sideways warmth. A breeze with an undercurrent of chill began to rustle the grasses around them. Nell leaned toward Charlie, and he lifted his arm to put it around her shoulders. "Charlie, almost everyone here could have an evil motive, even if they appear to be normal."

When he said nothing, Nellie continued. "How do you stand it? Auto crashes and even robberies seem more like accidents. But, ever since I arrived, one way or another, I've been involved in murders—seven of them now? Surely, that isn't normal. Every way we turn, we discover a person is complicit in one way or another. The money. The child. Multiple marriages. Is it like this everywhere in the West? Has it always been? Are small towns rife with evil? Am I evil?"

His laugh was loud. "No, Nellie, you are not evil. Even if your camera seems like a magic tool, there is an explanation for how it works. You are good-hearted, and that is why all this seems evil. Small towns have as much evil as big cities. It is human fallacy and weakness—money, greed, drugs, jealousy, even love." He shrugged and pulled her closer. His laughing voice changed to somber. "It is my job to stand it. That does not keep me from being sad sometimes, mad other times. Solving some of the mysteries of our community helps me continue, especially if it helps people I know, and I know most everyone in this valley."

They held onto each other, each with their individual thoughts. Nellie felt closer to Charlie than she ever had. Perhaps he felt close to her, too. She couldn't bring herself to ask, so she just enjoyed being next to him, even if it might not last.

CHAPTER 25

Several knocks on the boarding house door drew Goldie Bock from her kitchen. When she opened it, Peter Banks stood on the threshold with the woman Goldie had seen at the pool. She was the one who tried to peek into the men's pool.

"I took care of the baby," Goldie said. "She is in good hands for now. What else do you need?"

The woman stepped into the house, forcing Goldie back. Her short skirt and cloche hat confirmed Goldie's earlier opinion of her. "That child is my sister's. I need to find her—and the clothes you have here . . ." She sounded as if she would continue but stopped.

"And who might you be? And if your sister is the mother, where is she?" Goldie wondered how this woman knew about the knit baby clothes that sat in a box in her parlor.

"I'm Euphemia Thorpe. My sister, Harriet Thorpe, is dead, killed out in the lava fields by a crazy man." She pulled a hanky from her sleeve and dabbed her eyes. "Where's the baby?"

"How do I know she's your niece? This man here found her on the church steps. You could be anyone, cozying up to Mr. Banks here and wantin' a strange babe for yourself." Goldie wanted to close the door, but Peter stepped in, too.

"Mrs. Bock," he said. "I lied to you, and I'm sorry. I brought that little mite to the church myself, because Effie here was too distraught by her sister's death. She couldn't take care of it in her state. I called on you because I wanted the baby to be safe, and I didn't know what else to do. Surely, you understand."

"And the money," Effie blurted out. "It's mine, and I want it. That money was for my sister, Hattie. It's mine now. Give it to me." She tried to move past Goldie.

Peter laid a hand on Effie's arm, restraining her. "We're sorry to barge in here like this, Mrs. Bock. Effie is concerned about Hattie's baby. We need to find her. You were kind enough to be sure she was safe." His manner was the same as it had been at Guyer, friendly and brotherly.

Effie grabbed Mrs. Bock. "Tell me where she is. I want the money. Now. And the clothes." Her voice wasn't sweet any more.

"I can send you to the doctor in Hailey who made the arrangements." The doctor could decide if this woman, this Effie, was on the up and up. "You can't have the money until the sheriff decides who it belongs to."

"It's here?" Effie released her hold and ran down the hallway, poking her head into side rooms—the dining area, an office, and then the parlor.

"Here now! You can't just run willy-nilly in my house! Come back here!" Goldie took off after Effie but didn't catch up until Effie stood in the parlor and now studio door.

There, on the floor, stood two empty boxes and the small box with knit baby things scattered half in and half out. Goldie opened her mouth in disbelief. Just that morning, the boxes had been tidy and stacked on each other, the small one on top. A few bills stuck to one of the boxes, but, otherwise, the money was gone.

"Oh, my goodness," Goldie exclaimed. "I'll get the clothes for you." She packed the little garments back into the box and handed them to Effie.

"But where's the money? I can see it has been here. Peter, you must search this house. This woman took it and is hiding it somewhere."

Goldie stalked to the window to see if it had been opened. It was stuck shut, just as before. She looked at Effie and Peter. Had they come in while she was in her kitchen and stolen the money? Had someone else? The last she knew, Nellie had scooped up some of the money to place in a sack and take with her to the Craters to lure Mr. O'Donnell into telling his secrets. "How did you know about the clothes and the money? Who told you? You probably arranged for whoever that was to sneak in here and take all the money. You are bad people!" Goldie pointed at both of them. "Get out of my house. The sheriff will take care of this. I know you're staying at Guyer Hot Springs. I'll send him there as soon as he returns! Shame on you—using a tiny baby to break into my house and threaten me! Out! Out!" Goldie shouted the last order.

Peter Banks grabbed Effie's arm and pulled her back to the door. "We did not steal any money," he said. "Mayor Tom said he turned it over to the sheriff. I assumed the sheriff had control of it. Effie thought it was here. We are sorry to disturb you." He pulled Effie out the door and closed it.

Charlie and Nellie and Rosy stopped at the butcher's morgue, and Rosy and the butcher carried O'Donnell in. The sheriff swore the butcher to secrecy and then telephoned the coroner and told him what had happened and what he needed. They then dropped Rosy at Charlie's house. They didn't go in. Nellie didn't think she could face Effie again, if she was still there. She could see Charlie was exhausted and needed to lie down. When they arrived at Goldie's, Nellie helped Charlie to the parlor. He dropped onto the couch, lifted his leg up, and almost immediately fell asleep. Nellie tip-toed to the kitchen.

"We're here," she said, not wanting to startle her landlady.

"Oh, thank heavens. You won't believe what has happened while you were gone!" Goldie pulled a towel off the handle of the icebox and wiped her hands. "Someone stole the money. That woman Effie and Peter Banks barged in here, saying they wanted the baby that Mr. Banks brought to me and I farmed out to someone in Hailey. Who knows who? Only the doctor. How do I know they were telling the truth? What're we gonna do about the money?" For the first time Nellie ever saw, Goldie plunked herself down at the kitchen table and began to cry. "I even gave that woman the baby clothes!" She almost wailed.

Nellie placed her arms around Goldie and hugged. "Now, now. We'll sort this all out. Effie's sister did have a baby, and the one Mr. Banks brought was surely that child. I suspect they wanted the money more than the baby, so at least they didn't get that!" She didn't add that the money might belong to Effie, now that Cable O'Donnell was dead. Who else would claim it? Well, maybe Ben would, if it really had been furnished by his father. Goldie stopped crying, but Nellie didn't stop hugging. She followed her last thought—why would Effie get it?

"What is going on in here? Cannot a man get some shut-eye?" Charlie stood in the doorway. His smile softened his words. He leaned on his crutches.

Nellie stood up and patted Goldie's shoulder. "Effie and Peter Banks came here. They demanded the baby, the baby clothes, and the money. They got the baby clothes and may have gone to Hailey to get the baby. The money is gone."

"Gone? Did they take that, too?" His smile disappeared. "I was afraid someone would try."

"It was stolen. The boxes are empty." Goldie still huddled on the chair. "I'm sorry, Charlie. I'm not a good person to trust. I don't know who came in when I was working in the kitchen." She looked up. "For all I know, it was those two and then they went back out and banged on the door."

"They're not that smart," Nellie said. "And why wouldn't they take the baby clothes at the same time?" From Goldie's description, they had been scattered around—not wanted or needed. She tried to recapture her elusive thought about Effie, but it wouldn't come back.

"Where are the boys?" Charlie asked. "It is like a tomb around here—just like the old days."

Goldie stood up. "I don't know. They were playing upstairs last I knew. Where is Rosy? The boys should be in school, but we were afraid Gwynn would kidnap them to the ranch. Esther and I decided they should stay here for a few days. Oh, dear." She hurried out of the room. Her steps sounded on the stairs, still in a hurry.

"That wasn't much of a nap," Nellie said.

"With the caterwauling here in the kitchen, I could not sleep. Then I noticed the boxes were stacked empty." He crutched into the room. "I was afraid of this. At least Goldie is safe. I worried someone would hurt her while stealing the money, after the conversation about it at Craters of the Moon. Rosy did not call Goldie or mention it to her when he took Effie to Hailey. He didn't want Effie to hear."

A muffled scream came down the stairs.

"Oh, no!" Nellie dashed past Charlie and climbed the stairs as fast as she could. The door to the boys' room was open. She stopped, stunned. There on the floor were the two boys, each with a stack of bills beside them. Playing cards lay around them.

"We're playing poker!" "Just like the cowboys!" "I'm ahead!" "No, you're not. You cheated!"

Goldie stomped into the room. She grabbed an arm of each boy. "You boys stole this money from downstairs! It doesn't belong to you! If Rosy doesn't whale on you, I will!"

The boys' eyes grew round. "We didn't know. We opened the boxes and thought it was play money, so we thought we could use it! Please don't tell our dad, Aunt Goldie. We didn't mean to!" Matthew spoke for both of them while Campbell cried.

"We were playing in the studio and used the boxes as our stage coaches. One came open, and the money fell out. We opened the other one. There was so much money, we thought it was play money." Matt pulled his arm loose from Goldie's hold.

"It's all right, boys," Nellie said. "You kept it from being stolen. Now stack it up and put the cards away. The sheriff will take the money and put it somewhere safe." A bank, she hoped. She retrieved the boxes from the parlor after explaining to Charlie what they had found upstairs. When the money was re-packed and re-sealed, she put the boxes in her room until they could be delivered to the sheriff's office and thence to a bank. By then, the boys were happy again and playing another game with the cards.

CHAPTER 26

Ping, ping, p-ping. Nellie awoke with the sound. *Ping, ping.* It was still dark. A few moments passed before she realized little rocks were hitting her window. *Ping, ping.* She climbed out of bed, wrapped a shawl around herself, and stepped to the window. Of course it was stuck tight. She tried to see who was tossing the pebbles but could not. She knocked at the window, then pulled on her pants, a shirt, and boots, grabbed a jacket, opened her door, and crept downstairs. At the kitchen door, she unlocked it and peered outside.

"Who is it?" Her whisper sounded loud to her. Moonshine had followed her, but she bade him stay inside. She stepped down the stairs to the side of the big, old house near where her window, upstairs, looked down on the side yard. There were no street lights. The only ambient light came from the kitchen, where Goldie kept a small lamp for boarders who came in late or sought a late-night snack, plus a porch lamp at the front of the house.

More pebbles pinged. Nellie edged closer, trying to figure out who wanted her awake. Whoever it was, was accurate with his aim. "What do you want?" Her whisper was louder this time.

"Nell. Miss Burns. I need your help." A narrow figure in dark clothes rose up from behind several shrubs. "Again."

"Effie! What are you doing here?"

"I need you to come back with me. Just for a little while." Effie reached out and grabbed Nellie's sleeve. Nellie jerked it away.

"Why? What's wrong? Can't this wait?"

"No. My sister's baby is going to be kidnapped tonight, and we must stop it!" Again, she grabbed at Nellie.

"But where? Why? I don't understand." Nellie let herself be pulled toward the street. "You were right there with Rosy. He could help. He's a deputy." She dragged her feet. "Let me get the sheriff."

"No! I need you. Please. I'll explain in the auto. We must hurry!"

Effie opened the back door of a long, black automobile and practically shoved Nellie inside. She stumbled onto the back cushion and at the same time smelled something sickly sweet. Nellie pushed herself up and tried to back out. Too late—a cloth covered her mouth and nose, and she knew no more.

Sometime later, Nellie began to hear voices talking and felt herself moving in the auto. Her hands and feet were tied. Her head felt like a big balloon, and she was dizzy. She kept her eyes closed. She doubted she could even open them. They felt stuck shut.

"Why go all the way to the lava fields?" Effie's voice sounded querulous. "You didn't find the money when you went back and looked. It won't be out there, that's for sure. The sheriff probably did take it to the bank, just like he said. Otherwise, you would have found it in Nellie's room, where the boys said it was."

A mumbled answer. Nellie couldn't distinguish any words apart from ". . . smart cookie," ". . . dangerous," and ". . . never find . . ."

"No! She saved my life . . . my father . . . me . . . I won't be part of this."

"Shut up." That was clear enough.

Nell didn't know the man's voice. It could be Peter Banks, but it sounded rougher. "Her father." Who could that be? Mayor Tom? Or Cable O'Donnell? Someone in Hailey or Ketchum? Not Tom, of course. Tom called the three who went to the lava fields all strangers. Unless he was lying.

"Check on her."

Nell tried to relax, as if she were still drugged. A hand touched her face, softly prodded her.

"She's still out. Maybe you killed her. I can't tell if she's breathing or not." The hands moved away.

"How do we know the little brats were telling the truth about the cash?" The voice was clear this time. Nellie was certain it was Peter Banks. Too young to be Effie's father.

The auto rumbled along. Nellie risked one eye open. A pre-dawn light glimmered through the windows. She couldn't see anything but two heads in the front and the upholstery in the back. It was an expensive automobile. Cigarette smoke floated around.

"I told you. We don't, but they didn't know I was listening when they told their aunt about what happened—the play money, Nell's room. They'd already told their father, I think, on the way back from Ketchum." Her head moved with her talking. "He told them to pipe down. It was a secret." As if the thought just occurred to her, she said, "Did you make noise when you went up the stairs?"

"Quiet as a mouse I was. No one heard me."

By the time the auto reached the lava fields, Nellie was completely awake and trying to get her hands loose from the rope. When the auto stopped, the driver climbed out, saying, "I've got to find . . ." His last words were lost. Effie still sat in the front seat.

"Effie," Nellie said. "You have to get me out of here!"

Effie swung around. "I can't."

"Yes, you can. You drive, don't you? Move over and start up the auto and drive away." Nellie kept her voice low. "Please, you must help me. What is Peter planning on doing?"

Effie screwed up her face. "I don't know. He said he would get the money back for me and then take me away from all this. He promised. I don't know why he wanted you!"

Nellie thought for a moment. "I think I know. He shows up in one of my photos where your sister was killed. Maybe he did it."

"No! That was . . ." Effie clamped her mouth shut. Then, as if to herself, she said, "I mustn't tell. I promised. Besides, he didn't . . . She was already dead, by that fiend." She shook her head. "The baby killed her!" She covered her face with her hands and sobbed. "I don't know what to do. Hattie was the one who planned, who always knew how to get out of a fix. That was what she was trying to do, you know, when Elder found her." Her shoulders shook. "Only he was a worse fix. That's what I told—"

The auto door jerked open. "C'mon. I have the horse." He turned to Nellie where she sat in the back seat, and he tossed away a cigarette butt. "Now, miss crime photographer, you tell us. Where is the money?"

Nellie stared at him, visible, as the dark had lightened up. "It is safe and beyond you."

The man's beseeching manner changed. "Tell me, or I will make you pay."

"Whatever you do, the sheriff will find out, and you'll pay." Her words were braver than her thoughts. This man may have killed all three—Elder, Hattie, and Cable.

Peter Banks brought the horse closer. "Help me get her on it," he said to Effie.

"No! You can't do this. You promised to help me. This isn't helping me!"

"You want that money or not, you cry baby? What did you tell her?"

"Nothing. I promise. I'm crying for my sister, Hattie."

"She's dead. Nothing you can do about that." Peter handed a piece of cloth to Effie. "Here. Put a blindfold on her. Now. We don't have all night."

"She said she has a photo of you in the cave with Hattie."

He exclaimed and then said, "Nothing to do about that either. By the time someone finds out, we'll be long gone, and so will she."

Effie climbed in and whispered to Nellie, "I gotta put this on you. Hold still."

Nellie shook her head and lifted her arms, tied as they were. She shoved at Effie, who fell backwards out of the door.

"You wildcat. I should take you and leave Effie here. I like 'em feisty." The man practically sat on Nellie and tied the scarf around her eyes. "Now shut up, or I'll fill your mouth too." He pulled at her elbow and legs until she stood outside the auto. While she couldn't see straight ahead, she could see out the bottom of the blindfold. She knew where they were—the side strip near the narrow trail that led to the tree molds.

Coins. Nellie remembered how they found O'Donnell. Did she have any in her pants? As stealthily as she could, she pulled her arms to one side and reached a hand into a pocket. Nothing. Around to the other side—nothing there either. She tried to reach her jacket pocket and couldn't. Peter called to Effie again to help get Nellie onto the horse. She hoped he would let her ride, but her bound feet told her he had other plans. She hopped to the other side of the auto while they argued and tried to scrape a word in the gravel of the roadside. She could loosen her boot, but that was it, when Peter grabbed her and slung her over the saddle of the horse. She couldn't tell if it was the same horse she, Charlie, and Rosy had been using. Where did it come from? Was Tom in on this, too? Peter took a rope and wrapped it around her and then the saddle horn. There was no way she could slide off and attempt to escape. She felt like a bag of bones.

"I'm not coming!" Effie shouted. "You can't do this!"

"Good. You'll only slow me down. You better be here when I get back, or you'll get the same treatment, and I'll get the money." Peter paused and muttered under his breath, "Maybe I should tie her up, too." He stepped away from the horse. "Nah. She's too scared to drive off alone." He began to lead the horse down the path, still muttering. "Why do I need her anyway?" He stopped. "Effie, come with me. You can keep me company. I want your help." His voice once more adopted a wheedling tone.

"Promise you won't hurt her?"

"I'll leave her tied up out there by the tree molds. Someone'll come along and let her loose. By then, you and I will be on our way to California, like we talked about. That money will keep us a long time." He sounded again like he did at the Guyer Hot Springs when talking to the boys or wooing the woman behind the changing wall.

That money would keep him a long time, Nellie thought. Effie, too? She doubted it. She decided to say something. "Effie, he'll just leave you there, too! Run away! Get help!"

Peter knocked Nellie's head. "Guess I'll have to shut you up, won't I?" He pulled another kerchief from his pocket and stuffed it in Nellie's mouth. She choked and gagged and tried to lift her head, without being able to. She used her tongue to push the gag to the front of her mouth as much as possible. She found a position where she could breathe through her nose. The horse began moving again. She couldn't tell if Effie were with them or not.

The horse was being led from the front. Nellie could stretch her neck and see the cinders immediately below the horse. They changed from black to shiny to gray to crystal prisms and back to black. She worked on her feet and loosened one of her boots enough to kick it off. If Peter heard it, he would stop and throw it from the path. If she made a noise, he would turn around and see the boot drop. What to do? She could feel her heart thumping in her chest.

The horse stumbled. Peter stumbled. She didn't hear Effie, so she hoped the woman had stayed behind. If she were smart, which was in great doubt, she would drive off and get help.

Their travel smoothed a little, and Nellie decided she had to leave the only clue that was possible—her boot. She slipped it off with her other foot and felt it drop. She tried to cough to cover up any sound, but the gag didn't help. Peter didn't stop. Then Nellie realized he would see it on his way back from wherever they ended up. Despair seeped around her heart.

An hour, more, passed. Nellie ached from her head to her toes. Being slung across a saddle with her head hanging low on one side, her middle on the hard seat, and her legs swinging with the horse's movement was the most uncomfortable position she had ever been in. Peter whistled from time to time but didn't talk. The ground beneath her began to change, from piles of clinkers to a path with pine needles. They were near the tree molds. Then Peter and the horse changed direction, and the path once again was lava rock, smooth for a while, and then filled with the lava detritus. Occasionally, she could see a lava bomb. Dread filled her. They were nearing the area where Charlie and she had found Cable O'Donnell. Oh, please, she thought. Not one of those spatter cones.

Peter stopped. His boots neared her, and he pulled the gag from her mouth. "I should have given you another dose of chloroform. I could feel you calculating all the way here," he said. "No one will save you now, picture lady. I don't care what your camera shows." He untied the rope from around the saddle horn and her hands and feet and pulled her off the saddle. She could hardly stand, especially with one boot gone. The man shoved her to the ground, where she landed on the cinders. Her arms were free now, so she pulled off the bandanna around her eyes. Effie wasn't with them.

"You were so nice to the boys. When did you become such a monster?" Nellie's mouth was dry as dirt, and she could hardly get the words out.

Peter jeered. "Best way to get to a woman—be nice to the kids."

"Is that baby yours?"

Peter had turned away but swung around to stare down at Nellie. "What do you mean?"

"Hattie's baby. The one she died delivering. Is it yours?"

"I never—" Peter stepped away. "None of your business."

"Are you and Effie going to kidnap that baby? Why did you put her on the church steps if she was your child?"

"It's one of those O'Donnells' baby. Why else would that old man be willing to pay so much to get Hattie back from those religious nuts?"

"She, not it." Nellie dug with her hands behind her back. Peter still had not noticed one of her boots was gone. That was good. She was trying to find a cinder or rock large enough to cold-cock Peter if he leaned down close enough. She remembered O'Donnell's head and Elder's head—how they had both been smashed with a rock. Did Peter do that? Would he do it to her? She could at least try to defend herself. "She has a name now, too. Eleanor. Isn't that pretty?" Nellie made up the name. Maybe a real child would elicit sympathy from Peter, even if it wasn't his, but Nellie suspected it was, although some complete stranger in Twin Falls or Pocatello could be the father. Her long ride had given her time to cogitate on all of these people. One way or another, they seemed to be related or connected, a co-incidence she had found often to be true in the small towns of Ketchum and Hailey and Stanley.

Two steps and Peter grabbed Nellie's arm and pulled her up. She didn't have time to react. "Time to tie those hands again. We're going on a short walk." Only then did he notice her stocking foot. "Where's your boot? I'm not going to carry you. You'll just have to scrape up that foot of yours." He jerked her around and once again tied her hands together in front. He shoved, and all she could do was hobble like a crippled goose being led to oblivion. Peter pulled a circled rope from the horse's saddle and hefted it onto his shoulder. In exasperation, he half carried her to one of the spatter cones—the same one where Charlie and Nellie had pulled Cable O'Donnell out.

"You'll find some company down there," Peter growled and then laughed.

Nellie was afraid he'd hit her first, apparently the same way he had bashed Cable. She remembered tossing a stone down the hole and not hearing it land. How deep was it? She lifted her arms and tried to push Peter toward the hole, hoping he would fall in. Although he staggered sideways, he jumped up and knocked her over. Her face scraped the globs of lava on one edge.

Tears sprang to Nellie's eyes. She could feel blood seeping down one side of her face. She tried to kick out at Peter with her foot. Peter took the rope and circled Nellie's chest with it. He lifted her bodily and used the rope to lower her several feet into the hole. The edges of the hole scraped her legs, and she worried her head would bang against a sharp outcropping. She had difficulty breathing with the rope around her.

"Where's the money? Tell me, and I'll pull you back up."

A stray thought about swimming making him strong crowded out Nellie's fear for a brief moment.

"The sheriff has it—in his office in Hailey—locked in a safe." Nellie panted, trying to sound calm. "You will never get it." She tried to laugh.

The man's face looking down at her suffused with red. His eyes widened, and he pulled her up a foot or two. "What's so funny, you harlot." He looked like an evil clown.

"All your and Effie's machinations about the money. And O'Donnell's, too. Except he knew it was counterfeit." Her laugh sounded less forced. "He was a moonshiner *and* a counterfeiter, as well as a cattleman. Did you know that about him? The sheriff does." Nell tried to keep her voice light. Maybe it was true. Otherwise, why did Charlie let it stay at the boarding house so long? Of course, he could hardly get around. "After the revenuer raid this last summer, his house was searched. Apparently, he hid a lot of the counterfeit money, but the revenuers took away the machinery. When we opened those boxes of bills, Sheriff Azgo knew right away where they had come from. O'Donnell wasn't really giving anything up to Elder for Hattie. Just phony bills."

"You're lying."

Nellie tried to shrug her shoulders.

"I've seen some of those bills. They were flat out real."

That meant he took the bills O'Donnell had swiped from the cave where Nellie stashed them. He must be the person who killed O'Donnell. That would be proof.

"How would you know?"

"Maybe I don't know, but I can find out. In the meantime, you get to find out how to get out of that hole." Peter slowly lowered her again, maybe to torture her with fear. It was working. Before Nellie could try to do anything to save herself, he let the rope go.

CHAPTER 27

Goldie fussed in the kitchen getting a picnic basket ready to go. A picnic in October struck her as faintly ridiculous, but she had promised the boys she would take them to Guyer Hot Springs and then a picnic on the lawn. Rosy had promised to bring them back in the morning for this treat. She hoped he remembered their swimming suits. She did not approve of those boys swimming in the men's side with no clothes on. There was no school, but she had already rung up the resort to see if the springs were open.

Rosy arrived, and the boys ran upstairs to their room. "Shhhh!" Goldie called. "Nellie still isn't up yet, and I don't want you pestering her!" She turned to Rosy. "She has never slept this late. Do you suppose she's sick?"

"The last few days were pretty hard, Goldie. Leave her be. She probably needs the sleep. Plus, she has to go to Twin Falls to get some film developed. We ran into a strange deal out there." He helped himself to coffee from the pot on the stove.

"What strange deal? No one tells me nothin'."

"Can't talk about it. I'm a deputy now, so gotta keep things quiet until Charlie tells me it's okay."

"What's okay?" The sheriff stood in the doorway. Only one crutch helped him stand.

"Keepin' secrets from Goldie." Rosy swallowed some coffee and then rushed to the sink to get some cold water. "That's damn hot!"

"Charlie, Nellie is still asleep, and Rosy said you all had a strange time out on the lava fields. Is she all right?"

"Far as I know. I think she crept up and down the stairway last night, so she might be extra tired." He turned to Rosy. "I have been thinking. I want to call the photographer in Twin Falls and have him come here. The sooner we get those photos developed, the better. He could help Nellie—ah, Miss Burns—and we may have some answers. Also, I think he has some photos he took as a portrait photographer that might be of interest to us."

"I know who you mean, Jacob Levine," Goldie said. "I can call the Olsens and get his telephone number. But maybe we should ask Nell first?" She knew how Nellie felt about her own work—her photos, her negatives—but she made the telephone call anyway.

The boys came tumbling down the stairs. If that didn't wake Nell, nothing would, Goldie thought. "All right. Let's go. Got your swimming gear?"

"Hi Sheriff," Matt said. "Want to go swimming with us?"

The sheriff lifted his casted leg. "I cannot. Another time."

Rosy herded everyone out the door. He glanced back at Charlie. "I'll meet you here in a couple shakes. We can take the money to the bank."

"Don't hurry. We took care of the cash yesterday afternoon."

Matt pleaded with Goldie to let Campbell come with him to the men's pool. Goldie gave in, after she had the steward check and see if it was crowded, which it wasn't. Only a few men were in there, and they all seemed to be guests at the hotel, he said. Goldie sank into the heat of the pool on the women's side. It was like being in a hot bath, but without the worry about using too much hot water. Plus, the minerals and salt made it easy to float around. Aspen leaves surrounding the pools quaked, their yellow color beginning to fade. The cottonwoods had already dropped most of theirs. Two other women lounged in the pool with her, but no one seemed inclined to talk, so she didn't either. After half an hour, her skin had wrinkled like a raisin, so she climbed out and changed. She asked the steward to get the boys so they could go out to the front picnic tables and have lunch.

"They ain't in the pool," he said when he returned.

"What do you mean? Didn't you check on them like you said?"

"I got busy, lady. Wasn't my job to check on them."

"Well, I could hardly do it, could I? I'm going around now. Better tell those men to sink down." Goldie strode around the dividing wall and stepped toward the men's side. She could see several men, but no boys. She walked in farther. "Where are my boys?" she called.

"They went out a while ago with a man. They all seemed to know each other," called one of the men who was cowering along one side of the pool. "You can't come in here!"

"What man? Who was it?"

Another answered. "That Banks guy. He was staying here."

Uh-oh. Peter Banks. What in the world had he been doing there again? Goldie spun on her heel and went out to the steward. "Peter Banks. Is he still here?"

"I can't tell you that."

"Oh, yes, you can, or I'll report you to the police. Running a lewd place of business. Letting one of those men run off with little boys."

The steward pulled out a register and ran his finger along it. "Yes, he's been staying here. His room number is eight." He closed the book. "Now go away."

Goldie hurried around to the front door of the lodge. She asked a woman cleaning the lobby area where Room 7 was and was pointed down a hallway. Goldie banged on the door of Room 8 until her fist hurt. No answer. She hurried back to the dressing room where the boys had changed. Their clothes were gone. Back to the lobby, where she found a telephone and called the boarding house. The phone rang and rang. Would no one pick it up? They all knew she was gone. "Keep ringing," she told the operator. "Someone is bound to get tired of the noise."

Finally, Rosy picked up. "Hello. Bock's Boarding House," he said.

"Rosy, it's me. The boys were taken away from here by Peter Banks. I'm stranded, and I don't know what to do."

Rosy blew his breath out. "That ain't all. Nellie's room has been torn to pieces, and she's gone, too. I'll get the sheriff and come get you now."

"Oh, no!" Two kidnappings in one morning? They must be connected. Goldie grabbed up her picnic and satchel and began to walk along Warm Springs Road toward town. When Rosy's car motored down the road, she waved, and he stopped. She climbed into the back and found herself sitting with Moonshine. She flung her arms around the dog and sobbed.

CHAPTER 28

When Nellie felt the rope loosen and herself falling, she covered her head, seeking to protect it from more lava scrapes. The chute was narrow, and, instead of her face, her elbows suffered. Maybe she would fall to the center of the earth or to burning lava and die in fire. But she didn't. Her legs crumpled under her with a searing pain, and she fell mostly sideways on hard rock. Her automatic thrust of her arms saved her face, but her teeth slammed into her tongue, and blood filled her mouth. Nell could feel her head give way, losing consciousness, but she shook it and spat the blood out. It was not dark like in the cave. When she looked up, she could see the open hole of the spatter cone and light from what might be the rising sun. It seemed so far away.

For a moment, she thought she had died—she couldn't get a breath, and, when she did, her chest screamed. Her moans echoed up the steep rock walls. She tried to cover her mouth so Peter Banks, if he were still there, wouldn't hear her. Let him think she had died. And, maybe she still would. Her arms, torso, head, face, hands, and legs hurt in varied degrees of pain, seven circles of hell. All she could do was lie still and breathe in short breaths, each one a stab. Tears seeped down her face. Gradually, her heart slowed, and she could close her eyes. She slept in snatches, awaking thirsty, falling asleep, moving and jerked awake again by spasms of agony.

After a while, Nellie didn't know how long, she inched up to a sitting position. Her hands were still tied but almost loose. She used her teeth to wrest the rope away, then held her ribs, for surely she had broken several. She felt her legs and found her ankle had swollen to three times its normal size—the ankle with no boot on it. A break there, too, or a terrible wrench. Her arms and hands worked, but her elbows were scraped almost clean of skin. Blood dripped from each; she could feel the liquid on her arms. Her tongue was swollen like her ankle. Talking would hardly be possible. She tried. "Help, help, help." It came out "heph, heph, heph." No one to hear her anyway. With care, she swept the ground around her. The lava felt like *pahoehoe*, not *a'a*, although there were big scratchy slabs. The rope was still tied around her chest and lay in a jumble next to her. She was sure rope burns covered her front under her shirt. She hoped her jacket had protected her back.

First, she thought. What was first? She could hardly think for all the needles and knives throbbing inside. First, get the rope off of her. Easier thought than done, she found. Lifting her arms moved her ribs, and she shrieked. Then she looked up. No face appeared in the hole. The man—the monster—must have left. Mouthing the hurt in short cries helped, and, at last, she was able to pull the rope over her head.

Second, stand up, she ordered herself. She rolled to her knees, her cries growing shriller, and then pulled herself up by grabbing a rough handhold on the wall. The hole above didn't look any closer. Her ankle would not hold her, so she stood one-legged. She and Charlie—a pair to draw to. She wished he were looking down at her. He would figure out how to get her out. The sun had circled higher, and more light poured into the hole, enough to see that the walls of her prison were anything but smooth. Nor were they dark. Brilliant red ridges and ledges and chunky pieces of lava shone in the sunlight, but the light only reached perhaps the top third of the cone in which she found herself. Below the line, all looked a desolate gray.

Nellie let herself back down in slow increments. Although her chest hurt as much as before, she figured her mind was getting used to the other pains, for they seemed not so piercing. Still, tears dripped down her face. She felt abandoned. She leaned against the rock behind her. This must be how Effie had felt in the cave. She remembered the night she and Charlie talked and his story. No one hurt him physically, but Lily's father had threatened him and forced him to leave all he had ever known. He, too, must have felt abandoned and alone, but he had recovered and gained in strength. She should have been more sympathetic to a man she surely loved. "Stop crying," she said out loud. Charlie had called her a strong woman. She must live up to that description.

Nellie took the rope and formed a ring in one end, tying a slip knot taught to her by Charlie. Once again, she crawled to a standing position. Her perch was too narrow to swing the rope around; only an up and down motion would work, and that not well. Nevertheless, she persisted and, with one giant heave and a sharp scream, threw the ring toward the hole and hoped it would catch on something, anything. She had to ignore the needles in her chest, or she wouldn't accomplish anything. On the third try, the ring caught. She pulled down on the rope, and it stayed on whatever it had caught. And then she realized she should have left the loop around her chest. If she climbed up, that could be her safety line, in case she slipped or something gave way. Over her head or up from her feet. Which would hurt the least? She played the rope out through her hands and decided the loop to go around her chest was too distant from the rope end, so she tied it close to the middle and slipped it down over her head, gritting her teeth to absorb the pangs rising up.

One foot was useless, but Nell found she could use the other foot and then her knee to clamber up the rocky wall, a slow step at a time. When she reached where the rope had caught on a lava knob, she searched for a level spot to stand. She forced herself to rest. Eventually, she could swing the lasso up and down again and flung it upward. Four tries and she was out of breath and losing her balance. On the fifth try, the ring caught. When she pulled on it, it slid but then stopped and stayed. As she slowly rose in the chute, she noticed the light from the hole was waning, but it was closer. In addition to her other aches, her one good foot began to tremble, tripping up and down like a sewing machine needle. She stopped to rest and stretch it out. The rock area where she had lain below had disappeared in her second climb. The distance to the top loomed in her head— maybe two more lengths or perhaps a total of forty feet from beginning to end. She must have dropped twenty, she realized, and was lucky to be alive. Keep going.

When she neared the surface, Nell realized escaping the cone hole presented a major hurdle. She needed to circle the rope around the lip. To do so, she must get herself almost up to the top and then lasso the lip. Every muscle in her body ached and throbbed. Her ribs hurt so much, she cried. The pant wool around her knee had shredded, and her skin was rough and bloody. Her foot had settled down, then tripped again, then calmed when she rested. Her hands were scraped and torn. She was too close to give up but so tired. She formed a large circle in the rope, took a deep breath, twirled the rope—and let go. Even in the shadowy afternoon, she could see the loop surround the lip and drop.

Outside, at last, Nellie assessed her injuries. Most of all, she was thirsty. If she lay still, only her ankle and the various scratches and bruises on her skin hurt. Her tongue had assumed its normal size, not that she needed to call out. No one was around. Someone must have discovered that she was not in her room. Her camera and pack were there, so Goldie or Charlie would know something was wrong. And Moonshine. Nellie had regretted not letting him out when she left the house, but he might not have survived Peter's machinations. At the very least, the man was guilty of attempted murder—hers.

The afternoon had cooled and darkened, and an evening breeze chilled the air. As Nellie pondered her next moves, she saw a dark shape move in and out of the trees in the distance. Oh, no. That was all she needed—a bear or a mountain lion. Maybe the smell of her blood might attract one or the other like a shark to prey in water. She searched around where she sat for a weapon—plenty of lava chunks and a lava bomb or two. The gun she had carried was still in her pack. She grabbed a piece of lava. The animal would have to be close enough to hit. Her aim was good, she knew, when she was standing. She gathered up two more chunks in case she missed. The animal moved with its nose to the ground. Strange. And then she knew. "Moonshine! Moonie!" Her dog lifted its nose and ran up the incline toward her. "Oh, Moonie!" He almost leaped on her, but she had to hold him off. Her ribs couldn't take his weight. She grabbed him around the neck and hugged him as close as possible. His smell, his fur, his hefty chest—all were so dear to her.

"Moonshine!" Rosy's voice floated to her. "Where did that damn dog go?"

"Rosy! Rosy!" Nell called. "He's here. I'm here!"

"Girl! We had about given up on finding you." Rosy stooped down to hug her, but she held her arms out to keep him away. "Are you all right?"

"No. Yes." Nell couldn't stop herself. She wept with loud, gasping sobs—each one hurting her. "Peter Banks stuffed me down that cone, but I am better now that you're here." Nell grabbed his leg and hugged it. "Oh Rosy."

He patted her head awkwardly. "We knew Moonshine could find you, if anybody could." He pulled a canteen over his head and opened it. "Here. You're pro'bly dyin' of thirst. Out here for hours."

Nellie grabbed the canteen and drank and drank. When she stopped, she said, "I'm sorry. I may have taken all of it." She handed it back. "How long have you been looking?"

"Hours." Rosy squatted. "Where are you hurt? I'll try to fix you up. We need to get you back to the road. The boys are missin', too."

"Oh, no! Did Peter take them, too?" Nellie tried to stand but fell back. She had forgotten about her ankle in the joy of seeing both Moonshine and Rosy. "Where's Charlie?"

"Take it easy. Lemme see where you're hurt and what to do."

"Where don't I hurt?"

Rosy dropped his pack from his shoulders. "Now, just sit there, and tell me what happened. Charlie and Jacob are goin' after the boys. Goldie's at home, waiting for a telephone call about all of you."

"Jacob? How did he get involved?"

"We needed to see your photos, and he had some to show us. He motored up as soon as we telephoned. Got to Ketchum 'bout noon." He poked around in his pack and fished out a blanket. "Here, let's wrap this around you. Don't want you gettin' pneumonia."

"But the boys? Who took them?"

"That damned Peter Banks. Right out of the hot springs. He wanted money for 'em. The same money ever'one's been fightin' over." Rosy studied Nell from her head to her toes. "Now, where do you hurt? Then, I'll answer your questions."

Nell had ceased crying, but she felt weak. "First, my ankle. It might be broken." She pulled the blanket off the unbooted foot, its stocking just strings of cotton. "Did you see my boot any-where?"

"Yeah, we did. Moonie did. That's how we knew to come this way. He carried it a long ways but dropped it." Rosy searched in his pack again and pulled out her boot. "Lemme look." With gentle hands, Rosy felt around Nellie's ankle.

She tried not to cry out but didn't succeed. Talking might help. "Peter Banks and Effie lured me out of the boarding house. Like a fool, I came downstairs. Peter chloroformed me, I think. It smelled awful. I woke up just before we stopped at the lava fields. He slung me over a horse. I tried to persuade Effie to leave. I don't know if she did, but she didn't come out with us." Nellie rubbed her forehead, trying to remember the sequence of events. "When we reached the spatter cones, he wrapped a rope around me and held me over this one. He wanted to know where the money was. I think he searched my room after he drugged me." She patted the rocks beside her. "He lowered me, and then he dropped me. I fell quite a ways. That's when I hurt my ankle. My chest hurts, too. I think I broke some ribs. The rest of my—my—"

Rosy put his arm around her shoulders. "You're safe now, Nellie." He sounded like he might be crying.

Moonie snuggled up to both of them, as if to say, "These are mine."

Nellie accepted Rosy's and her dog's warmth but after several minutes knew they needed to keep moving. "Tell me about the boys. I am so sorry."

"Goldie telephoned from Guyer and said they were gone, and Peter Banks had taken them. I motored along to pick her up. By then Jacob Levine was at the house, and he and the sheriff were cozy with the photos you took. He'd set up in the bathroom, just like you did. 'Course, he identified O'Donnell, and he had one of him, too, along with a wife and kids."

"Kids? Wasn't he a little old to have children?"

"They was grown up women. Two of them. There wasn't no Ben in there either." Rosy sat up and stirred around in his pack again. "Here it is. Charlie said you'd want to see it."

The edges of the photo were scraped, but Nellie could see the figures. "Ah. This explains a lot."

"That's what he said." He put the photograph back in his pack. "We made Goldie stay at the boarding house, even though she wanted to come along. Someone had to be there to get telephone messages and call out. Jacob and Charlie headed for Arco and Mayor Tom. They think Tom might have had something to do with all this, because he was the one who told Charlie where to leave the money for Banks. Charlie said he had no choice but to leave it at the cave where you found the first body. Tom said Banks gave him the instructions, and he complied, because he could see Banks had the boys. Moonie and I came this way 'cause Effie said you was left out here somewheres."

"Effie helped? How? Did she telephone? Come by?"

"Yep. Guess she got dropped off at Esther's. My sister told Effie and Banks the boys had gone swimming at the hot springs. After Peter left, Effie telephoned us. She was afraid for the boys. Nice woman, that."

"When did she tell you about me?"

Either Rosy didn't hear the question, or he was too busy cleaning off her scrapes. Nellie left unsaid some of the nasty thoughts she had suffered down in the hole and tried to think of how Effie, too, had been abandoned. "Do you think I can walk on my leg?"

"Not a good idea. Let me find a stick and then maybe we can figure out how to get you back." Rosy found his flashlight and left her in the gloom. Moonshine stuck with Nell, keeping her company.

After a space of time, when Nellie began to tremble again, she heard Rosy's steps. He crouched down to her and asked for the blanket. She handed it over and could see he was folding it on top of what looked like a branch broken from a tree—a makeshift crutch. Rosy helped her up, and, once she was situated with the crutch under one arm and Rosy on her other side, they began to hobble and walk, slowly at first, but then with more assurance. Nell's efforts kept her warm enough even without the blanket.

"Look over there, Rosy," Nell said. "Is that a fire?" An orange glow appeared to radiate from the lava in an easterly direction. Nell stopped to get a better sense of where a fire might be. There wasn't much that could burn on its own in the lava fields, but someone could light a fire as she and Charlie had done near the spatter cones.

"Sure looks like it. How do you feel about headin' over thataway? Maybe it's a signal fire from the sheriff. Maybe he found the boys." Rosy had already taken several steps in that direction.

"If you could leave me your flashlight, I could make my own way there. Go ahead. It's important to find Matt and Campbell. Maybe the sheriff needs your help!" As tender as she felt, Nellie didn't want to hold Rosy back. She took the light and pointed out that the stars were beginning to sparkle and could help illuminate both his way and hers. Rosy left after a brief hesitation. "Yeah, Matt and Campbell."

"Take Moonshine!" She urged her dog to follow Rosy, and he did.

Alone in the dark and surrounded by cool air, Nellie hobbled along the path that Rosy had taken. As she crutched over and around rocks, she was beginning to feel as if she were part of the night sky and the dark lava fields. The smell of dried grass, the rustlings of small animals, the brilliance of the Milky Way, and the harsh moonscape of the Craters had become integral to her knowledge of self. The horror of the deaths that had taken place there began to recede and be replaced by a trust and calm she rarely felt. There were evil actions in this Idaho back country, but good and caring people would overcome them, perhaps not at first, but in the end. The boys would be all right.

Even if all the bad people surrounded the fire, she hoped Charlie had them tied up and that he didn't need Rosy's help. But why else would he start a fire? Or maybe Peter Banks had lit a match to the dry pine needles and shrubs. Maybe he planned to burn out the sheriff and Jacob. There was nothing she could do to help, as banged up as she was. Maybe it would be better to stay away and just await the outcome, whatever it was. Still, the thought of the two boys in trouble galvanized her to keep gimping along, as slow and sometimes painful as it was. She could throw rocks.

Another glow diverted her attention. A round moon, at first pink and then blood red, rose behind the orange radiance that was the fire she aimed toward. As the moon rose higher, the stars began to fade, and the night orb lost its carmen sheen. It would soon be bright enough to help Nellie stick to the path, probably an Indian trail in olden times. Before long, she could see that the fire had been built. It wasn't growing as a wildfire would. Bulky shapes hovered nearby, the flames making them dance like monsters. But no, they were two horses—one to carry the sheriff—and who else? Peter! Nellie decided to stay back until she could figure out who was who and what was what. She didn't see two boys or even their shadows. Rosy must have done the same thing, as she didn't see him or her dog either.

"Whoooo-ooo." Was that an owl, or Rosy, or the sheriff? Nellie hadn't heard an owl the whole time she had been in the lava fields.

CHAPTER 29

Nellie waited. And waited and then decided it was an owl. She limped toward the fire and saw Matt and Campbell poking at it with sticks. The wavering light shone on the faces of Mayor Tom, Effie, Ben, and Pearl all sitting on the edges like a campfire party. A brown bottle made its way around the circle. A surprise and a relief. No Peter Banks. But Rosy and the sheriff were nowhere in sight.

Effie jumped up as Nellie neared and helped her with an arm around her waist. "Rosy said you were on your way."

"No thanks to you," Nell said and removed Effie's arm. Don't touch me, she thought, but forebore from saying it.

The woman's face crumpled. "I know. It's my fault. I'm so sorry, Miss Burns." She covered her face, and her shoulders shook.

Nell wondered if her tears and sobs were real or just a part in a play, so she could be the victim. Pearl looked at Nell and gasped. "Your face! You look terrible!"

Mayor Tom hurried to Nell and helped her to a stump seat. "Do you need a blanket?" he asked.

"Of course she needs a blanket," Pearl said. "And water and food! Can't you see how bad off she is?"

Tom hurried over with a blanket and a canteen. He unscrewed the top and held it to Nell's lips. She drank greedily, and some of the water slipped down her chin. Nellie lowered her crutch and stretched out her legs, the blanket around her shoulders.

"Where is Rosy?" She supposed her face was bruised, as were her arms. The heat from the fire eased some of her pain.

"He and the sheriff and another man are off looking for—"

"Peter Banks," Nellie said, interrupting Tom. "The only one missing from this group."

"My father is missing, too," Ben chimed in. "We think he may also be after Banks, who has the money my father paid for—"

"Harriet Thorpe," Nellie said, interrupting again. "Otherwise known as Hattie." So, none of these people knew that Cable was dead.

Effie lifted her head from where she had curled up like a question mark and stopped her mewling. There were no tear streaks that Nell could see in the firelight.

All the faces turned to Nellie, except the boys. They were arguing over one of the burned sticks and appeared oblivious to the adults. The smoke from the flames, crackling softly in the night air, traveled up. There was no wind.

"Where were the boys?" she asked.

"Peter told me where to go," Mayor Tom said, "once he picked up the money. He left them with Ben and Pearl in the cow camp." He gestured to the west.

Was everyone in these lava fields also connected to the murders as well as the kidnappings? As Nellie looked around at each of them—Effie once again curled over; Tom rifling in his pack for food, she hoped; Pearl as usual avoiding looking back; and Ben, his face frowning and looking like his father, as if he had just discovered something—she realized she might be in more danger, except for the boys' presence. Even as that thought crossed her mind, Effie stood up.

"I'll take the boys back to their aunt," she said. "We can all three ride one of those horses." She motioned to the dark space outside the circle.

"No. If anyone goes, I go," Nellie said. She grasped her makeshift crutch and pulled herself up. "Pearl, could you help me?"

"Me?" Pearl sounded surprised. "Why me?"

"Because you're the only one I trust." Nell figured if Pearl had been involved with the others, she could easily have hurt or even killed Nell when they had traveled to the cow camp and back. No one would have been the wiser. She was also worried about Pearl's safety now that Cable O'Donnell was dead. Even though they had parted, maybe on unfriendly terms, O'Donnell had owed Pearl for not exposing him. Nell suspected he had seen she was protected from harm by the moonshiners by sending her to Ben.

And then they all heard rocks slipping and sliding, the unmistakable sounds of something or someone outside the circle of light. More than one. Rosy appeared and Moonshine along with him. The dog saw Nellie and trotted to her. The sheriff followed, using his crutch and leading a man whose hands were tied with a rope and, behind them, Jacob Levine. Nellie could hardly have been more surprised. All the good men in her life. She wanted to rush to them, except the man in the middle was Peter Banks, who had tried to kill her. His head hung down and didn't lift, even as they shuffled toward the fire. Jacob carried what looked like a heavy pack.

The sheriff pushed Peter, and he fell down, his back to one of the stumps. His feet were tied, too, with just enough slack in the rope that he could walk but not run. Justice, thought Nellie. She wanted to kick him. He looked up and around at the circle of people. When his eyes lit on Nellie, he gasped and scooted backwards. "All I wanted was the money," Peter Banks said. His voice again sounded like the charming man from California. "I needed it to finance the fight to make these lava fields a monument. Tom knows. He feels the same way." Peter then saw Ben.

"I needed it to fight the O'Donnells, who just want grazing to continue, to ruin this rare place." He sounded eminently reasonable, and Nellie could almost find herself nodding with him.

"Oh, no, Banks," Tom said. "You wanted the money to go to California. You may think this place is rare, but you've no love for it, or you wouldn't have used it for killing and hiding people. Besides, it's nigh on to becoming a monument without your help!"

Nellie crutched toward Banks. "And the boys? And me?" She tried not to screech. She wanted to sound as reasonable as he did. The sheriff came to stand beside her, as did Jacob, on her other side. She pointed her crutch at the man who continued to push himself backwards. "You're a liar and a murderer." Effie sucked in her breath behind Nell.

"No. He's been trying to help me get our baby back. The money was for me. It's mine!" Effie approached Peter. "Where's the money, Peter? You promised!" No tears this time.

"He took the boys to ransom the money," Nell said. "The sheriff paid it to him for the boys." Nell pointed at the pack on Jacob's back. "I suspect it is in that pack now, but it may not be yours. Or, at least, not all of it."

"What do you mean?"

"You think it's yours because Cable O'Donnell was your father, wasn't he?"

Effie's mouth dropped open. "How do you know that?"

"Rosy showed me Jacob's photo of you and your sister with your mother, Henrietta Thorpe, and Cable O'Donnell, her husband. Your stepfather, I believe. You and Hattie were stepchildren, but Ben was Cable's real son."

Ben stood up. "I thought Hattie and Effie were my half-sisters. That's what you said." He snarled at Effie. "From my father's second wife, who was Henrietta. My mother was devastated when she found out about the second wife when I was a teenager. I don't think she knows about Hattie and Effie."

Pearl made a disgusted sound. "See, I would have been his *third* wife!"

Ben turned back toward Nellie. "What do you mean 'was'? Where's my father?"

The sheriff answered. "Cable O'Donnell was dropped into one of the spatter cones. He did not fall down into it, as his murderer thought. Miss Burns and I found him and pulled him out and took him to the morgue. From the photographs that Miss Burns took, we could confirm that his head had been bashed in—just like the minister's head, the man who killed Harriet."

Ben looked down at Peter. "You did that. I saw you do it."

Nellie interrupted again. "Peter killed Elder. I thought maybe you did it because you were out here with your sisters and Elder before all the mayhem. And then you arrived too late to protect them. You helped Peter carry the dead Elder to another cave. When you approached me, you knew who that dead man was." Nellie sagged. "If you thought Hattie was your half-sister, not just your stepsister—. Was that why you didn't want to claim that baby as yours?" She pointed to Effie. "She lied. She wanted the baby and Peter Banks, but she wanted you out of her life."

Ben looked back and forth between Peter and Nellie. His face had turned ashen, even in the firelight. His eyes closed to slits, as did his mouth. Surprise or anger. He took a step toward Effie. "I loved Hattie. Her child is my child! She wanted to leave because she thought we were related. And so did I."

Rosy stepped between Ben and Effie.

"I didn't know Hattie and Effie growing up," Ben said and threw his hands up. "Father never said he had another family until I was working the cattle around here. When I went to Twin Falls, I met Hattie. She said her last name was Thorpe and didn't say anything about my father."

Nellie could only feel sorry for Ben. "Even though Effie didn't like your father, he must have loved Hattie." Nell ignored a small cry from Effie. "He apparently responded to Elder's blackmail with the money to get her back. I don't know if he knew she was pregnant. Effie may have told him. She was the one who picked up the cash and delivered it to Elder." A new thought occurred to Nellie. "Maybe she even kept some of it back for herself." She swerved to look at Effie, whose face turned grim and then flushed.

"When I saw Hattie in the cave with the ice pick in her, I couldn't believe it," Ben said. "I didn't know she had had the baby or that Elder Joshua, that crazy polygamist, had stabbed her. I would have killed him, too. Peter did me a favor. I left because I had to get back to the cattle. Peter said he would give Hattie a proper burial and tell her mother. Effie just cried." He motioned to her, his face rock-hard. "Just like she's doing now. I don't know how much of this is her doing, but she is no innocent." Ben grabbed the bottle from the ground and took a huge swig. "If you know so much," he said, turning to Nellie, "who killed my father?"

"Peter Banks and Effie came out here to search for the money," Nell answered. "Cable ran into Effie, is my guess, while Peter had gone into one of the caves. A shot was fired. I heard it and thought it was Cable shooting at an animal. Instead, it was Banks. His shot missed Cable and hit Effie's leg. Cable took her to that last cave to protect her, I believe. Maybe Effie will tell us. That's when I saw him, and he took money that was stashed there." She still didn't want to own up. "Banks must have seen him and, when he came out, attacked your father, killing him in the same way he murdered Elder Joshua. I know how strong he is." Nellie glanced at Peter. The hate on his face gave her pause. She was glad Charlie and Rosy were both there. "Peter told me he'd seen the money when I tried to convince him it was counterfeit. That was the only way he could have seen it—in Cable's hands. Banks killed your father for the money. I took a photograph of one of his cigarette butts outside the cave where Effie was with me. I don't know if she knew O'Donnell was dead or not, but she had no love for her stepfather. She did help Banks try to get rid of me." She swayed and turned back to Ben. "Your baby, a little girl, is in Hailey. Goldie knows where she is."

Nellie was wavering on her crutch. She was so tired, and her whole body ached, not just her chest and ankle. "And you, Mayor Tom. You were too helpful. You knew all these family ties, didn't you?" She didn't wait for an answer. "You helped Peter hide Hattie, didn't you?"

"Hide?" Effie stepped closer to Peter. "They buried Hattie. They said."

"No, they threw her down a hole. I found her. The sheriff and Rosy pulled her out. She is in the morgue in Hailey. You can bury her."

Peter Banks appeared to hop onto his feet and lunged at Nellie, his tied hands grasping for her neck. "You bitch." His voice lowered and once again he sounded like the man in the car, the man who held her over the spatter cone and then dropped her. The sheriff pulled on the rope, and Peter was upended, close to the fire. "Sit on him, Rosy. Tie his hands in back, and pull the hands and feet toward each other."

Nellie had almost fallen, but Jacob moved as fast as Peter had and held Nellie upright, his arms around her back and sides. She sank into the luxury of safety.

CHAPTER 30

Nellie lay back in her hospital bed in Twin Falls. She had protested, but all three men overruled her. The doctor who saw her said it was a good thing. She was dehydrated, and all her cuts and bruises, along with her ribs and ankle, needed care along with bed rest. He treated her like an invalid, as did the nurses. Even Gwynn came to see her and held her hand. Mr. and Mrs. Olsen brought a picnic basket of food—the first real food she'd seen since before her ordeal began. They brought a message from Goldie, telling her to stay in bed and mind the doctor.

Jacob visited and brought some of the photos he had printed from the negatives he had developed at Goldie's house. He laughed about the primitive conditions she had been forced to use early on. Along with those of O'Donnell were several of her "art" photos as he called them. Craters of the Moon looked spooky in several of them. "Very effective," Jacob said. "I would never have thought that those lava fields would lend themselves to light and dark as you have captured them."

Those words were as healing to Nell as anything he could have said. And, she thought, he was right.

"Nell, Miss Burns, I wish you would consider moving to Twin Falls and going into partnership with me. My workload is too heavy for me. You do such wonderful photographic work, I know the town would welcome you, too."

She wanted to ask, what about his fiancée? She would not

welcome Nellie, of that Nell was certain.

"You do flatter me, Jacob. And no 'Miss Burns,' remember? This is something I would have to give some serious thought to. Going by train back and forth to Twin Falls to use your darkroom, which you so kindly have permitted, is difficult. But now, I have such ties to Ketchum and Hailey, I am not sure I could leave." She thought of Goldie and Rosy and the boys and how little she would see of them if she moved to Twin. But the sheriff loomed largest in her thoughts. He hadn't even come to visit her in the hospital since dropping her off with not much more than a wave good-bye. Rosy had lingered longest, until the automobile horn had pulled him away.

"My fiancée is not returning," Jacob said, as if she had asked. "She has decided the West is not for her. She has asked me to move East, but I cannot do that. Idaho is my home." He squeezed Nellie's hand. "Perhaps Twin Falls could be yours, too. We have worked together well."

"Yes, we have," Nellie said. "I have to think about this, Jacob. Thank you for asking me." The lowering sun sent shadows through her window. She closed her eyes.

When Nellie opened her eyes, her room was almost dark, and she was alone. No, someone sat in the chair near the door. Jacob?

"You slept quite a while," Charlie said. "I did not want to wake you. The doctor said you needed as much rest as possible. How do you feel?"

The sheriff stood and used his one crutch to come to her bedside. A light in the hallway outlined his figure.

"Like I've been roped and tied and branded," Nellie said and tried to smile. "I do feel better but still aches and pains here and there. It may be a little while before I can be your photographer again." She gestured to his crutch. "Aren't we a pair? Did you learn anything more? I hope Peter Banks is in jail." She shuddered to remember her time in the spatter cone hole.

"Banks is in jail here in Twin Falls. He will be tried for murder and attempted murder. You will have to testify. We are not sure yet if Effie will, and she knows the most." He shifted to get more comfortable on his crutch. Nellie patted the bed to indicate he should sit, but he stayed on his foot. "Effie—Euphemia—told us more about what happened with Elder. He had found the ice-bound cave and herded Hattie and Effie into it, saying that was where the child should be born. He also expected to sacrifice the baby as a bastard."

"What a terrible man!"

"It gets worse, although you heard most of it at Guyer Hot Springs. Effie laid Hattie down where we found her and helped deliver the baby. Then Elder stabbed the stalactite into Hattie. He had planned something like that all along, Effie thought, although Hattie believed she was going to be redeemed for her sin. Effie grabbed the baby and began to run out of the cave, but slipped. Elder grabbed for her, planning to kill the child— 'spawn of the devil' he called her. It was then that Peter Banks appeared. Effie had telephoned him from Mayor Tom's filling station. He shoved Effie out of the cave with the baby and grabbed a rock and killed Elder. He didn't die immediately, as he had bruises all over his chest and neck, probably from Effie kicking at him. Ben arrived, too, as he had grown suspicious of Elder when he rode over to see what was going on. And then Tom. They helped carry Elder to the cave where we found him."

"What a tragic story," Nellie said. "No wonder Effie was almost hysterical half the time." She shifted in the bed, trying to ease her ribs. "That sort of explains why she did everything Peter Banks told her to do. He was a frightening man, it turns out. Will he be charged with Elder's murder?" Nellie reached out to Charlie.

"I doubt it. Self-defense, or at least defense of Effie and the baby, would probably stand." Charlie took her hand and sat down on Nellie's bed.

"And what about Mayor Tom? He wasn't exactly innocent in all this." She wanted the sheriff closer to her, but that was as good as she was going to get, she thought.

"Tom will be a witness against Banks about the kidnapping, so, no, even though he was tangled up with Peter, partly because they had both been on the earlier expedition. I do not think he had anything to do with O'Donnell's murder or the attempt to murder you. Banks was just a packer and part-time guide for the real explorers, even though he made it sound like more."

"What about Pearl? I don't think she was involved, but I hope she does go to Oregon."

"Oregon? Why there?"

"Ned Tanner, the cowboy."

Charlie nodded. "So that was what she meant. She did sign a statement about last summer, although it doesn't really matter anymore. Not with O'Donnell dead."

"At least he tried to save Hattie." Nell slumped against her pillow. "What is going to happen to that baby? Will Ben claim her?"

"Effie and Ben have decided they will raise her. I do not know how that will work, but at least two people will take care of her. Effie's mother will help, too."

"Are Effie and Ben getting together?" That seemed like a twosome doomed to failure.

"No, I think they are approaching this task as brother and sister." Charlie shrugged his shoulders, as if to say it might work.

Nellie sat up taller. "How is your leg? Scooting around on the lava must have been hard on it."

"It is healing. I get the cast off next week." The sheriff

continued to hold Nellie's hand. His wide palm and long fingers dwarfed hers, and his calluses, hard and rough at the same time, made her hand feel fragile. His darker skin contrasted sharply with her paler skin. "You and I have made good partners against criminals, Nell. You solved more than half these crimes, and your photographs are invaluable."

He sounded like Jacob. All work and no play. What about as partners? In life, say, although that might be a challenge with either of them. Jacob would be more willing to accept a "working" wife than would the sheriff, she suspected. She could no longer even imagine a role as a traditional wife, a life she could not and would not accept. Her sense of oneness with the sky and rocks had not left her when she was taken to the hospital. She wanted to feel it again, to capture it in photographs.

"I can wait for you." Charlie lifted Nellie's hand and kissed her palm with his warm, soft lips.

ABOUT THE AUTHOR

Julie Weston grew up in Idaho and practiced law for many years in Seattle, Washington. Her memoir of place, *The Good Times Are All Gone Now: Life, Death and Rebirth in an Idaho Mining Town* (University of Oklahoma Press, 2009), received an honorable mention in the 2009 Idaho Book of the Year Award. Her short stories and essays have been published in *IDAHO Magazine, The Threepenny Review, River Styx, Clackamas Review,* and other journals. Both an essay and a short story have been nominated for Pushcart Prizes. Her debut fiction, *Moonshadows,* a Nellie Burns and Moonshine Mystery (Five Star Publishing, 2015) was named a finalist in the May Sarton Literary Award. Her second Nellie Burns and Moonshine mystery, *Basque Moon* (Five Star Publishing, 2016) won the WILLA Literary Award in Historical Fiction in 2017. Weston and her husband, Gerry Morrison, now live in central Idaho where they ski, write, photograph, and enjoy the outdoors. www.julieweston.com

The employees of Five Star Publishing hope you have enjoyed this book.

Our Five Star novels explore little-known chapters from America's history, stories told from unique perspectives that will entertain a broad range of readers.

Other Five Star books are available at your local library, bookstore, all major book distributors, and directly from Five Star/Gale.

Connect with Five Star Publishing

Visit us on Facebook:
    https://www.facebook.com/FiveStarCengage

Email:
    FiveStar@cengage.com

For information about titles and placing orders:
    (800) 223-1244
    gale.orders@cengage.com

To share your comments, write to us:
    Five Star Publishing
    Attn: Publisher
    10 Water St., Suite 310
    Waterville, ME 04901

31901065094015